Solomon Kursh is a work of fiction. Names, characters, places and businesses are either the products of the author's imagination or used in a fictitious manner. Any resemblance to actual persons, living or dead, or actual events is purely coincidental.

Wintner, Robert

Solomon Kursh / by Robert Wintner

ISBN: 979-8-9855513-1-0

1. Cult—Commune—the '60s—Fiction. 2. Life Crisis—Cultural conflict—Fiction. Nazi—Auto Sales—Fiction. Printed in the USA

Layout and design: Keith Christie
Cover art: *The Return*, 5x7 oil on panel, by Bonita Barlow
https://bonita-barlow.pixels.com/ for more lyrical works
and bonitabarlowlight.com for reflective abstract works.

Contact at RobertWintner.com or Robert Wintner Author on FB.

Twice-Baked Books

$15.00
ISBN 979-8-9855513-1-0
51500>
9 798985 551310

D1598781

Solomon Kursh

a novel

Robert Wintner

Also by Robert Wintner

Fiction:
In a Sweet Magnolia Time
Lizard Blue
Whirlaway
The Modern Outlaws
Touch of the Unknown Rider
Reefdog
Was Is
A California Closing
Homunculus
The Prophet Pasqual
Hagan's Trial & Other Stories

Memoir:
1969 and Then Some
Brainstorm
The Ice King

Reef Politic in narrative and photo/video:
Dragon Walk
Neptune Speaks
Reef Libre, An In-Depth Look at Cuban Exceptionalism & the Last, Best Reefs in the World
Every Fish Tells a Story
Some Fishes I Have Known

Memorium:

Perline
mother, confidant and friend

Such a Nice Boy
Such a Promising Young Man

Stanley Harold Sokolov, of the later baby boom, developed conventionally for twenty years. Like many kids in suburban Chicago, he learned the values and lessons paramount to Jewish history: raise a family, make a living to support them and be a *mensch*, a complete man, with charity and compassion.

The darkest time in Jewish history was recent, so he learned Jewish practicality foremost. The elders who witnessed those times shared their dictate with grim resolve: *Never again!*

Those same elders moved directly to other lessons and lasting values, eager to move on, to focus on the brilliant future. Young Stanley's burden was predictable and common to boys of glowing promise and good manners. He shone in all things. By virtue of sheer will power—not his but that of the fawning *mishpocha*, the family—he would rise to greatness. The future glistened in the *shayna punim*, the golden boy. Only the evil eye could dim such light, but nobody thought it would, not on our Stanley. But, just in case, to be sure, they tore at their clothing and spat sincerely, "Feh!"

They didn't actually tear anything; no need to waste quality goods, and the epithet alone was believed as effective as could be, without tearing. Not to worry anyway; Stanley was such a good boy, even if he dabbled in devilish ways. Comforted and confident, they beckoned, "Mm . . . Come here. I want a pinch of that."

Expectations stacked up, as if Stanley would strap on a harness and pull his forebears into greatness. They rooted for the home team; a win for Stanley would be a win for them.

He seemed resistant, as a kid might be, preferring independence. The elders chuckled; such were the ways of pups and kittens and kids. The elders saw inner strength that sweetened prospects like icing on cake. They believed in a future as he would shape it, in heroic contrast to recent misfortune. They referenced the dark time in oblique terms, avoiding detail as Jews may do; no need to dwell on calamities past.

Back to pogroms, to King Achashverosh, back to the philistines, Goliath and the whole Jew-hating panoply, anti-Semitism spanned the aeons. Some Jews remained steadfast. Others changed their names after World War II, to fit in, as if the horror discomforted them. The horror gained distance but stayed open and raw. Mere mention would get them sucking their teeth and wringing their hands. Dark time would linger, and some remembered in fear.

As a bright boy with wits, Stanley thought the elders weak, conforming to type and platitude. So much *kvetching* and zealotry seemed made to order, a set piece for older Jews. They could take shelter together and sustain each other. He wondered what they knew of conditions in Poland, France and Germany from 1938 to 1945 and when they knew it. Sanctimonious in Chicago, they seemed distant in response as well, and he also wondered: *What did they do? Were they relaxing on a plush sofa with plastic covers when they learned of the camps? Did they rise? Or merely shift to the other buttock?*

He would not ask aloud. He anticipated the stock response: "Put a roof over your head and some brisket in your belly is what we did, you little . . . *schmendrik*!" But a schmendrik is a fool, which they would never call him for fear of the evil one making it so. They would change the subject, to protect him and cover themselves, just as they'd covered the plush sofa. What they had done came to *bupkis*. Pressing the issue could bear nothing but bitter fruit. What? Done? From Chicago? They had survived as Jews; that's what they'd done. And then, Mister Know it All, they did not put him on the street and send him on his way. Well, Jews don't usually do that, but the elders would have bristled at any hint of ineptitude. They endured. They lived and worked for a better future for their children, which is not for a punk kid to challenge. So, he didn't.

They knew of their inconsequence, no matter the melodrama playing out on the plush sofa, where they still relaxed, wringing their hands, victims. They played it like arrival in America fifty years prior made for a very close call. It didn't. A good boy played along. A good boy knew the difference between a point and a hurtful opinion. *Shayna* means pretty, and *punim* is face, but *shayna punim* gilds the frame on the boys of glowing promise. Filial piety comes natural as sunlight into day.

A *shayna punim* will embrace tradition. He will aspire to the law or investment banking, to medicine or the arts, but not so much the arts, unless the law or medicine or banking don't work out.

Stanley Sokolov's striking looks got second glances from an early age. Sephardic angularity with a Hashemite olive hue set him apart, set him up for a dazzling grin. He might glance back, wondering why glances had occurred. He didn't mind and took family effusions in stride. Hope for fame, fortune, robust health and a direct connection to God seemed part of the package, his package, and he went along to please them. Would he bear compassion for all things with intelligence and articulation like Einstein? Would he succeed as expected, in a corner office with a view? Would he thrive like a wise man, rich and famous, a brain surgeon or heart surgeon, a great arbiter or judge, or a master of moolah with huge caches of cash? He would, he reckoned, with good cheer and bright countenance, as a shayna punim should do. *Why the fuck not?* He giggled.

Gifted and destined, aware and well mannered, Stanley feared what he alone was willing to recognize: that he could fail—*Feh!* He felt failure lurking, even as the family invoked: *kina hora*!

Cast out the evil eye!

For years he thought kina hora a supplication to the forces of fortune. Like *mazel tov*, mazel meaning luck and tov meaning good. Kina hora is meant to fend off the evil eye, to block any negative force that would undermine full potential or whatever part of it God might be willing to grant.

Bubbi and *Zeda*, the grandparents, muttered and mumbled at all times to keep the evil one at bay. It appeared to work.

Stanley studied adequately for decent grades to enhance prospects; Ivy League not required. It wouldn't happen, because a scholarship based on academic excellence or financial need would need a bit more of both to lure a top-drawer university. Straight-A students were common, and Stanley Sokolov was rare, a genius who never really applied himself; he got by so easily on no effort. But if he put his wits to any task, *oi!* And he would. Just you wait. Besides grades that did not reflect true intellect, he didn't test well. He left the Scholastic Aptitude Test a short while in because, "It felt wrong. You can't test me."

Never mind. He went long on common sense, and that was his potential. What could be so wrong with a middle-class background, middling comfort and a monumental mind that might meander? Nothing was the correct answer. Stan Sokolov had his health, which was everything, and he would achieve greatness at a school closer to home, where a good boy should be.

Morris Sokolov had taken pride as a provider and did fairly well in the rag business, until he dropped dead when Stan was fifteen, leaving many accounts waiting for service to no avail. If only Morris had spent more time servicing the heart that gave out. If only he'd eased up on nicotine and *schmaltz*—cigars and rendered chicken fat oozed over toast and sprinkled with salt. What is it about nicotine, fat and salt to calm nerves? It just goes to show how a man must take a day of rest, must stop to smell a rose. He must reflect on the air he breathes, the color in his cheeks, some exercise and the power above.

Never mind once again. Stan would excel at a state university, as necessary, and fulfill his legacy of doing well, of taking a wife and having children of his own. He would matriculate into the law or medicine, accounting or research science, business or diplomacy, banking or the arts—*Acch!* The arts again, with the deprivation, the tatty clothing and ass kissing, if you have no connections. Better to pursue the Sokolov-Epstein sphere of connections in quality dry goods. It wasn't for nothing that Pearl, the mother, had been an Epstein of the dry-cleaner Epsteins, or that dry goods and dry cleaning should wed for obvious enrichment to society. Stanley would benefit from this stability and prosperity, no matter where he went to college. Better he should stay close to home and marry in his own backyard, sooner rather than later, to enjoy the fruits of life to the maximum. Better to do what a man has to do, like a mensch for all seasons. Better to live long and prosper.

Pearl thought Stanley would do these things, and so did the aunts, uncles and cousins. He was such a good boy, after all. Who could imagine that a tiny cloud on the horizon would change life on Earth? The Summer of Love in 1967 seemed remote, an oddity, foreign and forgettable. When California symptoms showed up in Hyde Park, they seemed anomalous, amusements for wayward youth having fun, a brief sidebar on the news.

Stan liked books and music: comic books, the odd novel and Top-40 pop filling the bill. But rock 'n' roll became anti-social with political stuff to tip things over, spill them out. Thrumming a downbeat that felt tectonic, the hard-driving music got things rolling on a talent cavalcade coming on in waves. Rock 'n' roll revamped to jumpstart a generation and Stan Sokolov. Sixties music proclaimed a new future. Potential had felt like money in the bank. Growth was foregone, slow but certain, like a seed, germinating. The new emergence, unforeseen, came on irrepressible sounds hinting new life in and out. Stanley's heart opened, and so did his mind.

A pilgrim on the bellbottom byways was presumed irreligious, a pagan refugee. A great wave of youth sought asylum in something so simple as a frame of mind, rethinking what had been forsaken: nature and love. And peace. Stanley knew religion from bar mitzvah training and High Holiday services with Pearl. He'd fasted for Yom Kippur; those things fulfilled her. He didn't get it but didn't press.

The Jewish things had been easy. Pearl knew he went along to please her, and she hoped that going through the motions would establish a pattern of enrichment. She extolled Jewish strength and endurance as characteristics as worthy as sporting attributes often glorified in media. She reminded that recent challenges had roots in history, spanning generations of persecution, scapegoating and random acts of hatred. The Holocaust was made worse by complacence and denial. Her key lesson: those who ignore history are doomed to suffer again. And if people are ordered into two lines, one will be for Jews and the trains bound for Madagascar. The other line will be for non-Jews.

Any young Jew knew that Madagascar was Third Reich soft talk for Bergen-Belsen, Birkenau, Buchenwald, Dachau, Ebensee, Flossenbürg, Gross-Rosen, Janowska, Kaiserwald, Mauthausen-Gusen, Natzweiler-Struthof, Neuengamme, Nordhausen, Plaszow, Sachsenhausen, Ravensbrück, Stutthof, Terezin, Westerbork and more, concentration camps, midway layover often bound for the dead end: Auschwitz, Bełżec, Chelmno, Majdanek, Sobibór,

Treblinka and Trostenets, extermination camps. Jewish youth did not usually memorize these names, but Stanley did.

Madagascar was a tropical paradise, where honest work would shorten the war, and everyone was well fed and would soon go home. Madagascar was a figment. The Reich propagated the promise. Most Jews are smart enough to read the writing on the wall, but what could they do? They could resist and get shot.

Stanley Sokolov researched in his *Encyclopedia Britannica* and crunched the numbers: six million Jews into twenty-four concentration camps funneled to seven extermination camps and gas chambers and ovens. The Final Solution pipeline ran daily for years.

Pearl said, "That was a few years ago. That's nothing in history."

Stanley said, "Well . . . It's . . ."

"It's nothing in time. A blip from then to now."

Stan knew the score, more or less, but wasn't concerned. *What? The Nazis are comin' to Chi-town to take over the trains?* He thought it but wouldn't say it. He didn't feel righteous, not theistically, politically or personally. He thought Israel evolved by necessity, do or die, but the Jewish state was not Chicago, except maybe for similar Jewish density. He could not begrudge her fear or feel the threat. Power and money ruled the world. The Third Reich used Jews to mobilize hate in German people, who went along because others went along—because hating others absolved the pain of being themselves, and a loud voice encouraged hatred from a podium. The lesson of those darkest hours came from a new angle, when *Bubbi* admonished in orthodox certainty and grandmotherly obscurity: "You can change your noses, but you can't change your Moses."

What? Change his Moses? What an odd phrase. And who would want to change his Moses or his noses? Stan had a big nose, angular and distinguished, more Roman than Jewish, actually. Such was the genetic difference between *Sephardim* and *Ashkenazi*—between Jews of North Africa and those of Europe. His nose hooked handsomely, like a nose of conviction and Roman lineage. How could a Hashemite nose genetically descended from North Africa be Romanesque? Well, the patrician view required a bit of imagination. And a young Jew in profile could make them wonder. In any event, Stan would not change his nose. But he wondered what the hell she meant.

He understood Bubbi's little ditty before too long. It wasn't so stupid, considering her life of practicality. She came off the boat from Austria in a former century with a bowl of sugar, as if to sweeten prospects. They snatched it from her little grasp, to hear her version. Introduction by way of theft stuck in her craw. Life would not be so sweet in the New World, and she still demanded, "*Gib mir meinen zucker zurück!*" She wouldn't get it back but dug in for traction in teaching. Stolen sugar and the Holocaust defined reality. Noses and Moses underscored the harsh truth. He got it. A Jew who denies his blood will board for Madagascar—he may board anyway, but in that case should be blessedly cleansed with that blood and rage.

Germans at the epicenters, Berlin, Munich and Dresden, denied Nazi affiliation by 1946. What? Nazis? Not us! *Nein!* But Jews had been rounded up, easily at first; they were so obviously Jewish. The rest got flushed, like game in hiding, down to a single drop of Jewish blood. No denial, connection or nose job could save them.

He would ponder Jewish endurance, but in that rare time of late youth, he sensed more godly presence in the music of the day. Guidance felt more natural from Dylan, the Byrds, Janis and Jimi. He saw the world anew, perception refreshed. Magic glowed on a simple directive: dig it. Long hair with headbands, beads and bellbottoms defined the Young Turks of the New Wilderness. As a force of nature, youth minions ditched the bullshit to join the flow. Psychedelic drugs sped things along like rapids heading over the falls. Chaos and grace struggled for better or worse, with vision.

Youth held the promise. An acid drop delivered the goods: the rock legends rainbow and original rhythm at sundown, sunrise. Days and nights became extraordinary. Rare time had begun. Sokolov, now, here, got down to quarter notes, sixteenths, eighths and on in to the first tone, which was *Omm . . .*

It didn't happen overnight but in a brief span of seasons. Did he transcend or transmute? That answer took a season or two more. Stan Sokolov went beyond, to nowhere and everywhere, morphing inside out. Every cell in a human body changes in a seven-year cycle. Calculating the makeover as a percentage function of the last seventy-seven minutes, from gantry to launch pad to liftoff, he concluded: *And in the end. . .* He laughed like a hyena without end.

He saw perfect meaning in a *Zap Comix* adventure, eight frames of Professor Natural, beginning with a fly-swarm on dirty dishes, ending on a sparkling sink and dishes stacked in a rack. The last talk bubble said, "Don't mean shit." Stan laughed again at pure wisdom; it didn't mean shit, if only we would let it, and he could.

What? Did I just think something?

Or it could mean shit, which made him giggle again. The uncles and aunts dismissed Stan's sad change. "It's a phase. He's gung-ho for now. Just wait until you know what." They longed for his return to normal aspiration for girls, grades and getting ahead, even as they saw him too far gone. Jews have long factored anxiety as cultural, measuring severity at each depth. Past farmisht or confused, *verklempt* or overwrought, beyond *fablunged* or tilting off his rocker, their Stanley, the golden boy, who would not shed his heritage like disposable packaging, loped headlong for *meshuga*, which is crazy and no two ways about it.

Tanta Flossie put a finer point on it: "*Meshugana hünt* is what!" Even with no two ways about it, a little spice helps clarify. Crazy dog translates literally from Yiddish and cast Stanley in greater doubt. Tanta Flossie was miserly, critical and worse. She would die in solitude, which just goes to show . . .

Never mind. Those closest saw that Stanley was crazy, off the margins. All the family loved dogs but could not deny the *hüntische* aspect of Flossie's indictment. She pointed out that a hyena is part of the canine thing, like a dog with an evil laugh, like Stan.

"Have you seen him lately?"

"Seen him? Have you heard him?"

"Did he study hyenas at the state U?" They'd seen and heard and assumed hyena research. They didn't snigger and took no joy.

Stan erupted in shrill falsetto when Bubbi rolled her stockings from her jellied thighs to mid-calf. It wasn't funny. But Stanley shrieked, as if a *dybbuk* was in the wheelhouse. The malicious spirit howled again when Bubbi kneaded dough for baking and tore off a clump to throw in the trash for the poor people in Israel. It wasn't funny. And when she mumbled prayers before and after eating, using the bathroom, passing a doorway, hearing good news or bad news . . .

Stan couldn't explain her behaviors or his, but the times they were a changin'. The suburban lie was over, and so were religion and superstition. He went hyena because of or in spite of or lack of. He laughed loud. People stared and winced.

Hey, *some people know about it, some don't . . . nitty gritty.* Rhythm and blues could quell the beast, could move his mind on rock-a-beatin' boogie with funky lyric of no meaning. He'd well up to a shiver in the shoulders, as aunts and uncles ignored or denied him. He knew they could feel it, some of them, but they suppressed it. Who couldn't feel it? He'd been assured of superior intelligence. His genetic pool was deep. The family had a basis in perceptiveness and fear. This new stuff seemed unholy and nuts.

Some prayed for rehabilitation, for Stanley's return to the fold and normal daily life. Alas, the genie would not go back in the lamp. Stanley did not resist suburban stability but raged against it. The new generation saw the world of complacence in a rear-view mirror. Self-satisfaction in a void yielded plastic-covered couches, highballs, country clubs and cookie-cutter houses. Success had no soul. Affair, divorce and remarriage on the cul-de-sac got what? Another round?

Change felt ambient and profound. Questions sprouted like spore growth. The Holy Grail was fun now here. The oldies could be dead and not know it, but not the youth brigade, getting down in the goodness abounding. Cost no longer tallied in dollars but in constraint; how much glory might I lose on holding back? *That* was the revolutionary question. Moorings parted. People drifted to the astral plane. Plastic-covered furniture, shag carpet, little rooms still as mortuaries, a scent of old flesh, the common prescription for life and death—no adventure and nothing unplanned—all that and more bobbed up from the muddy bottom, flotsam of the forlorn time. What a goof. Hair grew like seaweed on thousands of sisters and brothers newly bonded in revolution and nonprescription stimulation, natural, free flowing and unemployable.

Stan Sokolov took a while to gain shoulder length; his hair was so curly. Girls fingered his dangling locks, called them cute and whispered want. Sok blushed, and that was cute too, open and vulnerable and so tall. When a girl reached, he would bow to deliver. Giggles and curls could go to whimpers. Stan didn't mind. Touching felt natural in passing, free of constraint, alive and fun.

Moving from home, from neurotic family stuck on his recovery, he went forth, into the world. Roots shriveled. Indifferent to material loss, he pondered essence, thin air, dust, sky and so on, often defaulting to raucous laughter. Could a hyena howling in a solitary forest indicate nothing funny? He laughed short and chewed on the paradox, that former home and family had come to feel outside of everything. That seemed severe, a denial of blood and trust, until he laughed louder than a hyena should, as if urging all into all.

With practice, he could ignore distractions, like hunger and sleepy time, where and what. Free of mundane coordinates and chronologies, he drifted. One day he rose like a nymph with four wings and big eyeballs and soared to blissful heights in a purple haze.

Shirtless and barefoot in pink pantaloons, he danced on a street corner to no music. Passersby shouted platitudes of the day from the other frame of mind. The war in Viet Nam had caused a rift in America. One side yelled that he should love it or leave it, or that he looked like a girl. Stan laughed from across the divide, staccato and crazy. That shut them up, moved them along. His gangly size seemed hazardous, too, like crazier yet, for better and worse.

Stan Sokolov took solace in a society of peers. Decades later, the general population would smoke dope for medical relief or harmless fun or as an alternative to alcohol. Dope became familiar. In those days, pot blossomed from the bohemian core to the new generation. Sokolov's social set gathered at the Friday potluck with lids of Mexican laugh reefer: Acapulco Gold, Panama Red or Michoacán. A Morocco sojourner might offer hash spirited home in the freewheeling time, before sniffing dogs and x-rays. With pipes, chips, nuts, cookies, rolling papers, Boone's Farm Apple Wine and the *pièce de résistance*: the latest Zeppelin or Jeff Beck, Joe Cocker or King Crimson, they sat around the fire in their soul. Giddy in reunion, they rolled, loaded, poured and savored survival one more time. They shared a sigh on the brief hiss, until the needle hit the downbeat. They smoked and drank, ate and loved, passing out of Friday to Saturday, when they smoked and played in the sun or rain. Some played on to blessed Sunday, stormy Monday, ruby Tuesday, Wednesday and the other, because they could, for freedom and momentum.

Simple repast, like spaghetti with Chianti, could cut the edge when the LSD came on. Familiar forms of lysergic acid diethylamide felt like new family: Electric Neon Jesus, Owsley, purple microdot, orange barrel, blotter, and Stanford clinical. Time slowed to particulate reality and infinite measure.

How can the infinite be measured? It can't, which came around to everything. Or some shit, leading to hyenas calling in the forest.

One night, Stan Sokolov discovered kitten love when two walked onto his chest like spirits. At orbital altitude, Stan cooed, "Kitty, little kitty, little bitty kitty, kitty caat . . . Keeeteees!" A longhair rolling on the floor in his jammie bottoms with kittens on his chest seemed unhinged. But it was only Sok, tripping on a goof. A few compatriots laughed at kitty love and the wonder of it all.

In another galaxy, Pearl Sokolov prayed for a return to Earth. A mother knew: Stanley's apparent madness had not displaced his presence of mind. His practical concern proved it. If a kitty got spooked, Stan went still and purred. He got it on with kitties at the state U or in Pearl's apartment, when neighbors brought their new kitty, and Stan went to the floor. Was he whimpering? Kitty romped among his curls and came on board to challenge his nipples. The neighbors didn't like Mrs. Sokolov's son beaming maniacally and drooling along with kitty. They chuckled nervously.

Pearl observed with hope.

Stanley had got good grades in chemistry, physics, rhetoric, price theory, metaphysical poets and prose and the rest. He'd been coherent and comprehensive as a freshman at the state U. Most of his profs said Stanley could do better. He'd grinned or laughed, until subjects became irrelevant, outside of everything, and the process grew tedious. Who could teach better than the greatest teacher of all?

For him, the bigger subject was identity, clarification of self in a new context. He and it came in and out of focus. Another subject was destination, though he felt well on his way, down the road.

He quit. Good grades unnerved him. Formal education threatened a loss of presence in the blissful ether, where minimal needs, no schedules and righteous sounds felt eminently correct. He wanted into the best place, not the worst.

Stanley kept his nonstudent status to himself. He didn't inform the university or Pearl but holed up in a rambling flat in town. If asked, he was still a student, a transfer to the University of Life. Ha! Questions were rare. He got on as a pearl diver at The Hofbrau House and thought it karmic. The new cosmic order had rent and groceries covered for merely washing dishes. The job was so rote, he could do it on mescaline, and if the trip went higher than the dishes got stacked, he could stroll into the night, let them wait, the dishes and the job. Expendability seemed perfect in the firmament.

Besides washing dishes and serving pizza, he seldom got out. He spoke less, a goofy kid who laughed alone in public. Nothing changed in his social circle when he quit school. He'd been fading anyway, attendance spotty, often leaving class early, by request, after giggling at a bird in a window or a wrong point of view. Fellow students saw the error, as Sok preempted Professor Tedious with, "Gheee . . ."

Friday gatherings relieved much of what the week had wrought, until those hallowed eves were so loved, they went daily. The best of life in amazing times, like all else, would one day pass. Until then, the pilgrims flocked to a house near campus for joyful ablution to the spirit upon them. The orbital life felt lovelier with acidnauts suiting up together, caring for each other and drifting from the mother ship to wander in space, each according to need.

LSD, mescaline or psilocybin led them into the night, to seek and find. Weekend tripping seemed prudent for conscientious students or draft avoiders still enrolled in the real university, who needed good grades to get ahead in life or passing grades to maintain life, away from Viet Nam. Weekend psychedelics allowed Sunday for reentry.

Sokolov was flexible. Fridays were beautiful, and so were Tuesdays, on campus at the University of Life.

Boyish frivolity did not fade but gained depth. He could gaze off any time or blither like a fool or expound on the modus operandi by which a rational society could fuck itself in the ass. Mordant or talkative, extreme, logical and troubling, he begged the question. Who behaves erratically and speaks profoundly but a nutter? Or a professor addressing his single student: himself?

Sokolov stared or muttered. He rolled on the rug with kitties.

JoAnne Johnson, a classic beauty with raven hair, striking green eyes, a brilliant smile and dazzling figure, pointed out one sundown that Sokolov's *schlong* was hanging free of the yawning fly on his jammy bottoms. At twenty-six, JoAnne's allure was that of a glam elder, a vintage beauty who fit in, despite her age. He followed her gaze to his member and came back up with a "Gheee!" He seemed crazier than minutes ago and drifting.

The tale would be told among college boys: "JoAnne Johnson? Are you kidding?" The boys ogled JoAnne and thought of her often in private. What's the difference between a coed and a woman? JoAnne Johnson. She had a boyfriend. So? Many women had boyfriends. Even more had former boyfriends. So?

Again, a mirthful essence released this circle of friends from former boundaries. Joints circulated for life support, buffering new times, setting the haze for whatever. Clowns of the Round Rug matched the ratty furniture, wobbly lamps, stained shades, paisley cloth hung from the walls and beaded curtains on an alcove. Tassels, trinkets and symbols filled in, perfect décor for Revolution in a nation of no nation, on the front lines, in the trenches.

Sok lay there like anthropomorphic spore growth.

JoAnne stared in an odd tableau: the Age of No Reason. Mexican dope made most things funny. In another classic goof, truth unfolded out front. Sok looked timid and wild, lovably crazy, clean and correct.

JoAnne leaned to grasp and hold it up. "God, your schlong is huge. And dark. Why is it so dark?"

Sokolov grinned like a pooch who may have erred but couldn't tell how. "Gheee!" He didn't know why it was dark.

She leaned closer, as if to engorge, but sang into it, synced to the music on the box: "You can't always get whatchu wa-ant . . . But if you try sometime . . . You find . . ." JoAnne harmonized with Mick Jagger, taking a joint with the other hand and putting it to her lips. She paused, deciding which missile to kiss, joking, kind of. She released Sokolov's schlong and took the hit best suited to the moment, even as the circle felt primed for the greater beyond.

Billy Keene laughed loud, happy in the world and JoAnne's boyfriend. Billy loved Sok for his total removal from desire, greed or deadly sins. Sok demonstrated freedom from want. Sok was advanced in real life and shored up the fringe at Billy and JoAnne's.

Also twenty-six, Billy had stayed on to finish his doctorate. What else could he do, get a job? Eligible for the jungle war until his recent birthday, he'd sweated it out, as the body count climbed. The kid had helped, because the government hated drafting Daddy. Billy and JoAnne's baby girl had been relevant to Billy's survival.

She whined. JoAnne went for crackers. Billy said, "Three already. Thirteen years till her first beer run." He torched a bowl and sputtered that it was a breath of springtime next to a hot mop any day.

Billy no longer sweated the draft or his PhD dissertation. He sweated over a tar bucket instead, for a few bucks more. He called his doctorate in history good as done, once he could figure out what to do with it. Meanwhile, he'd make better dough pitching roofs. He said he'd marry JoAnne, too, once he figured out . . . Billy and JoAnne were old, grad students, but in the groove.

Stan Sokolov was unique among sideshows in the cavalcade of freaks, prophets and casualties whose trips seemed one-way. His view set him apart. He was slovenly but not dirty, casual but not careless, crazy but not stupid. A few burnouts seemed blocked on returning, never to be seen or heard from again. Not Sok. He didn't return and went gaga as any burnout but came around in wee hours with cogent news from stellar planes. Or so those who trekked that cosmos perceived. Sok told of what others called indescribable. He turned on a light, so they could see. The coherent agreed: *Man. Sokolov.*

Among the circle of friends, two poets in the graduate creative writing program agreed, that a graduate program for an art form was a goof. Yet they dressed to type, black berets over beards, neckerchiefs, baggy shirts and pants, all beige or gray, blue or black, with white socks and beater shoes from Goodwill. Also sweating the jungle war, they smoked *Gauloises* or *Gitanes* or Camel straights in a pinch, confident their mystical, lyrical views would earn 4F deferments easy as iambic pentameter.

One nodded in a set piece, keeping the beat on imaginary bongo drums, scatting the rhythm.

The other rhapsodized: "Sok is like a . . . like a pupa, man. Yeah, cocoon emergent, shedding goo, spreading wings. Fly away from dew-damp dismal swamps of bacterial-borne society sinking in woeful woes and woe is us."

The bongo guy stopped, went snake-eyed and said: "Mindscape rolls to distant plateau. A tree in moonbeam makes shadow where possum hang out."

Nobody suggested that Sokolov was ordained or preordained or destined or karmically derived, least of all Sokolov. Rhyme, reason and Sokolov drifted in space, frozen solid until thawed to fluidity. Sok articulated what defied verbalization for many, replacing doubt with laughter as a grammatical form. And he was, simply, a form of being.

Things were and would be.

A few friends got the joke, or the supposed joke that triggered his laughter, no matter how subtle, softly touched, amorphous or invisible he was.

Some laughed again later; joke on us . . .

Hima Lujans

HL had been around, a communal klatch on the fringe of the fringe, a wet spot under a slow drip with a small radius. Hima Luja would gain momentum as these things can, offering direction in a wayward world, its perspective unimagined for some, a homecoming for others. As a cult or a commune, HL would become a black hole in the fringe galaxy, drawing remnants from other groups as they disintegrated under pressures of practical reality.

Transcendent or transmuted to suit your needs, Hima Luja's stardust emissaries also embraced the transferrable plane, by which assets gravitate to the core, until personal value is weightless, the best way to be. Greater glory takes more time. Fun and work can pave the way. New wealth includes singing and dancing, loving and forgetting.

Sok blushed on first sight of them, swaying and chanting, finger-cymbals tingling, as they beamed with viscosity. When a man yelled from a pickup that they should get a haircut and a job, they oozed like flapjacks swamped in syrup, cloyingly sweet and gooey. The man called again: "Yer lazy, and yer dirty. And by God, ya piss me off!"

Even a dirt farmer could see through this bunch. He got no response but more happiness, so he called again. "Ya ain't fooling nobody with that happy hippie horseshit. Bunch o' fuckin' draft dodgers is all ya is. Oughta get yer asses over to Viet Nam. That'd teach ya." The Viet sentiment gained momentum, as blissful Lujans pressed the book at airports, calling it free! The book would reveal magic. "Please donate," they softly said, proclaiming the title like news clarions: "Hima Speak!" Nobody wanted a three-pound book of obscure fragments—make that a compilation of thoughts from Hima Luja. Among the nuggets: *The light within can be without.*

And: *The treadmill mouse runs circles up and down.*

And, for a brief time: *Be what you is, not what you is not. . .* Wait! Cut! Cut! That one got removed, by hand, as it were, with scissors, after missives on corporate letterhead from NBC in regard to copyright laws and *Mr. Wizard*, with respect to Tooter Turtle and pending litigation. Ah, well. Not to worry; real wizardry would prevail. Meanwhile, a few passersby now and then accepted the hefty tome and donated as requested. And so it came to pass that Hima Lujans in orange jammies were like any hustlers; the book wasn't free. HL grew, soliciting in public places, but taxpayers don't need that crap, even with aery-fairy finger dances. Especially when the song-and-dance sideshow included males eighteen to twenty-six and eligible for the jungle war. Public perception throbbed in a nation fighting tooth and nail for liberty, somewhere, somehow.

A smaller gap separated frolicking goofs and a used-to-be-brilliant kid, watching in awe. Blind to lame antics or feeling connected at last, Stan Sokolov stared at something stranger than himself, something niched in society. Hima Lujans had each other. Taking their joy at face value was like seeing kittens at play, and he called, "Gheee!"

They saw him on the verge, curious but tentative. They wiggled the fuzzy yarn, so he could pounce and knead and know he'd gone around and come around. He didn't spook. They matched his squeals and giggles, feeding his freedom from rationale. They laughed with him and at him, daring to be offensive. At one in oddity, they bonded.

Stan Sokolov grew up in secular times. World War II ended with soldiers coming home and the war machine going commercial. Exceptional victory spawned exceptional affluence and babies. Zoysia grass made for exceptional yards. Exceptional split-level homes had modern appliances and air-conditioning. Filter cigarettes, highballs, automatic transmissions, power steering and brakes, rocket-ship fins, social prestige and more, more, more seemed exceptionally overdue.

The Sokolov household went along as it could. Suburban comfort put distance on ghastly times. Distance and comfort felt remedial to horror and deprivation. Jews felt secure in a stable world, but with crimes against Jews so recent and personal, they knew: the trains to Madagascar could roll again—unlikely in America, though Charles Lindberg ran for president as a Republican after being asshole buddies with Herr Hitler in the newsreels. Lindberg lost but got thousands of votes; no discussion required. Lindberg faded, along with the *Time/Life* WWII Book of Horrors. It went to a drawer in the hutch. Nobody needed to see it again.

People knew but didn't dwell. Some Jews sought a cleaner fit in society. They'd been sullied for no good reason. They adapted for greater distance on Holocaust association. Not exactly changing their Moses, they called him regular Joe. Londsman Rosen became Rogers; Goldstein became Goodson; Shapiro hid behind Shipley.

World War II happened. A few years was time to heal and forget, time to deny. Viruses don't go away but into remission. Holocaust denial was a symptom. How can something that happened not have happened? And why say it didn't happen? The *Time/Life* WWII Book of Horrors came out of the drawer, but dwelling on morbidity seemed morbid. The Jews took a header. It was over; back to the drawer.

Spiritual paths of the '50s and '60s attracted young Jews seeking an alternative to what had failed, seeking meaning in crazy times, present and past. Buddhism made sense, Tantra, Rinzai, transcendental, and so did Veda, Sufi and Whoyou.

Hima Luja felt familiar, like Hasidic Jews who followed the *Baal Shem Tov,* the master of the good name. The Baal Shem Tov founded Hasidism to remedy ghetto confinement, oppression, pogrom and scapegoating. The Baal Shem prescribed song and dance to cure suffering. Jews could have asked: *What? Are you nuts?*

But the Baal Shem's compelling example discarded asceticism for real world joy. He made lemonade from bitterness. Where did he get the sugar? Just dance and sing, heart and mind. And so they did, embracing the removal thrust upon them

Money lender was a job suitable to Jews. Nobody prohibited

international banking. *Oy gott!*

Jews couldn't own land in Eastern Europe, never mind science, the arts, literature, painting and music.

The Holocaust banned Jews from living on Earth. But they do, excelling further in medicine, diplomacy and stand-up comedy.

Sokolov laughed, as prescribed. Did the Baal Shem experiment with magic mushrooms that rise on cow patties after a light rain? He could have. He was out there, like Sokolov.

The Lujans sang and danced as well, gaining distance on suffering. Was this a Jewddhist path? Well, no. Jewish blood is a condition of birth. These Lujans were born into something, maybe their own private Moses. Could they or Sokolov have turned out otherwise? Hima Luja was their man of the good name, showing the way to everything as everything. Why not watch the show?

Panhandlers, uninhibited and goofy, Lujans had fun instead of doubt. Who could call them fringe lunatics, as the world wallowed in jungle war? Perfect strangers were shooting each other in Southeast Asia—these people took drugs to distant galaxies. So what? Billowing pantaloons in citrus shades, shaved sidewalls and topknots like Samurai felt better than camo-fatigues and automatic weapons, agent orange and napalm. . . No, not Samurai but soft and flaky, in your facey, strange players but hurting nobody, as war waged to make East Asia safe for Coca-Cola and burgers.

Most Lujans didn't stink, in notable distinction from those who did. Up next to a smelly one, Sok winced at the pungent combo: patchouli oil and road-kill goat. He moved away. The stinker pursued. "Why do you avoid me?"

"You stink."

The others stared, and one called out, "Stinky!"

A gawky guy with a shaved skull stepped up to play a ditty on his finger cymbals and sing. "Hima Luja. Hima Luja. Luja Luja. Hima Lu-uh ja." Transferring two little cymbals to Sok's fingers, he led a refrain. Sok got it. The gawky guy said, "I am Viga! Great Viga! Viga grandé!" His accent sounded *Español*, and all his finger cymbals went to Sok. Viga pulled a kazoo from his folds for another round.

It felt like nothing but fun, removed and questionable as all else but fun, worldly, jolly fun. The gregarious Viga did not seek formal recruitment with an oath, a signing bonus and benefits contingent on surviving the jungle war. Hima Luja did not point a finger from a poster: *I Want You!* Viga wanted anybody who didn't fit but could fit in. Recruitment came to singing, dancing and kazoo!

Sok stepped up and back, left and right, tinkling cymbals, beaming beatifically, not seething but unhinging to carefree connection at last. He looked silly, detached but bonded on arrival at last to one heart.

Best of all, like the shortest or longest journeys, this one began with a single step, and step two went to the wild funky chicken ad infinitum.

A Frat Boy from Hoosierville

Finger cymbals, saffron jammies and giggling seemed a sure fit, but to call Sok a short circuit in the great schematic would understate what became of him. He'd given up conventional modes of development, beginning with formal education, ending on denial of expectations, his own and those of others. Family and friends expected conformity, as if by rights. Stanley declined those tenets deemed normal, begrudging happiness to none and all, himself foremost. He followed his calling.

He ditched the ballast to rise again. Clothing, posture and movement had been at odds with social norms, even in those days of bellbottoms, long hair, beads, brocades, conchos and fringe. Sokolov never looked conventional but like a lost nutter in his own private wilderness. Hima Luja fit, no adaptation necessary.

Speech patterns commonly default to jargon or slang, to buzz phrasing of a subculture or demographic. Sokolov's patterns articulated the inner core, flowing forth. He wondered if cliché and platitude abounding could indicate earthly attachment or weakness in so many others. Right on, far out, dig it, lay it on me. Sok kept silent as the better part of syntax. Silence comforted, though few of his new housemates responded in kind. A rock group called Blind Faith seemed ironic; blind faith had steered the world to a ditch. But Blind Faith hailed truth and beauty, too, as a basis of artful pursuit, a means of redemption. He sang along on his fave, "Can't Find My Way Home."

JoAnne Johnson had stared at his dick and grasped it. He'd watched it like a foreign movie with no subtitles. Did he desire so little? Could he be so indifferent to a young man's desire? Could his hormones be dead? Probably not. The little joke with JoAnne had caught him by surprise. That was all. As an older woman, a vintage classic and iconic beauty, she seemed worldly and wise. She'd dismissed another taboo, the blessing in hand granting insight on mild shock and laughter.

Some people are asexual by nature. Stan Sokolov had pondered co-eds, technically women but much younger. His experience in genital contact was rare and long ago, when he owned a blue blazer for formal wear and a madras sport coat for fun, along with penny loafers and a button-down shirt in blue oxford cloth. He'd worn the fun ensemble to a fraternity party, his fraternity, in a set piece, all the brothers dressed like birds of a feather, pouring gallons of grape juice and grain alcohol into garbage cans for commitment. A soul band and co-ed dates, some from "the best" sororities, rounded out the pursuit. As a freshman, he'd learned that seniors were cool, and so were some juniors. Upperclassmen could look like carbon copies—clones were still decades away—but madras patterns and colors could vary. Some boys wore white shirts instead of blue, and some substituted paisley for madras, daringly but sparingly, to avoid jeers and slurs. They all wore khaki pants, with or without cuffs, depending on inclination to tradition or trend. Stan Sokolov giggled at khaki variables, these early tremors signaling the quake to come.

He had a date with Sally Tompkins or Eleanor Thompson or Mabel Thomas and after the bash went back to the frat lodge and the back room, the lounge, as instructed. Fifty years of brotherhood photos festooned the walls of that hallowed den. Sofas lined the perimeter, spaced so groans and whimpers remained anonymous, in the spirit of discretion as befitting a high-class outfit. The sofas ranged from mottled beige to mottled mauve, mottled gray green and mottled brown, with the lights on. Lights off took a bit of memory, but finding a vacant section of sofa, a brother and his date could sit.

Stan's date breathed on his neck. He giggled until she planted her lips onto his. A senior brother had been on a date with Sally or Eleanor or Mabel and counseled Stan that she would choke the chicken, if properly warmed, with the patience and poise befitting a true gentleman. Most fraternities maintained themes, like animals, science or math geeks, spooks, nerds, jocks, wealthy Christians, upper-middle-class Christians, practicing Christians, Christians with Polynesian pretense and so on. Stan's fraternity self-framed as Jewish aristocrats, as if a bunch of young Jews could claim aristocracy in the heart of Hoosierville and behave like upper-crusters. The brothers were "poised," their actions "befitting." Pledges carried two hankies, one for nose blowing and the other to wipe up the goo. Rest assured: the goo could happen from a hand other than their own, and they would soon learn how. Such were the benefits of brotherhood.

Among fraternities in the traditional animal niche, none admitted bestiality, but all seemed barnyard ready. Sok's fraternity scorned lowbrow behavior, so he giggled at guidance on getting his chicken choked. Giggling could indicate bad attitude, but pledges were so unseasoned, he got away with it. He giggled again on advice to carry three hankies on his date; she was poised and willing, as befitting a woman associate of the gentlemen brothers of Zeta Iota, any of whom would serve her needs with the poise and style . . . The debs could count on them. Stan packed a third hanky with another giggle, making attitude a possible issue yet again.

Alas, she knew the lounge in back. He felt good, following her lead, after all. She set his hand on her breast. He squeezed gently and firmly, quickly and slowly. "Wait a minute," she said. "You'd never get this." Her brassiere hooked in front, an innovation he considered new and possibly unbelievable. That is, he worried that a front loader would be a hard truth to sell later, when the brothers convened to share tales and challenges. But sure enough, she unhooked and peeled. Concern gave way to gratitude. This was it! College! He cooed and twiddled her nipples. She arched her back with hot, hurried breath. He giggled. Never mind. She freed his *schwantz,* squeezed and stroked, breathing faster.

"It's chafing," he said.

"Oh, God," she said, going down for less chafing. A young man could plainly sense a door opening on the meaning of life. First blow job gave rise to visions down the aisle and life ever after in holy matrimony with the deepest devotion a man can feel for a woman, an extraordinary, most incredible young woman—make that a fairy princess who could grant any wish ever dreamed. In soft shadow, he knew that this was love, and he was in it, and it would be eternal because it could never end. In mutual exhortation, he called God by name, as she groaned encouragement, "Mm hmm. . ."

Old Faithful changed everything back. Sok struggled against a squeal from deep within and lost, as a young man with pent-up love may do. She came up gasping, "God! What is wrong with you?" Stanley Sokolov didn't know what was wrong with him but felt embarrassed and awkward at the formidable mess he'd made. Worse yet, love forever had ended in a blink, or three blinks or five. He wished for a few more hankies.

Later that night, as the rowdier brothers straggled in and down to the dining hall to compare notes, Steve Schmultz reached his apogee: "And I'm begging her, please! You gotta help me out with this thing!" The show ponies whinnied, and Schmultzy turned to pledge Stanley. "Did you show her how a Jewish princess eats a banana?" Schmultzy, a very cool senior, casually grasped the back of Stan's head. Stan jerked, resisting an aspect of hazing as yet unanticipated. The older, cooler brothers laughed again, some of them patting Stan on the back, assuring him that the man-to-man bonding process was the real nitty gritty; it's why they came, but no, they did not blow each other. And it was on, the gristle and bone of frat life and men becoming brothers.

Stan felt marginally relieved and knew they had to be guessing about his date, even though he'd untucked his shirt to cover the crusted mustard. Shirttails showing were strictly *faux pas* at all times, except to cover gusher stains. A pledge might think of untucking as a convenient comfort after hours, but he'd be wrong!

Or untucking could have been a ruse. But would the quiet, reserved young Sokolov be so brash as to untuck with no mustard to cover? He seemed sincere, so maybe the shirttails gave him away. Two other brothers had their shirts untucked, something a Zeta Iota simply would not do, but both of these brothers had regular girlfriends and were getting serious, one pinned and the other more serious still, lavaliered, both on their way to matrimony, so a hand job or blow job would be nothing for them. But Sokolov? Surely, he would not untuck unless he had to, with the discretion and poise befitting a . . . Shirttails showing verily underscored a frontline engagement. Untucked? At ZI? What else could it mean?

With a manly laugh, Sok said he hadn't asked for anything. From around the room, skeptical eyes zoomed in, disbelieving, challenging. Let them guess. Oh, they wanted to know, but he knew that sharing his Sally/Eleanor/Mabel adventure would fill her dance card six months out by sunrise. A surge of distrust rose like bile. He thought he'd get over it. But he'd get no second date, because her soaring popularity would leave him high and dry as befitting a poised blabbermouth. He also gained status in the clan, his prowess perceived; only a man earns the curious admiration of others. He would one day hang in the hallowed lounge.

The frat brothers, in low, manly tones, reminded the frosh that it wasn't smart to hoard the riches. It was selfish and stupid. He couldn't fool the brothers. Did he really think he could? Besides, the truth had to come out with so many cool veterans watching. Stan felt his defense crumbling. They knew what he'd done. They knew that he knew that he'd have to share the riches, short of giving her his fraternity pin, which he didn't even have yet and would hardly leverage at this juncture.

He spoke around the riches, avoiding specific details. "There was no love," he said. "No love." The brothers laughed lowly: this up-and-comer had nailed it, maintaining the poise befitting a pithy truth, admitting the emission of no admission. One brother walked away, reminding the others that a man needs his space and earns it when the bird dogs sniff a bit much. The other brothers played it cool, trying to remember her last name or sorority or dormitory or any lead available to facilitate a call ASAP without sounding too eager, maybe for a study date in the morning or something.

A scientific fact of frat lodge life: it could get no better than with regular blow jobs, ideally from a co-ed. Studying came easier, time freed up, recreation fit in, and things in general rose to a level of relaxation as yet unknown. The brotherhood would pursue dates with Sally or Eleanor or Mabel, who had been known for hand jobs. But this . . . This marked Sokolov as a pledge to reckon. Or some shit.

Sok thought about her and did absolve his distrust by moving out of the frat lodge on Tuesday, ditching his blazer and madras sport coat, his button downs and penny loafers on the way. He kept the khaki pants. Why not? They'd break in soon enough.

Two elder brothers tracked him down to advise that he could not quit Zeta Iota; the mere act of quitting actually violated fraternity bylaws. Sok didn't giggle but closed the door, the new door to his rambling flat in town.

Hold the Mayo

Twelve years down the road, rock 'n' roll turned to new wave and punk, the Eighties already. Sokolov lived in *The Hima Luja Temple for the Sanctity of Souls Having Fun*. At thirty, he sensed the person he would become. A young man of few words seemed wise; youthful innocence felt fresh. Foolishness was part of life. Females admired this olive-skinned, gangly guy with thick, black curls. Looking into his sparkle, they dropped in slow scan to make him blush and giggle. Sok went along in his way, silly and shy, which encouraged them no end. Hima Lujans called open sexuality natural, simply natural or purely natural. Calling an appetite natural could reassert essence, as necessary, like poised and befitting, but more relaxed. HL women and men assured Sok that loving freely was a beautiful, honest part of life with Hima Luja. Foremost among them: he who first eased the kid into rhythm and flow, who slipped little cymbals onto the willing fingers and offered solace in a gentle song and wild kazoo.

Viga was older and would have been a grad student when Sok was a freshman at the state U. But Viga was bold, not cool. Sok reflected on women, circumspect to the point of circumstuck. Viga encouraged him to jump in. "*Vamos, mi amigo! Esas mujeres son deliciosas*!" Viga was from *el sur*, and he laughed, "What, you think I would talk this way if I came from Booneville?"

Sok wagged his head. "Why are you Viga and not Vigo?"

Viga raised his kazoo: "Viga! With great Viga! You know? Like JFK?" Sok went along; Viga was so ebullient and friendly.

More casual than boisterous, Sok took intimacy in stride. He didn't often think it grotesque or graceless but anticipated regret in casual sex. Love could be natural and beautiful, but naked abandon seemed foreign. Mom and Dad had been casual in life, which seemed natural to a child but not beautiful. Mom was anxious, balancing her lot with hope for a better future. Dad was melancholy, his regret suppressed in his drive to get ahead or break even. Happy on the surface but sad just below, he lived the delusion, that material gain could have spirit. Sok blushed to imagine Pearl and Morris getting it on with viga or vigor.

He'd looked up to Billy and JoAnne. He'd admired and loved them. Why not? They took him in, accepting who he was, no matter who he'd been or might turn out to be. Sure, things were simpler then, including love in an age of discovery. Friendship evolved on experience and light rather than fraternity affiliation or family connection. Billy was an early scout on the new frontier, curious and willing to *break on through to the other side*, like The Doors lyric. Billy had no regrets, setting his dissertation aside to make a few bucks in the roofing business. When the business made more money than an associate professor ever could, or when JoAnne got preggers and soaked up every dollar he made, he worked harder. No regrets? Billy didn't give a shit! Billy reached for another swig or a smoke, a joke and a laugh at this, the life we have.

Family connections and fraternity affiliation could make a difference in life. But Billy ended up teaching acceptance instead of history, as if by choice. Billy was a mentor and perfect host. JoAnne went along, setting doubt aside, depending on Billy for strength.

Sok waited to feel that kind of kinship and love among the Lujans but was wise enough to know that certain feelings of the past would not be duplicated. He had sex once in a while, more or less in polite exchange. He had no intimate with whom to share. One-on-one with himself seemed a good match but most often ended in stalemate. Others watched him find his way, lost in space before joining their orbit, a smiling, bright-eyed guy who spoke rarely and didn't mumble.

Twelve years on the scene, he moved easily through the HL Cosmos, steady as a stellar object. Love? Who could tell about love? Love would come from within and out. Meanwhile, other needs awaited. Giving felt natural and necessary, whether giving a book or a moment, in love or a facsimile thereof.

Years melded, their count superfluous. But rare moments stacked up to make a man wonder. Sok counted insights as a measure of time. A movie outing with his mother, to please her, lingered. A boy of eight didn't take well to musical romance, and *The King and I* was no different, slogging hopelessly through one dance and another. He endured, as Pearl lit up, enthralled and whispering, "She's in love!"

He replayed it, her escape to the big screen and epiphany, that dreams come true in movies.

She'd marveled. The magic was scripted, with sets, costumes, casting, caterers, directors and producers, with grand lyrics and a masterful score, a bevy of full-flounced dresses and a massive cast breaking into song and dance from easy conversation. Pearl had a vision, a miracle come to life.

Why did love at ground level seem so different? Why were Pearl and Morris in their Chicago flat so removed from Siam?

Well, Stanley was a kid when Deborah Kerr gave her heart to Yul Brynner, when Pearl sighed at the meaning of life and fantasy and that rare, blessed confluence of the two. Little Stanley thought the mushy parts tedious, but twenty-two years later, at the domicile he called home, he still thought romance a trick of nature. The gravitational pull of Slot B for Tab A must lead beyond courtesy and gratitude. The exchange should be neither clinical nor dependent on flirtation, and potential should be more than a cul-de-sac.

Or maybe love is a delusion, self-imposed.

His failure left him doubtful, especially with a naked woman. An imposing phantom had brought them together, but if she had bad breath or a coated tongue or body odor or motor mouth, or none of the above but seemed perfect in every way, it didn't work out so well. In coming years, he would accept his limits, for better and worse. With tolerance and understanding, he might become detached from these petty concerns and be a better person for it.

He remembered, as some men don't, that judgment goes both ways. He observed new women, as if newness might bear different fruit. His infrequence in the mating act made some females crave his attention, to see if their wiles could gain it. He laughed at that, too, to himself, having learned that random laughter can give a woman pause when momentum seems best.

Sok's cool view was known but not discussed. Was he aloof? Or gay? The women concurred: not gay. But why would he decline the hot buffet? He didn't decline, but rather than belly-up to all-you-can-eat, he opted for the exotic entrée and saved room for dessert. Or he preferre a book or a project, alone. He took comfort where he could. Would love come along at random? It could but didn't.

Time passed on courtesy, respect and mutual admiration. He couldn't return admiration all the time but appreciated the challenge. All the world was a cult compound, and he strove to make it better. Was his emotional shortfall the same absence that haunted Morris? Maybe, but solitude seemed better than strained compatibility on a recipe called marriage.

One evening led to the next, lights out and thoughts flowing, *merrily, merrily, merrily, merrily, gently down the stream.* Daily life ran the gamut from comedy to drama, according to him who knew best. Hima said: "Things are. Things happen."

Hima Lujans thought their guru brilliant as sunbeams, which, like God, should not be faced directly. But they basked in the light.

Hima isn't God, but then who is? Sok laughed short at the God within, reaching stalemate again and again keeping mirth internal.

Hima was everywhere, like God but with more tangible presence. *Would that be like Jesus?* Sok laughed aloud, couldn't help it.

Hima Luja, the man, took note of Stanley Sokolov, his big eyes and cool head bringing logic and less crazy to the scene. Wait a minute. Less crazy? No. Sokolov fit right in, another chronic fuck up, a howling hyena who could out-goof the goofiest. But he had another side, where he often divined what he couldn't deduce. How did he do that? What was he up to? Others wondered, until the next sideshow got their attention. Did Sok have something up his sleeve? He knew things, intuitively or mystically or maybe from school—not likely, but it didn't matter. He looked busy, alone and thinking. What he didn't know, he found out. He searched to solve, mundane problems mostly, hangnails on daily life. Applying logic to unhinged situations, he stayed above the fray, a cool mechanic in a melee of mystical fun.

They called him Doctor Webster or Professor Britannica for the dictionary and encyclopedia in his cubby, where he brooded until emerging, informed. He shrugged off those names, neither aloof nor superior but blessed with a practical nature. In that phase of rediscovery, he descended to terra firma and rose in the social order. He loosened knots, freed logjams and dilated the impenetrable. He didn't stop in the middle for a quickie or a nap or idle chatter leading to a quickie and a nap.

Innately and obviously smarter, he took the lead. With growing confidence, he ingratiated those long gone from real-world challenges they could not meet.

Tainted sandwiches became a milestone. Years before veganism evolved, a vegetarian diet was fringe radical. Mayo was key. Salmonella hits mayo at room temp. People in the world knew this. Imron and Zinco worked as a team, pumping gas and cleaning windshields, even as self-service gas pumps came in. They made the world a better place. They alternated cleaning and pumping and spoke of the fine points of each. As airport all-stars, they set up near Pan Am and alternated again, dancing and jingling and selling books.

Pan Am people flew farther and had more money. Imron and Zinco did okay, until paying the price on bad sammies, hurrying home on gut sounds and pressure.

Sok sleuthed it to salmonella, recalling Morris yelling down the hall to "use some goddamn sense!" Somebody left the mayo out. Sok solved it, and a wise aura shone like a halo.

Imron and Zinco revered Sok for assurance of nonpossession. No dark spirits or bacteria remained. That same week, heading back to the airport, they stopped for new protocol: a bag of ice. When only half the ice fit in the cooler, Im and Zinc looked to Sok, who took the bag to a truck pulling in.

The guys in the truck said, "Fuck" but did not say "fuckin' fruitcakes" or "what the fuck you lookin' at?" Already 1982 or '84, the hippie days were gone. Guys in a truck and cultists could still bristle. But the truck guys put the ice in their cooler. When one of them laughed short at the orange jammies bunch on a second glance, Sok laughed back, full hyena, to make a point of no point. The truck guys left. Another resolution had saved the day. Nobody got salmonella or beat up. The Pan Am outing went well on thirty books at ten bucks each. All agreed on beauty in nature.

Back at Central Compound, an old house in a blue-collar area, Sok lay down for a rest. Sheila came with flowers, a grand bouquet she'd gathered from the neighborhood. She lay beside him and rubbed his thigh, praising his beauty and love. Easing up to the pendulous essence, she chirped. She revealed him and made short work of relieving him.

He groaned and rolled over. Sheila was a physical therapist, known for her skills. He didn't ask for shoulders and neck, didn't need to. Nor did he ask who else made her beauty-love roster. He relaxed into a terrific rub. He'd viewed her physically and mentally but regretted the exchange. He loved her hands. She looked good, smelled good and felt great. He thought he would revive soon and try to please her and fell asleep.

Love and rubs were given, like compensation. Or Hima Lujans were happier than most, trading the world for frolic. He felt part of a great experiment in making things right for those who'd felt wrong, who didn't fit. Could a child of middle-class entitlement, who'd never gone hungry or homeless, fail to fit? He could. He'd failed the social norms aptitude test. So-called rational society could not adapt to his world view. He was a bad fit, or a good fit for a different society. He feared that comfort and convenience for a single species would rule the world until both ended. Hima Luja was refuge.

Insight happened and got him down the road. Lujans infused their days with a dose of crazy to better resolve their pasts. Having given everything to the cause, they were burden free. The future upon them felt secure. Hima called them "our people," affirming them home in the Land of Never Never. He spoke in loco parentis, in place of parents, and they listened like children. Our people, in their thirties and forties or younger and older, saw the world as he did and took HL as the antidote. Silly shit cured them. Nobody gets out alive. Lujans could be happier than most on free sex, no hunger or fear.

Sok wondered one day where it could lead, catching himself on a reach for too much practicality. Why must anything lead anywhere? He knew progress was a myth, a delusion, a pit with bamboo skewers below a thatch covering—he laughed, as Viga entered.

"He beckons." Viga grinned, having stated the obvious, and he clarified, "Hima wants to see you."

Sok sat up. "Hima wants to see me?"

Viga slapped his back, assuring that reality could include a personal chat with Hima Luja. "Hima sees you. He likes you." Viga deferred to Sok's shyness. People loved Viga for his energy and strength. Even Hima cheered Viga's antics. "Come. Time to visit."

Rising from his futon felt like the old, giddy liftoff, back when a ratty sofa was the launch pad, LSD was a Redstone rocket, and he blasted off, searing the stratosphere to inner space.

"What did he say?" Sok asked.

"Bring me Sokolov." Viga looked grim.

Sok followed, leaving the capsule for the deep unknown.

Hima Luja lived at the Summit, sanctum sanctorum of deific vibration, adorned with mystical totems, osmotic absorption and yard sale treasures from many outings. He loved his stuff and regaled the compound with tales of bargaining skill, Jewing them down like Hymie. He laughed, "Hymie. Hima. I dunno veah it comes from!"

Sok noted these slights, a sensitivity of the birth condition, but set them aside, as all laughed in good cheer, after all.

The Summit was an add-on bedroom with a high ceiling and private bathroom, connected to the main house via hallway. Doors at either end made for privacy. Few mortals had been to the Summit. A sign outside the door said: *Our Leader*. Hima's accent, starched German, was hardly sinister, given his great good cheer. He'd ordered signs to read *unser Führer* but got corrected and translated to a better nickname: Mr. Wizard. Hima loved it and had the accent long before the cartoon guy. The Mr. Wizard sign was sweet vindication on NBC and its tyranny over what should belong to everyone. Beyond that, Hima was no cartoon. He was real; only wizardry could get these tumblers falling into place, opening the doors of life as it could be lived. Hima Luja created joy and mirth and made it work, a private society in beauty and love. Viga often asked through his kazoo, "Who else could do that? Jesus? Maybe. Buddha? I think so. Mohammed? Hmm. . . Cat Stevens thinks so." They laughed.

Cat Stevens was somebody, another headliner up to snuff, keeping historical company with Jesus, Buddha and Hima, proving the point one more time. Belief in magic helped make magic. Hima Luja—the man and the institution—made sense at that elusive level called perfect. The sexual gravity of the place also bonded, providing the glue to hold things together. So? What was up?

Viga backed off at the hallway. Sok entered with trepidation.

Hima Luja greeted like a wizened elder. Silk strips in white hung around the chamber from the picture molding, billowing to the oscillating fan. Sok was six-five by then.

Hima looked up from down at six-one and nodded. "Success comes to tall people when others admire those they look up to." He mumbled about midgets and dwarfs. He scorned short people who tried to control. He said basketball players, even the Black ones, *jene schwartzich reisen*, don't do that. They just play. He laughed at Sok, *der klutzy Jude*. Sok laughed too, couldn't help it, even as phrasing stung. Sok took it as a joke, insensitive but not malicious, if he could lighten up. Let bliss come in. HL worked his magic. Sok felt the higher power. They embraced in the breeze, until Hima eased back and said, "You iss von."

Sok said, "I am von? Ah! I mean one!" He blushed.

Hima was familiar with emotional breaks in proximity to his radiance and pressed on. "Gratitude is a great thing to feel. We feel it. Your gratitude gives me warmth."

Sok nodded for the truth of it. "Hima . . . I know who I am."

"You do? And you are?"

"I'm . . . home. I am one." Sok laughed again, not a chirp but manly. Hima squinted at the source of Sok's bravado. Sok's forehead bunched, and he laughed again for no reason in baritone, a self-defense that recalled the old frat lodge.

Hima nodded. "Let's take a minute. Please." He directed Sok to a cushion close to his own, form-fitted to contour. Folding so many big feet and long legs in the narrow space between them could have triggered the old, shrill eruption or worse, the calamitous tumble, rolling about and worse yet: squealing and drooling. Or that silly shit could have been magically blissful too. Or not and never mind; they sat like craftsmen weaving a wicker sculpture.

Hima led in silence. Sok followed easily, as eyelids lowered. Sok thought about giggling but held strong.

After thirty minutes or forty, Hima Luja sighed.

Sok followed, opening his eyes to Hima's scrutinous grin.

Hima said, "You are Sok."

Sok nodded.

"Stan Sokolov. I think you are . . . Jewish?" Hima actually said, "I zinks you ah Chooish?"

Sok had an ear for it, the German lilt similar to Zeda and Bubbi's Yiddish but different, with the jackboot . . .

Let it go . . . Sok nodded again, relieved to have the Jewish factor behind them or at least out in the open, where they could laugh as necessary. Silence reigned a minute more, until Hima Luja declared that the blessed man before him would forevermore be called Solomon by all who knew and loved him.

Sok wondered who in the compound loved him. He counted Viga as a friend over the years and asked, "Solomon?"

Hima stared, until Sok gave up a chirp, more like a chicken than a hail-fellow, fidgeting but not upending the rare balance at hand. Putting his mind elsewhere to ease the pressure, Sok recalled Uncle Sol, who died of rectal cancer after complaining for years holding bowel movements for hours "because the *vacocta* rag business won't even let a man relax for a good BM. I wait so some *schnook* won't have to wait for me to answer the phone. I wait for meetings to end. What are you gonna do?" Uncle Sol died of what Stanley and his cousins called asshole cancer, agreeing that they didn't want any asshole cancer and swearing they'd never hold a dump for the rag business or schnooks or meetings. Sok didn't mention Uncle Sol or his big fat gut and stinky cigar that he chewed for hours, unlit.

"Solomon," Hima said.

"Sol Sok?" asked Sok.

Hima said, "Not Sol. Solomon. It's marvelous. It's wise, like the Hebrew king. It's you. I've been saving it. For you."

Sok looked up. "Solomon."

"Solomon Kursh," Hima said. "You have your one-name people now, show biz and media types, artsy people. It's a big part of what we do, the entertainment thing. Exposure makes it fun. But you have the Kursh in case you need a last name. It's best, if, perhaps, we want to do something in another country. The one-namers play hell in immigration. Why fuck around if we don't have to?"

"Why Kursh?"

"Don't question. No. It's okay. I'll tell you why. You know what I do? What we do? Don't you think? I do. We turn words into actions. Actions do the work. You might say the actions are the work. But we follow through, and the work takes care of itself when the actions are properly executed. No! I don't mean executed! When the actions are implemented. Yah! Implemented." Hima went to inner dialogue, mumbling the mother tongue to get it right. "*Nachsehen bie der klasse führer im geschichte . . .* Yah." Peering again at Sok, he translated: "Take the class leaders in history. Actions get what they need. It's like you, working all week for a paycheck on Friday. You don't. I use workaday as an example. You avoid that treadmill by choice. You make choices from first steps to last, from far away to coming home. People confuse our work, but the work keeps us. That's more than I've explained to anyone. How do you do that?"

Sok blushed again and said, "I don't know."

"I know how you do it. You are the Hebrew king. You can split a baby or get it wholesale. Yah, Herr Solomon?"

The young man before him could neither split an infant nor get it wholesale, but Hima let his dry wit sink in. "Creation began with a word, and the word was Om. All other words fade in the wake. Mish mash, bubbles! When words find harmony, we feel meaning. I feel Kursh. It sounds right. You see? You get the phonetic overlap as well. Krishna. Kursh. We'll take it. I don't begrudge much, but those Krishnas want it all. So, we take some back. Okay? Good, Yah?"

The young man formerly known as Sok gazed upon his master. He smiled, emotional, sitting taller, blinking like a guilty man, trying to absolve his cult mentality, his simpering capitulation, mindless obeisance and failure of fortitude. In accepting a new name from this man, he preempted comprehension with faith. Blind Faith?

Buckling under the years and what they'd wrought, he sobbed.

Hima mumbled more mumbo jumbo about pupation and emergence, dewy wings and flight.

Solomon Kursh felt soggy and limp, waiting.

Hima stood to help his ward up.

Solomon stood, dabbing his eyes.

Hima Luja laughed a manly guffaw to clear the air.

The younger lowly intoned, "I'm Solomon Kursh."

They embraced, until Hima sat again to talk business. Solomon would oversee the Central West, Northwest and Southwestern Regions on travel coordination, sleeping arrangements and meals for HimaCon, the upcoming Convergence. Hima gave him a clipboard, paper and pen. "You're like Moses. These are your tablets."

Solomon received and, like Moses, kept his yap shut, constraining the fact that Moses' tablets weren't blank.

Hima said, "This is the beginning. Our people work. I look at our Sokolov—now Solomon—and think why he's not working. And I think, Oh! He is! You are a Jew! Very productive people, always working . . ." *a Chew . . . alvays verking* . . . "and getting into trouble, mit der mischief unt der money." Hima nodded sanguinely, skipping the part about banking in specific regard to *Deutschland über alles*. "You're thinking. You meditate and contemplate, and you know. But! A Jew must have management. Lucky for you and me." He paused to let the load settle. He perked. "Some of our people seem *verrückt—meshuga*, you would say. Maybe you're crazy too, but you'll be in charge, as long as I'm here. Maybe longer."

Solomon knew exactly what to say, which was nothing.

Gentle understanding sustained him. Coordinating travel, rooming and meals felt tedious and rote. And dull, but when he sighed, Viga admonished, "All you have to do is don't fuck it up. Come." They joined a bunch headed for a mall to sell books and sing and dance. The mall was worse, a hub of foolish pursuit, not the stuff of life but flotsam after the blast. He wrote his thoughts down and offered the orange book. He let it go if they took it or not if not. They paid or didn't and kept it or left it on a bench or the floor or a trashcan. He bagged the money and shagged books left behind to sell again and shag again. "Maybe you're crazy too." He said, going to mantra, "tomaybeyocra zytomaybeyo crazytomay beyocray . . ." Hima had a point. May be.

Viga cavorted out front to draw attention and boost sales, dancing the airy-fairy funky chicken, blissing out, making no sense of it all, underscoring the wicked truth. In two hours, they left.

Back at Central Compound, Solomon sat up, wondering why, how and when, when a fissure emitted light to the high plateau. "Maybe you're crazy too," he said. A mouse on a shelf stopped to stare. "Selling stupid books over and over is foolish."

He'd blushed, and he blushed again, for sobbing, for guzzling the Kool-Aid on cue. He'd surged on being chosen but recoiled on review. He sensed a pattern. Three hundred dollars was a casual take at the mall. A Pan Am outing bagged a grand in March and April. Roadside fruit stands were ripe all summer, colorful, lively and bountiful. The HL system brought in the moolah but never enough. Hot in the summer, cold in winter and don't get sick. Medical support was a tube o' goo and a sticky strip, generic. But they'd stopped for necessities: beer, old produce, marked down, cleaning agents, toothpaste, bread and mustard—oh, and a pair of Dingoes for Viga at the specialty boot shop two doors down. Total cash out: three fifty. Nobody said boo; he was such a great guy and worked so hard, traveling so much and needing to look sharp.

Why did Hima make a point of promoting a Jew and urging him to keep the common touch with book sales and floor mopping?

He scratched the shayna-punim head, no longer brimful of potential but aching on a new disjunction: Solomon Kursh made no sense. The puzzle filled in by intuition and phone chats, comparing notes, regaling satellite compounds with tales of Hima, himself.

The people loved their guru and craved color and more color. Compounds were spacious, dingy dumps, paid off long ago. Safe haven from anxiety and refuge for the spiritually advanced, they endured on food stamps, govment cheese, good cheer, no maintenance or upkeep, no payroll and no rent. And no tax, because religion is sacred in America, and HL had no money.

Hima Lujans lived on sandwiches and yard work. Book sales and tepid showers. Yard sale clothing and furniture. Casual sex made the world a beautiful place, along with dancing and singing. Jobs or small concessions balanced their time. Viga set the pace, traveling to other compounds to validate joy in life.

His three duffels seemed odd. Shirts? Clean skivvies? He didn't wear skivvies.

Solomon pondered mischief, defaulting to type.

Hima's routine was rote: lunch and defecation, *mittagessen unt eine scheisse* in the vernacular. He ate, belched and counseled regularity for a happy life. He used the toilet off the dining room, for expedience and windows. Lunch and a dump ran noon to one.

Bubbi said Tuesday was lucky, because light was mentioned twice on the third day. Bubbi seemed relevant in a default of her own.

Tuesday noon, in the Summit, Solomon cleaned like Columbo, feeling baseboards and windowsills, moving furniture, rolling rugs, dusting shelves, peeking behind an expressionist nude. He tilted vases and lamps and removed the duct grill. Sorting fabric remnants, old reports and ratty towels, he found a book, *Women in Love*, hollow. Beside the book: a journal and ledger wrapped in a rag.

Each line showed numbers and letters: dollars and people. He needed a sounding board. HL accounting felt wrong, but what wasn't? What was a jungle war? Or a weapons deal? One man's morality and all that—Hima Luja morality was better than war, or had seemed so.

Solomon had viewed his new job as a path to a position. He would manage for efficiency and growth, which felt, uh, corporate. Never mind. The money had gone away, as life got colder and hungrier. Hima Lujans scoffed at affluence, as Hima assured, "You are earning the wealth you can take with you!"

Solomon thought he might ask if the accounts needed balancing. Who better than a Jew with management? He might say nothing. Either choice would measure him. He could keep his yap shut and tap the cash flow, calling it reallocation or misc expense. He could ask Viga. As the wild and practical yin and yang of it, they could talk.

He mopped, pondering former potential in nuclear physics and think-tank economics, hedge fund trimming and astronaut training. He could have been a surgeon, a judge or president of the United States of America. He mopped. He already had the astronaut credential. Glowing like a heat shield on reentry to Earth's atmosphere, he would begin his descent to normal life. He sensed inner vision turning out in a mirror universe. He mopped and felt better. Viga would know what to do. Wouldn't he?

Hima shuffled in for his lie down.

Time and the mop sloshed onward. Money flowed and vanished, like the mountain that was but wasn't. Solomon said,

"Donovan still has it, don't you think?"

Viga raised his kazoo for the refrain, "Oh, Juanita, I call your name." The mountain stayed gone.

On a practical note, Viga confided that it was no secret: Hima Luja the guru had been Henry Lawrence, private citizen. So what? Names get changed. A private citizen crossed the great divide to make magic as a guru.

Solomon blinked at the HL phenom, an epic play in one act. Could the fall guy, formerly known as Stanley Sokolov, get caught out, holding the bag, while the guru crossed another divide to thin air with the contents of said bag and Juanita?

Puzzle parts drifted into place. Solomon went down the road, for perspective. Parnelli drove a taxi, graveyard mostly, where he could relate to other weirdos. Off-duty, he drove the limo. Solomon said they needed a better mop bucket and wrote the requisitioned for the deluxe model with a levered squeezer for mechanical advantage and easier compression. Requisition documents, dated and stamped, were part of the new Purchase Order Protocol developed by Solomon K. He stamped the form **REC'D** and stamped it again **APPROVED**. He filled in the date and headed out with Parnelli. The limo had been a hearse and got reincarnated as a rock 'n' roll bandwagon prior to life with the Hima Luja. Solomon sat in back for the brain room most available there. Parnelli asked, "Tunes?"

"No."

No reason had been a code to live by, but the rationale of no rationale ran amok. Was he only paranoid? It happens.

The people had grown older. Some drifted off. New people

were fewer but seemed smarter, more in the world. Hima had wrung his hands over so much chaos. Viga played Hima's complaint on kazoo.

The headlights came on. Who would steer with a rocky coast drawing nigh? Had they put a Jew in the wheelhouse so the officers could steal away in the lifeboats?

Solomon had granted his guru the benefit of all doubt, deferring to cosmic alignment. He made an awkward turn-around at the industrial supply place where he got a new mop bucket. He threw it in the trunk, and they cruised home. "Parnelli. Tunes."

Hallefuckin' and Hima Luja

Life got better at Hima Luja. Solomon worked it, singing, "First there is a mountain, then there is a mountain, then there is."

Viga blew it on kazoo: "First there is a mountain, and nobody took it away, so here it is."

Hima asked, "Vudju hoff der Grey Poupon?" He laughed loud for the benefit of those who didn't get the joke.

Hima's good cheer would survive him. Meanwhile, the people felt secure, grateful for Hima's guidance, for Solomon's management, Viga's strength and for Grey Poupon for affirmation. Stupid stuff be gone! Let a guru be happy.

What had Solomon seen, cruising down the road? Hima asked, after seeing him go in the limo.

Solomon said he'd seen the need for a better mop.

Hima waited.

Solomon blushed, caught in simple truth. "I saw hope."

Hima smiled. Solomon Kursh had learned the play.

Solomon smiled back. "Vision happens." *Whatever the fuck that means*, he thought but didn't laugh or smile.

Hima nodded wisely on an oblique glance; trying to see.

A ramshackle house for misfits hadn't changed but for morale; it was up. Top-drawer mustard was in. It cost more, but what price love? Solomon said it cost no more than sunbeams and seemed a bargain at twice that.

"Hallefuckin' and Hima Luja!" called His Radiance from the billowing Summit. It felt like another sideshow.

Solomon pressed on.

The frolicking fuck-all begged a remedy. The people wanted the wonder years redux: youthful innocence, year in, year out, with family support. They wanted feelings of well-being through sexual anarchy, to have their cake and eat it too. But anarchy has practical limits, and sexual abandon became something less than magic among them. Beyond that, they bandied radical terms like "sexual anarchy" and "free love" to support the notion of radical independence—as they flirted, batted lashes, held hands and courted like kids. The single difference between this warm-up and the one of the ages was the end result, in this case every time, at least once. Repetition indicated good.

Beyond sexual anarchy as self-proclaimed superiority, no kids could have nonstop sport fucking or develop stable psyches if they had. Most boys stroked the fantasy, but that's all it was. Solomon introduced with structure. No, not structure, but loving options. What a circus it had been! Kids love a circus, until they puke from too much cotton candy and realize the animals out front are abused.

Many Lujans shared a bedroom in youth. Some shared a bed. Snug rooms and beds were part of middle-class life when the people were kids. Many kids in the '50s and '60s had little room to spare. And here they were, all grown up and sharing a bedroom. A person could lie down and sleep, if moaning, groaning, don't stop and calls to God allowed. It worked for some, not so much for others who needed rack time, undisturbed.

Solomon split the baby, making peace and quiet a viable option. Complaints against communism and fascism led him to explain how opposite ends of the political spectrum actually meet, end to end, full circle. "Yeah, yeah, yeah," he got for his trouble, but the problem was solved. Rooms in Category 1 allowed frolic by choice. Those who just needed some fucking sleep went to Cat 2 for women or Cat 3 for men. Gender distinction seemed extraneous but helped mitigate spontaneous love disturbance. It happened, though rarely in the gay quarter, where room sharing deferred to logic and taste. Cat 1, or romper rooms, were short term, experimental, in the tradition of free love. If good, consensual lovers could move to a room of their own. A love date seemed far from anarchy and required arrangements, awkward and not spontaneous but more stable after dark.

Common sense carried the day. It wasn't wizardry, that sleep through the night yielded blue-chip returns. All categories tingled at dawn with yawns and stretches and nary a whine or whimper. What was that sound? It was golden silence lapping the beautiful shores of our dreams. The sense of it seemed easy and obvious, even in Cat 1, where free lovers got to it, got on it and got to sleep without the usual fuss, repeating in the night as necessary. Cats 2 and 3 also chugged like locomotives but on the Sleepy-time express.

With no orgasmic eruption to waken the slumberous and no complaints, they slept like babies or sensible adults.

Solomon's simple solution brought solace to all and to all a good night. Peace settled as well on the select one, Hima, or Henry, as Solomon had playfully experimented.

People aged, as they do, and mostly grew into a world of proprietary beds, made up with clean sheets as primary occupants saw to it. Even anarchists, Solomon explained, need a bit of responsibility.

On another lap around the sun, Solomon took a few grand off the top each month for the Better Living Fund. All compounds pitched in roof repair, lawn chairs, a window-unit AC for a cool room, area rugs, dishes, pots and pans and so on down the line for comfort in life.

Viga said comfort is not the way, on his way out. He traveled first class. He stopped playing kazoo and got scarce. He grew dour when once-willing women tired of his tireless thumper. He could arrange a Cat 1 room but had no reason to, really.

A message emerged in the ledger that year. Deposits were noted but not made. Solomon asked permission to audit, to be safe. Hima took a moment and said, "Yah. Vy not?"

In honors econ, Stan Sokolov had learned inverse variation on dollar value, depending on a dollar's origin, whether it accrued as savings on overhead or came in as revenue. How could a dollar be worth more than another dollar? Easy: one dollar was retained with no expense, while the other dollar cost ninety cents to earn. He first saw the difference in Price Theory 404. The calculus depended on a constant ratio of overhead to cash flow, with overhead fixed. If the ratio fluctuated, a small business could fail. He'd summarized the paradigm in lay terms, advising Professor Bow Tie that, "On a 10 percent margin, a dollar saved is nine dollars earned."

Most lecture attendees saw the professor shake his head, but Sokolov saw something else. This erratic student had refuted a price corollary that he, Professor Bow Tie, had strained into three semesters of analysis for the last forty semesters. Alas, Bow Tie had nothing to add. Class dismissed.

Revealing numerical truth in a single sentence was satisfying, but Bow Tie's embarrassment was not. Young Sokolov did not seek one-up but to correct what had no basis in fact. Bow Tie recovered on realizing that Sokolov's theory had been his own all along. Sok missed the remaining lectures by way of youthful indiscretion but heard that Bow Tie came out of his funk to ramble the point to submission as he, Sok, drifted to the wilderness, no longer a student, neither employed nor employable, seeking nothing, laughing insanely, seeming lost. Besides all that, the other students cared not for savings or earnings or differences in value beyond the value of a good grade to secure a stable future.

Ironically insight on fluctuating value with regard to cash flow and overhead *and* pricing was out of character for a hippie, back in student days. But as the '90s gained depth, Solomon applied his overhead/revenue formula to cash management at HL with effect. Any money manager will sharpen his pencil sooner or later, and he wondered how fine a point this #2 might take.

Economic cycles turn like seasons or fortune. *First there is a mountain, then there is no mountain, because somebody took it away.*

He'd been a fool by design, in spite of his brain. He'd traded a frame of mind for no mind. Like a fool on a hill in a world at war, he'd found a niche. What changed? He loved chaos and chance and incidents of no coincidence. His niche changed. He'd seen the inner workings as a watchmaker sees a movement. This movement could deliver. *Because let's face it: Twenty million is a load o' coal.* Money moved with the precision of German engineering. *Do I see something by staring at it long enough?* Yes, situation clarified.

Solomon imagined himself in a bow tie and cheap suit, up front. He was the student as well. *But here's the thing. Everybody called him a genius at this or that, but all he did was get good grades without doing the work. The subjects were hard sciences. And college courses are not the real world. And he got an F in expository writing—he didn't attend writing classes either and faked that one too on a genius summation at the end, but . . .*

Okay. What's your point?

My point is that I have known things without trying, seen things without looking. And here I am, knowing and seeing in the dark.

Can you clarify your meaning?

I mean that this Hima Luja organization is a timepiece, wind-up or electric or self-winding, a mantel or wall clock or an overbearing grandfather—there's what that smelly fuck would glom onto, the self-deluded, self-inflated guru.

Wait a minute.

This inner repartee led to another difficult truth and another movement. Call it a movement in stealth. No, discretion. Better yet: discovery. Discovery included three military medals, each with a swastika and eagle on top, all snug in the hollow book, *Women in Love*. A swastika flag rolled and stashed in a cardboard tube had leaned in a closet corner. A bayonet rolled in burlap lay hidden under floorboards in another corner, where nobody stepped, unless he did. And an odd needle, crude as a nail, along with wooly rags, was stuffed under the mattress with two small jars of dark green sediment.

So? Hima had been a German soldier, as seen on a photo ID: Heinrich Lohrenz. Any German his age could be suspect. But if a nation elects a maniac, are all its citizens culpable?

Solomon had wondered what to do but couldn't know, beyond biding time on making life better and waiting to see. Hima seemed less threatening as a grandfather clock than as a war criminal. And who could say he was a war criminal? Germans denied participation; they'd only followed orders. They hid their Jews in the basement. They meant no harm.

But a young man becomes a grown man on a test. Stanley Sokolov had challenged his elders on action. He'd heard of the Holocaust and browsed the ghastly photos. Years later, he stared at artifacts and felt catharsis, in which old questions are answered.

What is a war criminal? Hima wore a toga with no skivvies, as if a schwinging schwantz proved liberation. People ignored his odor and exhibition, surrendering mindfulness and income, as cultists do, oblivious to time ahead. But did raunchy habits make Hima criminal?

Could a brainy kid called Sok indict a man for being German? Did Solomon just compromise personal values for convenience? Had he betrayed his Moses by ignoring his noses? Or did he contemplate a violation of the most ardent Commandment?

Kill Hima? Should a Jew kill? Should a Jew kill a Nazi? Would a Jew kill a Nazi? Is germ the root derivative of germination?

German?

Hima has no worries? He's old, a bygone Colonel Klink put out to pasture, calling for more fun and skimming cash. Why did he change his name from Heinrich to Henry? Names get naturalized. But why did a cult run on a starvation budget?

Ah, the rub. Just as Jim had jumped into a longboat in long shadows; so could a cultist jump ship to the material world. A man called Solomon could simply leave this make-believe world. He had his health and his wits. Life begins at forty, so let it.

But this is not the Patna and I am not Lord Jim. Unless this compound is a sinking ship, and I am keen on survival. Life can imitate literature, but we have no fear or honor here. We have goofs and low voltage. Vindication intercedes in the shape of our noses, some of us. In our Moses, some of us, comes forth a notion that seemed far-fetched not so long ago. Or was it?

Noses and Moses when last considered had rendered insight. But Mr. Moses could walk in with his thumb up his tuchus and not know Solomon Kursh from Harry Fischimull. So?

So, Solomon contemplated growth and its converse, pro and con.

Timothy Leary's Dead

Viga split in '92. He called it a pilgrimage but didn't come back. Hima said he went south, maybe Mexico; homesick, to open a compound for *amigos*.

Solomon thought Viga escaped.

The puffy old man formerly known as Heinrich Lohrenz, took a downturn a few years later. He would croak and turn to dust. Make that ash and cinders in a beaded bag, to sit on a shelf, where the people could praise him.

Solomon pondered.

Wisdom and accountability will vest in me. I can kill him by all that's holy and unholy, moral and immoral, ephemeral and eternal and skip town. I judged the old Jews who sat on their tuchuses, wringing hands and gnashing teeth. I called them inconsequential.

Or, I can let evil pass away, return to Chicago and live in peace, another helpless elder. And what could a killing provide, a final solution? People kill in war, and wars wage on. Heinrich Lohrenz is jovial and loved. And we have the ultimate commandment. Thou shalt not kill.

Wait. Thou shalt not kill Nazis? Forget it. What else?

You'll always be a murderer?

Fuck it; I'm vegan!

He will haunt you?

Not! I disliked him from first hugs, his stink and baiting. I wanted to choke him last week. He'll go to hell or nowhere, either freely or with mortal fear. What else you got? Last call.

From where did this Jewish zeal emerge?

It's not zeal. It's survival, fight or flight, always there, never triggered. I heard his jovial voice, telling me to board a train headed you-know-where. I can decline as few could. I can render justice. Call it zeal, if you must.

Wait a minute. When did an acolyte in the land of arrested development become judge and jury on presumed capital crimes? Where are the evidence and motive? And testimony? Did Hima get the medals and flag on the fly? At a pawnshop? He's innocent until proven guilty. Do not rush to judgment.

He has the Storm Trooper tattoo.

Okay: guilty as charged.

The Chambers Brothers sing, "Time Has Come Today," and the prosecution rests, the evidence overwhelming.

Stan Sokolov could enforce and take cover in the ebb and flow. As a cult went belly up, he could vanish in thin air, like a storm trooper over South America. Hima had taken millions, leaving the Lujans out. Old Nazis leave a toxic legacy for a foul future. Should Hima pay?

Probably not; if a prime mover knew his true self: pussy. Yet he toyed with the mouse. What's to gain in revenge? Why kill a man so old, sparing him from difficult days? Why risk spiritual welfare on a crime of long ago?

He pondered paths not taken and glittering potential in politics, education, finance, commerce, science, the arts, economics or the esoteric. Scratch esoteric—he was there. Let the well-wishers be happy for Stanley the guru, a smashing success.

Does every path end? Surely murder is not a common milestone. He smiled at small irony and wondered what if . . . But of course, this was if.

Who was he kidding? Below the lowest rung, he would take a life to compensate others and rectify the past. From a wallow of dark rationale, he could crawl out or stay and kill. He could look back and laugh or cringe. The past loomed like a waste of time. What had he learned? That he could kill or walk away, with compassion as the better part of life thereafter?

A cult with a Buddhist/Hindi outlook depended on book-sale beggars in baggy jams with mostly menial jobs. They could endure no more than a caveman in Times Square. A caveman might, but Hima Luja was done. Bills weren't paid. The end was nigh. They could coast a few months, but cash was nil. Truth be told, under oath, Solomon Kursh had been inner sanctum, Your Honor, had consolidated five HL compounds. HL NE absorbed HL SE to cut overhead in half. Members migrated. Solomon made it happen as only he could! HL Hoosierville (Irreverence boosted morale, Your Honor.) continued, still a bargain on rent and groceries. HL PNW rolled to HL LA, on the bus, Your Honor, down from wet and cold and a heating bill higher than LA rent. Solomon cured chronic cult complacency on the path to solvency and decent stuff to eat.

Stringbean grumbled and came for clarification. Not so tall or humble as Solomon but more demanding, sallow and needy, he walked in asking, "Why is it always nature stuff when I want a war movie? We seen this one, all the bugs eating each other, and this movie is a classic, man. What's his name, his girlfriend shot him, after this movie. You know what I mean?"

Solomon stared at Stringbean's naked scalp and fluffy white temples, wishing he was somewhere else, and said, "Stringbean no more. You will be called Q-Tip by all who know and love you."

Q-Tip said. "Everybody knows Stringbean. What about that?"

"Find out the guy's name. Watch the war movie."

Q-Tip left for the TV room to lay it out, but all who knew and loved him laughed. Q-Tip wondered if a cultist could change careers at fifty-one and left again.

A woman who'd known and loved him followed with the remedy. He didn't care about a war movie anyway, and a matinee in her room made it all better. He and Jane agreed on want, and he smiled. "Me Q-Tip, you Jane."

Soon after, Q-Tip came again. The oscillating fan had stopped, so things hung limp. Solomon lay in repose, contemplating. HL was out for lunch and a dump. Q-Tip asked, "How much money you need, man? It's rolling in. How much you need?"

Solomon said, "Okay, Q-Tip. What's the difference between revenue and income? Can a cult save enough on nonorganic produce to pay rent for a month or two? Can we groom and dress for better jobs? Can we contribute to society, so others will donate to our cause? Well? Can we punk? Can we?"

"Fuck, man," Q-Tip sputtered. "Don't jump up my ass. I'm just sayin'. You're the smart guy. Write a book. You just said it." Q-Tip shuffled out, muttering fuck, man, what if and how much.

Solomon recalled a floppy young guy waving arms and spewing "Gheee!" Dividing years at HL by seven, he counted four and a half cellular makeovers over thirty-one years. He'd been a small crowd. He'd lost that time, but all time is lost. How many more people would he be? Who formed up in the cellular matrix currently known as Solomon Kursh? When had he returned to the rational world? Was this it?

Must the old Nazi die? Yes seemed most natural if not most beautiful. Hima only hustled a con on free sex and rent. A *goniff* or *schnorer* must make a living too. Had Lieutenant Lohrenz put a gun to anybody's head? Well, yes, he said as much. He lived again to steal the lifeblood of those seeking freedom from bourgeois needs and trusted a Nazi posing as a wise man. So?

Solomon's first step, calculated and bold, was a proposal, face to face, or rather facing the old man, who lay flat, perspiring mildly after lunch and a dump, giving new life to the old phrase: between a shit and a sweat. Solomon said, "Loans. A series of loans. If Central loans a million dollars to LA, then LA can lend that million to Hoosierville and so on round the bend."

Hima sat up for a listen. Solomon made no sense, yet, but came from crafty people who could clean up a mess as tidy and concisely as anyone ever could. Hima sniffed. "What are you talking? Why make loans? What you're getting?"

Solomon said nonprofit salaries are capped at four hundred grand for a CEO. "We spend half our take, as required, and a paper trail can keep us legal and go nowhere, liberating that million to circle back to you."

Hima gazed. "You think I want a million dollars?"

"I think we can protect that money or lose it. We could have it when we need it. We can spend more on . . ."

"No. We don't spend. It goes where we need it. Your way, they would track it."

"They may but probably won't. I factor seven to one against an audit. If they do, they can disallow and require the money returned. We pay it back to ourselves, no worse off."

"Penalties and interest," Hima said.

"A pittance," Solomon said.

"What would I do with a million? What do we need that we don't have? I think you're suggesting . . . money laundering."

"No. Money laundering is international. We'll only cross state borders. Money laundering is illegal activity on ill-gotten proceeds. We have donations. Our loans would put no cash into a foreign economy. Loans around the country would replace the second phase of conventional laundering, the layering. Layering isn't meant to be impenetrable, only thick. We're blessed with thickness. No need to make confusion. We are confusing. Lending the money to you, will bring it back to legal status, redundant in this case, never being illegal. If disallowed, seven to one against, the net is a payback. Meanwhile, we establish a thousand-year light!"

The old man gazed at a very clever Jew and the play—that by which he'd risen, on deceptively smooth moves. Testing his chosen one, he said, "You're dangerous. And the money?"

Solomon shrugged. "Offshore." The perfect setup had led to the operative word. A destination could indicate where the moolah might be. Simply precise, the gambit lured Hima to convenient enrichment as a frame of mind, and a fresh approach to cash laundering could yield more money.

"You said domestic."

"On the loan-go-round. Offshore on clean cash. It's done."

"Where would we . . ."

"Ah. You would know best."

Solomon waited blissfully.

The old man coughed and lay back down. Dead?

No, he'd take a month to die, muttering, "Ga . . . ga me . . ."

Solomon would probe, "Cayman?"

Heinrich Lohrenz would shake his head—or was that a spasm? He might mumble, "Ba . . . ma . . ."

"Bahamas?"

"Dah . . . me . . ."

"Dominica?"

"Ma . . . muh . . . Muh . . . yuh . . ."

"The fuck is muh yuh? Okay, sorry. I'm trying."

And on through the geographic panoply, in which Solomon offered money laundering capitals as translations for these sounds, to reveal the moolah matrix. Hima finally exhaled, "Sss . . ."

"Switzerland? Syria? Sarajevo? Sudan? Sewanee, how I love ya, how I love ya, my dear old Sewanee . . ."

And so it came to pass that Hima Luja lay ill as an old pope and just as mortal . . . but not so fast.

As dying people may do, he surged to wax nostalgic on life's adventure, on out-pacing what should have caught up.

Solomon knelt, arranging a machete, a bowl and a towel.

"What are you doing? Why do you futz? Where are my people? I want dancing."

"No dancing. You're dying. I'm going to open your eyes." He paused for a doubt. It passed.

Hima choked, "Foolish. Mein eyes iss hop'm"

"Not yet. We need this for my résumé."

"You're getting a job?"

Solomon shrugged. "Hard to say. I thought I'd cut your neck, here, so you could die in a minute. Then I thought better of the femoral artery, you know, for more time."

"You think you know. You know nossing."

"Tell me about the money."

"I will tell. First you listen. Then you chop me, and I die. You think I would leave my people in the cold?"

Solomon laid the machete across his knees.

"It was dark, *die flugzeughalle, nein lichten, mit der Fallschirmjäger, die elite der Wehrmacht,* three sides, ten deep, *und der oberst . . .*"

The hangar was dark but for lantern glow. The paratrooper division stood ten rows deep, as the colonel shouted about their last day on Earth. "Hard to think, *mit der* rage *unt der schpittle. Ist der* problem *mit* der fockin' Nazis. Yelling. Alvays yelling."

Yelling helped them hate. Hate got them going, but the Jewish resource got squandered. "We could have won! Look at you."

Leutnant Lohrenz reflected. None had gone so boldly as the Third Reich. He'd followed orders but sensed prosecution as things wound down. He'd served as an admin functionary, numbering and helping folks on their way.

He paused, so Solomon might envision *Leutnant* Lohrenz comforting his Jews. He said, "A Jew will not want a tattoo on the superstition that mutilation blocks the magic tunnels to Israel at death. No tattoos. Did you know?"

"Yes."

"Did you have your tonsils out?"

"Yes."

"You can't go! Maybe you won't mind. We tattooed little girls with pierced ears. I don't get it. A rabbi begged for the number with a pen, no tattoo, so he could get into the tunnels. I told him, 'You're going to get cooked, and you worry for a tattoo?' Okay, not so funny. You try stand-up on a crowd like that. What do I do? I tell him, 'I can get you in the tunnels. I swear it.' He didn't believe. Nobody's fool. I tried. We went fast; terrible pressure. But you know, thousands are not so many in six million. They say six million. I don't know. *Nacht und tag*. Too slow. They put me in a shed near the fence, where the lucky ones got my ink. You should know why. I answered to the main Jew, Sokolov, maybe not your cousin but surely your Londsman. You got my attention, Stanley. We made you perfect."

Hima paused again for perfection. "Look." He pulled his sleeve to show the small ϟϟ of the *Schutzstaffel*, storm troopers, inside, near the elbow. He called it nothing but show; he never pursued a police action, ever! "Solomon should belief, haffing seen ze antics around here!" Below the elbow: 20001 B. "So? No tunnels. Eh?"

"Why?"

"I told you: writing on the wall. Hell had to pay. I wanted to make a case. To be honest *mittchou mein freund,* I became a Jew. A rabbi called it my *mitzvah*. My lucky thing. You see?"

"Hima. Would you mind?" Solomon pulled his own sleeve and found the old needle and green ink, reconstituted.

Hima smiled weakly at the joke life can play. "Why?"

"You worked an extermination camp."

Hima kvetched like an old Jew, like family. "For you? What is one more?" He grunted, sitting up. "But why would you?"

"For the honor of the thing."

Hima poked away, rubbing an inked rag into the wound. "It must be deep. I still got it. Tell me: Do you know of vivisepulture?"

Solomon doused with alcohol and said, "Premature burial is a chronic fear for some Jews. We bury our dead quickly to avoid embalming, another mutilation, and so is cremation. Many things block the tunnels. We want to go to Israel when we're dead, so we live in fear of vivisepulture. But you know this."

"Yes. Do you see the foolishness?"

"Look who's talking. I had my tonsils out. Now I have a tattoo. But the God of Abraham understands practicality and Jews. I'm here for this. It feels correct."

"You are wrong."

"I've been wrong. I want to make it right."

"Yah. The God of Abraham hates to inconvenience His chosen ones. They don't feel good on Yom Kippur and cannot fast; no problem. *Vas iss los?* You think an SS man could skip an order if he doesn't feel good? How nice to be a Jew, except for a few tough years. What do you call that, the inconvenience that God forgot?

"*Mein* Solomon. My Jews knew me. I assured them, no vivisepulture! The ovens would not be their fault. God would understand. The God of Israel forgives inconvenience. Ach! To be a Jew, as good as dead and worried about form."

Pulled from his little shop near the fence and sent to the French coast near Normandy, Heinrich Lohrenz wound up loading aircraft for the big drop. The colonel ranted, as the paratroopers pretended acceptance, as one aircraft got loaded discreetly with rations and fuel drums for a flight to Argentina. Volunteer crew came easily on the spirit of survival, with vital equipment on hand.

Hima came alive in the telling. The Reich could have won, if only the Jewish resource got used instead of gassed, making more work and wasting fuel. He blurted: "I did not kill Jews!" Not like some—he might have shot one or two, a dozen at most, but it was war, shoot or get shot. Nazis were watching! He never hated Jews. No, he admired them, as he admired Solomon, for shrewd efficiency. He favored goodwill, unlike some. He sighed and lay back. "There. You are numbered."

Solomon dabbed with antiseptic.

Hima sputtered. "We ran out of fuel. How can you plan such a thing? We ran out!" They bailed out over Colombia, six inches shy of Buenos Aires on the map, feeling lucky to have many parachutes on board. "I felt like Jorel, going with Superboy, to Earth! Ha haaa!" A coughing spasm took him apoplectic but leveled.

And the world opened like a lotus. America fell asleep, drunk on victory. The beatniks entered, then the hippies. "I met other refugees like me, you know. We talked. Most stayed south. I sensed the north, for love, always my choice. I could be in Buenos Aires, teaching tango. But I came north to begin our work. You see?"

"You're a genius, Hima."

"That may be."

"Who do you have but us? We are your legacy."

"I have cared for you. Now you will care for them. The money goes where it is needed. You must believe my legacy is not hate. You may hear hate, but it's a stepping-stone, not a cornerstone. A tool for motivation. That's all."

Hima nodded off, perhaps recalling good cheer to soften a harsh situation. Coming to terms with his heir apparent, he rested.

Solomon lay back too, to dream of Hima on the pyre, and the people rejoicing: the stiff formerly known and loved as Hima Luja lived on. He sat up in his dream, as if to see for himself.

The people had built the pyre in the yard and chowed down on a favorite feed: cornmeal mush with scallions and cornbread, to commemorate the sad and joyous day. The people would need their strength. They woofed and hailed Solomon. He sobbed in his dream, as if to practice, and drifted downstream.

Hima moaned.

Solomon woke and eased over to shake the old man. Rummaging his kit, he said, "Thank you, Hima."

Hima groaned.

"I have news, good and, eh, the other.

"Mm..."

"I'm not going to kill you. I want to show you something." He held up a syringe, needle weeping. He set it aside to take a frail wrist and tap a vein. He paused for fickle meaning, briefly, and injected carefully, to keep the old man ticking.

Hima exhaled on stillness, eyes open.

Solomon leaned in. "Hima. You're not dead. That wasn't ink.

Or cyanide. It was the oxidase inhibitor phenelzine and the neuroleptic haloperidol. I mixed it. I love chemistry. Some of your best chemists are Jews. You know that. You're catatonic. If my Bubbi was here, she might say, 'I vant you should enjoy the show.' She was a cut-up, like you. I have to tell you, Heinrich, full disclosure: I'm getting signals that the God of Abraham wants to inconvenience an old Nazi."

He rifled his kit for a Q-Tip, a real one, and pressed Hima's chin to open the mouth. He swabbed Hima's cheek and sealed the Q-Tip in a specimen tube. "A few years ago, we got a technique, RFLP. Restriction Fragment Length Polymorphism. DNA testing. Who cares about an old Nazi? Well, *mein* lieutenant, a few Jews care. Okay, you're going to get cooked. We take this swab, because a Jew knows the value of info. It's all we'll have of you."

Hima might have had the last word, if he could. But he couldn't, and somebody called from the tunnel, not the Jewish tunnel to Israel but the hallway to the house. "Solomon? Open up."

Well, they worried and wondered, with Hima doing poorly. Solomon opened and called up the hall, "Rejoice! Roll him in silk. Not the head. He'll love the view." The people worked while he changed to formal saffron. A toga seemed suitable.

"His eyes are open."

"Yes. Hima sees. The vision lives," Solomon said, and in the familiar voice of authority, he jammed them into gear: "*Schnell! Gayen zee!* To ze pyre! Get him free!"

The pyre rose in the backyard, scrap lumber, old saw horses and signs over kindling, faggots, sticks and cardboard, buffered as best could be against stray smoke, sparks and prying eyes.

Neighbors watched. Some approached. The funeral pyre rose with to heights the world had never seen. The neighborhood had never seen such heights at any rate. And it wasn't even lit.

More neighbors watched from porches or yards, as Hima Luja got hefted up, up and up for the kerosene dousing. Who keeps kerosene? Ah! Solomon got kerosene, *mit der* requisition *unt der* approval, and he called like a clarion, "Let the light shine!"

The people lit the heap from many angles, and it soon crackled and hissed, until sirens announced county intervention. Hima watched from the catbird seat, as firemen sprayed. Cops arrived.

Solomon thought he'd got it right, after wasting a lifetime to date. Okay, not so much wasted. A wunderkind chem student had derailed but achieved small justice on crimes against humanity. He wished to share the moment with the long-gone *mishpocha* and willed them a sense of knowing in the ether, stretching on tippy toes to the man of the hour. "I know you're in there." Finding a pulse on the neck, he said, "There you are. I think you're right; a little light humor does help things along."

When the flames were out, dead out, Hima got dabbed and tidied for the ride to the crematorium, only a few miles. The masonry monolith seemed too somber, wrong for Hima Luja but zoned for incineration. The people adapted, dancing and chanting in the parking lot, as Hima eased into the furnace, a wonder of technical efficiency, until Solomon raised a hand.

He leaned close again, until eyeballs ticked sideways. It didn't feel good, prolonging agony for such a nice man. It felt like vindication, no better than the unfounded hatred of a camp guard. But he wished regret would go away, and it did.

The furnace can turn a corpse to ash at seven thousand degrees. A bonfire cannot. The people envisioned the solar glow, drank from jugs or bags, smoked dope, howled and cried in the richness of life and Hima Luja.

The crematorium director was tardy and called for the death certificate. Solomon waived him off. "What can you do, say he's not dead? Stop it halfway? The fire marshal approved this. If you need a death certificate, you should get one."

The exhaust flume belched on Solomon's retreat to the great stone portico, for perspective.

Up the steps to overview, he turned regally, like a Roman at the senate. He looked over the people. With one hand on his heart, he waved the other. They cheered and cried.

Local media honed on grief and the new guru.

A Tweak Here & There

Hima Luja faded like an epoch. With Hima gone, donations and pay checks could stick. Lo and behold, HL got media.

This Just In:

Guru Passes with No Death Certificate!

—Cult Claims "Divine Ascendance!"

Media begat media. Facts and figures jumbled on melodrama and dark potential. Adjectives sizzled: suspicious, malodorous, missing. A trailer-trash tabloid raged: Henry Lawrence had checked out in a backyard barbecue as the guest of honor if not the entrée.

Political candidates and nonprofits know that media means money. Name recognition is Step 1 in the Moolah Derby. But money following media was not to be. In a single news cycle, Hima Luja, the guru and the cult, went from name recognition to shadows. The same lowbrow tabloid shouted out: "Murder 1!"

What a joke, but alas: donations ceased.

Beyond the tabloids, Solomon was in the news. Uniquely tall and handsome, he went up the media food chain to *The Nightly News, Good Morning America, Larry King Live* and *The Garry Shandling Show*. Headliner time ended when he declined Tonight—

refusing to wear saffron jammies, ear bangles and a turban. The producer said, "You're making a mistake. You could be bigger than Tom Hanks!"

Solomon sighed.

Hoopla rose and fell. Money dwindled. Living in the moment remained a vanity but gained perspective: here today, tomorrow maybe. *The Hima Luja Temple for the Sanctity of Souls Having Fun* hung on by the hair of its chinny chin chin, as cults and communes inevitably do. Closed societies and cliquey clubs don't last forever. Devotees drifted, choosing filtered water over Kool-Aid.

Phillip Munson had arrived in 1980, an electrician who came to be known as Filament for his bright light. He left on a Saturday morning in 2000, saying on his way out, "Saturdays are my favorite. Here I go again."

Solomon wished him well, also wishing for stronger coffee or better coffee. He'd stopped trying to turn the corner or find the corner. Hima Luja might rise from the ashes. And what? Fly?

At forty-five, Solomon entered midlife, the age of crisis for some. Questions of purpose and value attended many tasks, treading water to stay afloat. Urging efficiency, he strove to break even, fending off feelings of futility. He spoke like a capitalist, managed like a communist, felt like a cultist. Oh, how far he'd come in versatility and staying alive.

What of guilt? Could a man shrug off mortal sin with Jewish rationale? He could. He hadn't killed. He'd opened eyes to poetic sense, what Hima loved most. It wasn't murder but reciprocity. A tad vindictive, but death was foregone and came quick. Hima loved a good joke and a view from the top. Solomon had granted perspective. One man's rationale could be another man's nightmare; the gate swings both ways. Hima got the Jewish view of choice as a matter of personal salvation.

Heinrich Lohrenz had killed Jews only as necessary and avoided prosecution. Solomon's response was fair play, abiding Hima's *mitzvah.* Solomon Kursh pondered pain and suffering, vindication and cruelty, as a clever Jew asked, and a cleverer Jew answered: *who gives a fuck?*

That felt convenient.

The more difficult phase was meditation. Thoughts were birds, flying away, until he lost access to the beautiful void. *This nothingness business is not what it used to be.*

Next up, fifty years old, making ends meet and taking solace as a Cold Case File. Fifty wasn't bad but for a nagging idea that life should hold more. Most people seemed disappointed, and then they died. He wondered when the longing began. Would it go away?

Fulfillment and its converse haunted his meditation—oh, he tried, until jumping on a stump like Little Black Sambo to watch the tiger chase her tail and turn to butter. Or ghee, as necessary, to get his brain unstuck and oozing down the way. *Om mani padme hum.* A bird flew in. He looked online. *Om mani padme hum: on a path of indivisible union of method and wisdom, your impure body, speech and mind can transform to the pure exalted body, speech and mind of a Buddha.*

Warmth in the glow felt better, not so wise or jolly as Buddha, not so much absolved as resolved in acceptance of self. Embracing the almighty fool who first crossed over from the rote path of fraternity life to the variable path of cult life, he wondered anew.

Was he meant to be the fool, to be a nutty/brainy kid escaping society for higher application? Was he there yet? Years of dedication to the belief of no belief had found the success of no success. Had a tree fallen in an earless forest? He knew the guru game, except for the doubts. What did he know? Nothing! In that void, he relaxed anew and grinned again; Buddha knew less.

Solomon Kursh at fifty-five felt okay about magic tasted and life wasted. The people hailed the age of Caesar, who also made fifty-five, barely. Carlotta used to be Joan and stepped up at the birthday party to wax rhapsodic over a great leader in the world of their making. "Without Solomon, we'd be fucked!" She stood tall, chest out, salacious as a woman in training for mixed martial arts can be. She shone in her unique callings: HL and MMA.

Squeamish in praise, Solomon bowed out on a mudra to hit his chamber for a joint and a beer, to work on a book, a new one on a subject of no subject, for gleaners between the lines. Solomon's books did all right, much better than the orange book. He was in demand, on TV again, cable shows for authors mostly, where he didn't get treated like a clown, and book royalties equaled the income of a solid menial job.

The people aged too, coming to terms with the world of reason, more or less. An awkward, pimply kid called Goofy had come in at about the same time as Solomon and grown up, his skin and awkward movements fairly smoothed. He was still Goofy to those who knew and loved him; that was his name. Goofy meditated. He focused on fundamentals and was likeable and not goofy.

Solomon recalled another Goofy from the frat lodge, also

awkward and pocked. He didn't wonder what became of frat Goofy but saw the differences between one cult and another. The frat cult valued social connection, money and material status, binge drinking and pussy, on the way to upper crust. Hima Luja valued wild, crazy, nonsensical fun, love and free-range fucking, now and forevermore.

Solomon searched frat Goofy, Barry Mehlman, and narrowed to the mug and crooked smile grown older and more confident, bolstered by ten million in annuity sales, and Golden Soaring Eagle status, the highest honor at Hoboken Life & Casualty. Barry Mehlman's bio did not mention Goofy.

Solomon couldn't remember HL Goofy's birth name, but it seemed incidental to value in the social/spiritual matrix. Goofy had more juice than Barry Mehlman or a maturing annuity.

How would fraternity brothers fare, staying on for life in the frat lodge? It wouldn't work: a frat lodge needs turnover, so new pledges can be scum o' the earth slaves, to learn the ways of cool from juniors and seniors, who move on to make room. Many frat brothers did stay rooted in fraternity values, a lesser cult, after all.

Tweety Bird, a petite blonde, had the cartoon voice of her namesake. People laughed at the outset and said, "I tought I taw a putty tat." Tweety shook her head, cleaning, cooking, baking and finding bliss, until nobody laughed or mimicked. Tweety made specialty pastries in the kitchen and sold to caterers at premium prices for the betterment of all. She wore an apron over a dress for business. She looked good and caught him seeing. They laughed and took a break. He thought it strange and didn't go again. She didn't press. He loved her indifference and soon wanted to go again. It was less strange, more loving. And that was it. Tweety said she loved him, gave him a peck on the cheek and went back to the kitchen. A frat might have blackballed her for her voice and no-girls-allowed. Solomon wondered how some cults endured.

Taz was short for Tasmanian Devil, for his gravel voice and twitch. Taz had no questions. He parked cars on weekends for a valet company serving home entertainments.

Q-Tip had chronic questions, pitching in to tasks at hand, as if to compensate. Q-Tip worked security at a mall.

Roses came as Sally, becoming Roses to tend the roses. She worked in landscape maintenance.

The cult cavalcade known as the people seemed average, like characters in a play of infinite acts. Tidbit, Jancie and Janet, Muley, Mambo, Mongo, Visquine, Celeste, Tumult, Cassandra, Inon, Imron, Bluto, Pluto, Zinco and X. And the rest who came and went or stayed and aged, developing into something more or less. If granted the benefit of a doubt, they weren't stupid but gave in to it, like frat brothers but colorful and carefree.

Brown rice and tofu displaced sandwiches as staples. Wok-braised carrots and celery livened the mix on Monday, bamboo shoots on Tuesday, kale on Wednesday, bean sprouts on Thursday, mushrooms on Friday and woo hoo! Water-chestnut Saturday! Sunday was chili beans and rice for three-part harmony. They laughed like chimps, getting it right, shooing inhibition, and at their age. On Sunday, Crème de la crème: lasagna, so good but saved for special occasion, to remain loved.

Solomon pondered holding back to remain loved.

Why such order on a menu for anarchists? Because anarchy adapts. On the edge of a society outrunning its headlights, the people went vegetarian, then vegan, for compassion among species.

Vegan meant no more eggs, honey or crème de la crème.

The people talked of leather and silk and left both where they belonged. They felt divination in God-presence, revealed when least or most expected.

Prakash dealt Tarot and read happiness in the cards. "Why the fuck not?" He'd come as Tom and would have been a shrink but couldn't fit in pants, shoes, shirt or a schedule but shed light where he could. He rejoiced on Death, calling it the golden time of rebirth.

The people became family. Solomon walked apart, not so joyous. He spoke of material peace when war waged for oil in Iraq. Desert war replaced jungle war and promised more war. The world dimmed to a dismal view.

He needed more. Liberal behaviors became passé and faded like romance in marriage. The people recalled the lust, the fuss and aftermath. They aged as families, when familiarity precludes discussion. Had they figured each other out or turned away?

Some said Janet was too skinny, but Jancie called her perfect. Janet could hide behind Jancie. They fell in for great good times and, presumably, to touch each other as nobody could or had. They had a cleaning service and worked it together, until they fell out.

Janet said Jancie was "tighter than a gnat's ass." Did she mean cheap? Jancie was plush, not tight.

Jancie responded, playful and hurtful, "There once was a woman named Liza, with tits of two different sizes. One was so small, it was nothing at all, and the other so big it won prizes."

"My name is not Liza," Janet said. Her different sizes were known, but she hadn't been sensitive till then. She said, "There was this skanky bitch, Jancie, who couldn't fit into her pantsie. She was so fat and sat on her hat . . . And went squat."

The Rodent laughed.

Jancie shook her head.

Janet cried.

Solomon said, "Looks like renewal." Nothing came of it, once they made up. Solomon loved their foibles and forgiveness.

The Rodent came in as Danny Shipley with a long nose over an ill-conceived moustache. A friendly fellow who'd survived a caustic youth, he volunteered the nickname, to get it over with. He laughed short, saying it would come out sooner or later, and he could take it. He took it. The name lasted years, until the night Solomon announced that the Rodent would thereby and forevermore be known to all who loved him as Danny.

Danny smiled and frowned, smiled and frowned, until Mongoose called, "Hey, Danny."

Solomon loved Danny's acceptance and endurance.

Mongoose carried the torch for Miranda. She couldn't see him, until an equinox meditation, when they joined hands under the stars and twinkled and retired to the Mongoose burrow. Solomon wondered who grasped whom and loved their grasp.

Among the difficult, Lucent, a handsome fellow and self-proclaimed genius with a bad diet. Lucent said weakness is for the weak, and he was strong, no worries. He went out for meat, extolling the glories of pork butt and ribeye and fouling the facilities soon after.

Also tough, as if to type, Miss Titty bellowed, "You expect me to breathe that? You peeled the paint in there!"

Lucent blushed, caught out like a stinky guy.

Miss Titty said it didn't have to be this way, and he came around to a better diet. Some thought it a ruse, that it wouldn't last. But Miss Titty showed her appreciation, and it did, for now.

Tasks filled days, but they changed. Idjits grinning, dancing about in orange jammies, pressing orange books on strangers and asking for money was an old regimen that wouldn't play. Seasoned idjits harked back and went to work and to good works. At the home, the hospice or county jail, visiting the handicapped or victims, they helped. Donations came. With Solomon's book royalties, they got by.

Central Compound got orderly as a small town in Kansas after a tornado. Community service fortified a sense of well-being.

Sanguine and steady as sunrise but worn and weary, Solomon went along on a picnic to the river. The people laughed, getting naked and helping each other with sunscreen, remembering when.

Solomon bared flesh. Clouds came in. He got chilled and dressed, and another change was official.

Stillness prevailed in the room at the end of the hall. Mice rustled in the refuse and stuff. He laid a trail of crumbs for them, asking if they'd heard anything on the money. He sat in the lotus and loved this following too, rodents to be sure, and honest. He cleaned the corners, closets and shelves to reduce habitat. He found Viga's kazoo in a plastic poncho, chewed like a cigar butt but intact. It went to Ziploc as the better part of nothing. He sat. The inner sanctum was, and so was he. Still-life with mice.

Why was Danny Shipley never so cute? He waited.

Heinrich Lohrenz had planned two legacies. The first was telling jokes and divesting himself of a cult, utilizing the *Juden* resource, as the Reich should have done. The second was sending money elsewhere for the legacy long lasting, for the nine hundred eighty-seven years remaining in the thousand-year Reich.

HL was a dump in a suburb, a cell of nothingness sustained.

Solomon rose to a fantasy lectern in the Reichstag to face a jackboot gang spanning the horizon. *Heil madness*! As *der neue führer*, he inhaled and cut loose: "Gheee!"

When stillness settled, he crawled among the boxes and piles again, one more rodent in XXXL groveling for crumbs.

Moolah as redemption felt like another aspect of failure, more time wasted on the wheel of desire. When the crumbs were gone, the trail cold, Stan Sokolov sat again to seek salvation.

So Long Ago

Pearl Sokolov died in 2001 at seventy-eight, young by modern standards but way past projections for stage-four pancreatic.

Solomon flew to Chicago to sit bedside and recall old times, friends and family who'd checked out or stopped coming around because they couldn't or didn't.

Pearl called her son Stanley and asked if death would be soon.

Warm and wise, he consoled, displacing anxiety with acceptance—and regret; such a lawyer he could have been. He didn't remind her that everyone dies; she knew, and his smile said it all. Incapacitated and thin, she didn't know what was worse, this or the other. Did she mean the last of life or the first of death?

As he explained that the other ends worry, she asked again, "When?" Despite a lifetime of muttering prayers in Yiddish, as her mother had done, she feared the end, finding little comfort in faith.

Stanley asked, "Do you mean for you or me?"

She knee jerked on a Yiddish mumble and admonished, "Don't talk like a crazy man."

"Sorry, yes. You will pass sooner or later."

She looked off, sadly. He moved in on a memory. "I call it my first memory, because I can't remember anything before it." He chuckled. She didn't, perhaps hoping for more than the nonsense that claimed her son so long ago.

"Do you remember bathing me in the kitchen sink? I don't have all the details, but I see a few parts, your hands under me, dipping me in the warm water. I splashed. We laughed."

She smiled. Tears rolled, as if splashed again. "I remember."

"I feel crowded in a hot tub now," he said.

"With your friends, it probably is crowded."

"No. I meant . . ."

"I know what you meant. You were smaller then."

Yes, but he'd grown in many ways and still rolled gently down the stream. "You wouldn't get me a bicycle until I rode that clunker hand-me-down from Suzie Gottleib? Training wheels. What do you learn with training wheels? She was such a nudge."

"Yes. She had a terrible crush on you. You rode that bicycle for her. You didn't know that? We took the training wheels off so you could fall down." She remembered.

He turned a page. "Remember Harry?" Harry the dog went to the park with Stanley early summer mornings to explore and find a hideaway for lunch from a brown bag, sandwiches, dog biscuits, fruit, cookies, a drink, chips, carrot and celery slices, olives, coleslaw or pickles, a napkin and chewing gum.

Pearl nodded, repacking the bag. "He was the best little dog."

"Still is," Stanley said, and she cried.

After a month of it, he had to get back to work. She didn't ask what work or question his lot or lost potential, or ask about Jewish girls who might be at that place or visit that place. She never said ashram or cult or compound or commune because she didn't want to. She said, "Don't come back. I don't want you to come back. When the time comes. I see you now. I love you as always. It's too much. I want you to avoid their talk. You can't. But . . . please."

"Avoid their talk?"

"If you don't come, they'll talk. If you come, they'll talk more. What kind of son you must be." She laid her hand on his. "They talk. You've been in their mouths since you changed. Let them talk. We don't care. I know what you are. You're the best son ever. Kind, compassionate, brilliant and handsome. The best."

She squeezed.

He didn't attend the funeral a month later, relieved that she'd spared him from those who could not know him. He sat for a day of meditation, sobbing intermittently.

It seemed so long ago that a young man stood at a kitchen sink pinching green beans. A kid mowed a lawn on another Saturday, sacrificed for five bucks. An adolescent roamed a park with a dog and lunch. Solomon thought, as he'd thought as a kid, a teen or a twenty something. More confident then, he'd known more than he currently knew. Where did certainty go? It equivocated with age. From twenty to thirty felt all grown up, an extension of playtime with heady access to the cosmos, until the Milky Way went blurry. Suburban values fell away like spent boosters. He careened in space on angles of being as yet unknown. Reflection in deep space has no compass rose.

Age thirty-five, Zen teachers advise, is the age at which the self is formed, more or less. Thirty-five is time for core development.

Zazen lasts three days or ten days for those who seek it. Zazen format is forty-five minutes of meditation, fifteen minutes of walking, usually in a circle, and repeat, with meal and sleep breaks, no talking. Zazen opens the core to what might been seen. Zen teachers say thirty-five is minimal age for zazen benefit. Solomon Kursh sat zazen for a day and three and six at thirty-five and forty and forty-five. He thought he'd know if he was ready for ten.

He didn't know and relished not knowing and sat for ten days at fifty-five. Heinrich Lohrenz drifted in and out on a whisper: *You're Solomon Kursh.* No, he wasn't but wasn't Sok or Stanley Sokolov as well. Nobody in pursuit of nothing, he felt invisible and relieved. Arrived, or on his way? That bird too headed over the horizon.

A lost youth in baggy jammies grooving to The Moody Blues seemed so long ago. The wise ones advise repetition. Do what you do. With practice comes virtue. Did they know that routine can grind to bare metal, the wise ones?

What's the difference between illusion and delusion? Illusion is perceived while delusion is imposed. One is exterior while the other roils inside. One is mirage, inviting from a distance, while the other is a trick played on the self. Why be born to no exhilaration? Why see love as a trick? What's left, if love fades on approach? The momentum infinitum of youth went upside down, inside out in a mirror-world of fun. A person with whom to conjugate on three levels might help, but alas.

He sat, unsuitable to the practical or impractical world.

Can a soul be measured? Can principles of accounting, like loss, capital gain or depreciation, apply to person management? How can life improve, if overhead is a fixed expense? Cold and heat, lumpy mattresses and gruel might build character, but comfort can allow for breadth of spirit. Comfort can raise spirits. Or would material gain displace spirit, like in the '50s? Yes, if HL sofas got plastic covers, and the people drank too many highballs.

Odd bits sizzled in a guru brainpan. Crispy on the edges, he twitched to mythical status. Solomon Kursh wrote books on a way of being, off the cuff with alluring lyricism. He got sales. He lived reclusively by choice, not ascetically but with a few beers, some dope and a TV. And a legal pad or a laptop for notes on being. He became the stuff of legend in a parochial circle of refugees from rational society, eager readers who fed their belief of no belief. Solomon Kursh became grist for spirit-nihilist mill. Tales of ethereal largesse got shared around the cosmic campfire. Sparks leapt from the flames.

A story emerged of Solomon's first date. The tale threatened his transcendental place, where sheer, boorish sex is not necessary.

Followers agreed online and off: "It never happened. He never had a date. He's not like that."

"He was in a fraternity. He had dates."

"Dating ended before Solomon's time. They didn't have dates back then."

Young and old women and men sought him for light or hope, an answer or a minute, a nod, a touch, an embrace. Did he bear up? Did he transmute or transcend? Yes, he did, taking cover alone, with fewer needs to fill. He preferred the airwaves, buffered and safer. Followers loved the discourse, and Solomon came forth, off the top, from deep within, or from literature. "Yes, he said yes, again yes," because the denouement of *Ulysses* was affirmative and became a sign off. He read excerpts from the Joycean masterwork as another meditative form, on the air and off, laughing aloud at certain passages. Could a narrative transmute? Or was it the reader? He laughed again at desire and cried again for falling off the first rung or making it to the second rung and falling off for fear of heights. He dreamed that psychiatric counseling might make a difference.

Modern times carry new diseases. Carnal exchange became casually hazardous, but HL would not be a monastery. Lust could trump sense, but friends could talk. Solomon supplied rubbers and literature on contagion and transmittal. Prevention seemed civilized but more of a milestone than a setback. Formal guidelines included the value of deferment until love, which can happen in a day or two.

Love makes the world go round, if you let it.

"Okay, okay," allowed Sassafras, a middle-age female, recently arrived and awestruck as a teen backstage. "Did you hear about Solomon's first visit to New York?"

What a story, proving the power of humility in the concrete jungle. Who else could roam freely uptown or down? Muggers stared in awe, she said. Several listeners stared off, imagining Solomon offering safety tips in the park, chatting the homeless. Oh, and turning his pockets out to show no change. Ha!

"Did you know he killed Hima Luja?" asked Carlos Leuganoff.

"You're sick," replied Nunchuk, an old Lujan who sensed a tourist or a parasite.

"Chopped his head off with a bayonet," chimed Maria, visiting with Carlos.

"How would you know?" Nunchuk asked.

"And you helped clean up the mess," Carlos said.

"You're not welcome here." Nunchuk stood.

"Solomon is Jewish," Carlos said. "He thought Hima was a Nazi."

"Solomon is not Jewish!" Ixis fairly sang on entering the room.

"Was," Maria said.

"Not," Ixis trilled.

"You're in denial," Carlos replied.

"Denial," Maria concurred.

Nunchuk led them out, as Ixis warbled, "So long, farewell. *Auf Wiedersehen*, goodni-ight!"

Never mind. Unpleasantry came from the negative world, outside. Like any cult, HL got old, its pulse weakened to a blip. Lujans needed guidance. Solomon hadn't been to New York but did smoke a joint in Golden Gate Park. The stories were goofs anyway. Nunchuk came back. "Man, the nasty people we let in here."

Bankruptcy got more media than a salmonella outbreak would have done. HL was good for color and fill as a white-elephant commune given over to good works and struggling to survive. HL going under led the news cycle. The Cold Case File warmed up when a candidate for county prosecutor called for a new investigation. News hounds followed the scent. Solomon welcomed them in, listing social contributions. But media didn't want warm 'n' fuzzy. They wanted failure, foul play and the death of a movement, or would that be murder? Solomon parried like a guru. "The kids aren't culting up like they used to. They follow handheld devices now, numb to their surrender. You think Hima Luja was out of step. Just you wait."

His words reverberated: "Just you wait!" It sounded like a plan.

Eviction approached but seemed like small potatoes on the firing line. "Did you kill Hima Luja?"

"I've done my best to save Hima Luja."

"The man. Did you kill the man, Hima Luja?"

"No." Solomon held firm, statuesque, removed. *Let them howl.* On Hima and consequence, he wanted to share thoughts and actions but did not. He'd bemoaned the lazy brains at HL but felt covered; they met the challenge with their dazzling brand of crazy.

Bills went to the round file. Rice, beans and tofu on hand should last two months. Everything would remain everything for a while.

He worried about the people, some growing old, some still giggling or staring, too long in captivity for release into the wild. He drew a blank on them too. Some could fake it in polite society. Many people do. Others not.

Anxiety rose and fell. He couldn't help and could no longer wait. They waited. He argued pros and cons of staying to the bitter end or leaving now, in the bitter moment. Practical and spiritual selves stopped getting along or trusting each other. They would go their separate ways.

He sent Hima's cheek swab on a Q-Tip and Viga's kazoo to a lab for DNA testing. It was a match. He'd known it would be.

Evenings gained weight. Solomon felt like a cheap date, two brewskies and two hits changing his mind for the better, easing things up but not out. He teetered, feeling decrepit as an old, empty warehouse. He stoked the bong till it billowed boom times, and from that blur, an image wisped. Amorphous yet radiant, the raven-haired beauty JoAnne Johnson stretched her lithesome self to grasp his idle essence and sing into it. *You can't always get whatchu wa-ant!* Her cameo face and pitch perfection conjoined the righteous and the mundane, the playful and profane. He marveled anew.

It seemed silly at the time, and he admitted in the future: *I guess I liked the way she held the micro-phone.* But he wasn't Mick Jagger, and this wasn't "The Spider and the Fly." Still, recollection gave him a laugh, a short one, and any harbor seemed snug. She'd eased him into an odd scene on the floor, challenging him to feel something or nothing. That was her gift, squeezing his dick playfully with love abounding, as yet and forevermore, fading away.

It was only the first rung, but he'd made the second rung plenty with JoAnne. They'd communicated as peers. They'd understood and loved each other as friends can. The top rung seemed an easy reach but wasn't. Youthful presumption could not allow the next step. Real life got in the way. Delusional, internal, self-imposed, based on physical beauty. Besides that, she was older, and he hoped Billy was still with her, or that she had love in life at any rate.

You Can't Always Get Whatchu Wa-ant!

JoAnne married Billy Keene. She'd grabbed Solomon's dick and held it like a microphone and sang into it—no, not Solomon's dick. She never knew Solomon; nobody grabbed Solomon's dick. It was Sokolov's dick back then. What a scene, and Billy laughed too, in the loving spirit. Sokolov loved them both as Solomon loves them now, as *mishpocha* of the wandering times, the spirit family who crossed that desert on a horse with no name. A man could wax nostalgic, remembering the desert, until realizing that the oasis stumbled into was a mirage all along. Would that be illusory or delusional? A man could laugh at his own joke, until wondering if he'd shuffled on through to the other side. How would he tell an old, dear friend what became of him? *I'm nothing, really. I share a house with friends, more or less. It seemed dynamic for a time, but I got stuck. They need me, so I stay. It's like an old marriage. And what about you?*

How many years had passed? Make that decades. Where might she be? Is Billy still around? How would it be to see them again?

He didn't wonder for long before the miracle of modern times and a search engine helped cast time and distance to the wind.

He wanted to rejoin the old social circle in the moment rather than wallow in shallow memories. He seldom relied on his computer for reconnecting; it seemed unnatural in a world of chance and convergence. He did not seek long-lost friends who'd no doubt become something else, eager to share tedious chronology, geography and genealogy, to count the years in which this or that came to pass or to the pass of no pass.

He didn't not give a snit who'd died or divorced or made a killing in the market or turned into nothing or vanished, never to be seen or heard again. Who cared? He wasn't feeling so great about his own résumé and its dead-end dilemma. And he frankly didn't care who begat whom or got begotten or sold the hardware store for enough money to buy an RV to follow a retirement dream to Arizona and beyond. Woo hoo!

He didn't want to trade memories like baseball cards. Both seemed inconsequential, without meaning, without hope. But people trade trivialities like it's all they have. It's what they do, often reflective of what they are. He weighed pros and cons of a call to his old friends from olden times. What if Billy and JoAnne were suburban, obese and dull? Ah, well, he could call to send his love because that's all he had. People do that too, so maybe he was coming around to being more . . . uh . . . normal. Things could go either way, tediously regrettable or wondrously reconnected.

He thought it might be a good idea and made a snap decision to make the call, perhaps one day soon. He wondered if love could fade as people fade. Or could it stay the same? Why not? Why not roll in laughter and roll another one? He thought it a thing to find out.

His love for JoAnne and Billy endured. As intellectually compulsive, they likely spiced the years with experiment, with open minds and honesty. He assumed so but knew that past friends can be unknowable in the future. He laughed at what had been.

But speculation on JoAnne and Billy seemed hazardous. Time and distance sort things out. The future arrives as it is. Solomon never knew two livelier, lusty people. Would they see him as alone in every sense? Could they fathom a like-minded female not coming along? Would his solitary nature underscore his failure in romance? No, not failure. Some things don't happen. He'd never climbed Everest and was no failure because of it.

He'd loved JoAnne and Billy in the most loving time, in friendship and trust, simple ingredients but rare. Did he imagine sex with JoAnne? No more than any boy on campus. She would have been a romp, a rigorous back scratch and then some. Or they could have killed what she and Billy had, no matter the love abounding. No, he could not love JoAnne that way with Billy in the picture.

Speculation seemed irrelevant. He longed for a change of scenery but couldn't go back. Nobody can. He rarely felt sexual arousal and rarely agreed to conjugation. He didn't pursue it. He thought it briefly fun but mostly odd. Was he a weirdo? No wondering required. Among his failures: he'd loved few people—meaning no people in romance. He'd loved his mother and everyone in the friendship circle of the golden, glowing time. Could a deep friendship of youth go away like first love, never to be replaced? It could. Yet his heart soared on Billy and JoAnne and could again.

Unless it couldn't. But he knew it could. A grand reunion would restore life with love and a yen fulfilled. Billy and JoAnne were older by six years, not so much. Some of the people were older than that, and so was the old spirit of natural and beautiful. As a subculture, HL attended to needs among like-minded people with courtesy and gratitude. That didn't seem crazy, not compared to Billy and JoAnne.

How had they aged? Did Solomon still love them, given his total eclipse of self? Loss feeds growth, by necessity. We let go in order to move on. Their paths differed. Would they bog in the mundane tedium he loathed and regretted?

The cover art for the music on his computer recalled the soft sibilance of a needle in a groove and that timeless interval that broke into the greatest music of all time. The groove was gone, and so was he. Ah, well, African harmony was another groove, rhythmic and reminiscent, thumb piano and drums scoring jungle foliage near a pool where critters gathered for a quench. He closed his eyes for a drink of youth, moist and lush, tinted green.

Oh, yeah . . .

Loving times come and go, but a first blush imprints like a gosling's first sight of Mama. Life can bring mobility and room service or not, but . . . A blush is a blush is a blush, and by another name is a memory of something sacred, or so it seemed, something gone that won't come back because it can't.

Solomon Kursh cried for such loss.

He'd cried for loved ones passing, but those tears dried up long ago. He sobbed anew for this loss, not so much of youth or zest or glory but in realization. People cry at funerals for their own mortality, and so did he. The loving time would not return, unless, maybe . . .

No, he could not and would not. Didn't have to.

He opened a search window and entered JoAnne Johnson. Many women came up, and many men went by Billy Keene. He tried Billy and JoAnne Keene and got Eloise Kessler Keene Smythe in a photo with Billy and JoAnne. The wedding photographer had day rates or hourly to fit any budget. One shot showed people behind a giant cake. The bride beamed, chest out, stomach in, smile flared, back arched, defiant in nature or life or long odds or something.

The bride was Eloise Kessler Keene Smythe, standing between Billy and JoAnne, two graying, reasonably fit and happy people. The post was eleven years old. He picked up the phone and dialed, but the wedding photographer was no longer in service. The area code was suburban fringe, south of Chicago, in the heart of the heartland, Hoosierville in HL jargon, part of the great scab. Directory assistance had no listing for Billy Keene, but JoAnne came up.

Five minutes from first denial, the phone rang. A robot voice gave a new number in 312, also Chi-town. He dialed and listened again, two rings and counting . . .

"Hello."

"Gheee!" He couldn't help it, laughing wildly and crying more. "Gheee!" The falsetto escaped like a jinni long constrained.

"Who is this?"

"Gheee!"

She hung up.

He called back.

"Look!" She yelled, all business, like JoAnne. "Stop!"

"It's me. Sok!"

"I don't know a Sok."

"Who is this?"

"Who are you calling?"

"Billy. JoAnne. JoAnne?"

"JoAnne isn't here."

"Billy?"

"Who is this?"

"I'm their friend from college, but I quit."

"Sokolov?"

"Yes!"

"I heard of you."

Sok wept, couldn't help it; the heavenly vibration flooded back.

"Billy's gone. Almost five years."

Out for smokes? To greener pastures? "Gone?"

"He had . . . cancer."

Sok got stuck in the larynx, choking up. He'd anticipated a celebration but couldn't speak.

"Is this your number you're calling from?"

"Yes."

"I'll tell JoAnne you called. She'll be happy. They talked about you. They thought you were the craziest guy ever. They heard you got involved with a . . . group. They loved you."

"I love them. I love you."

"Yes. I'm sure. Um . . . I have to go. Where are you?"

They exchanged coordinates, and the daughter said, "I have to go. Sorry. I'm already late."

"Late?"

She laughed. "I heard about that too. I'll tell JoAnne. She'll call you. Tell me something. Are you healthy?"

"Healthy? You mean physically fit? What did you hear about?"

"About back-quoting with questions. Until you made people crazy or made them laugh."

"When will she be back?"

"I don't know. I'll leave a message. Maybe an hour or two."

"You live with her?"

"Yes. For now."

"You look like her."

"That's mostly the hair and big tits. I'm taller. And thinner. I'll probably gain weight. People do."

"You're married. I saw your wedding cake. It's how I found you. It was huge."

"Nobody's safe anymore. I'm divorced. It didn't work out, in spite of the cake."

Solomon laughed. "You were a baby. I think two or three."

"I'm thirty-eight. I really do have to go."

She hung up, and he realized he hadn't given her his real name, his new name. Ah, well, the phone numbers were real and so was the warmth, rising with the old happiness. Billy was gone; that wasn't happy. That was life and death with giddy prospects for reconnection with JoAnne and those times. Yes, they were great fun, everybody too young to imagine challenges or loss, unwilling to accept life as mundane chores in series, like their parents had, dreamy enough to see the world refracted. Elation surging, he felt willing to go again.

Goodness and regret went around on another meditation, on memory and loss. Magic scenes and blessed times merged. He wanted to roll a joint and swig a jug o' Boone's Farm and drop a tab but merely trembled over a joint and two beers—okay, three beers. He waited an hour, got up to pace and sat another hour. He dialed back.

"Oh, Sok!"

Again, speech came down to a lilt. "JoAnne."

"Please come. Please."

"Come where?"

"Come here. So much has happened. I'll fill you in. But I don't mean just come to visit. I need you. I mean we have a situation you can help with, maybe. I think you can. I thought of you and tried to find you but you're gone!"

"A situation?"

"A beautiful thing, really. How's your health?"

"So much concern for my health. It's good, I think."

"No diseases or conditions?"

"Probably not. I get exercise, walking mostly. I'm thinking of jogging but haven't picked up the pace yet. I need the shoes. I eat well. I weigh more, but people do. I'm not fat. And you?"

"I'm fat, but you still love me, don't you?"

"I think you got me where you want me?"

"I'm not fat, but things change. Like you say, everybody fills out. Please come."

"What about Billy?"

"Oh, man. He died. He had AIDS."

"I heard that he died, but AIDS?"

"It's a long story but not really. He was gay."

"No, he wasn't."

"Okay. He wasn't, or he was. It doesn't matter. He's gone."

"I'm Solomon now. Solomon Kursh."

"Yes, you are. And we knew you when."

"You still know me. You knew of Hima Luja?"

"I hope I know you. *You're* Solomon Kursh."

"Yes. It's been fun. It's winding down. Could be dead, and I'm only a figment. I need a change of scenery, and you sound great."

"*Tie-eye-eye-ime is on our side.* Are you in California?"

"Oh, God. Yes. LA for the last few years, ten or twenty. Should I fly in to O'Hare?"

"Yes." He wrote madly as she gave the street address, even as it seared his brain.

"I'll call when I get a flight."

They said goodbye and hung up, as if decades were days, and Friday was coming on, and some hot new albums and reefer and Boone's Farm were queued up at JoAnne's. Did he actually expect to move in and stay? They shared a wavelength yet again, this time older with baggage. A beautiful situation? He got a flight for noon the next day on an iffy Visa that felt karmic because it worked.

He sat, not seiza or zazen but as a man at a desk, strolling the decades, beginning with midnight in the snow on LSD, trucking into town among huge snowflakes plummeting like tiny paratroopers and growing to life size to invade Earth. He lay his tired head down to rest and sort further but woke in the night, stiff and sore. Moving to the bed, he sank again in swarming recollections.

Up at dawn and packed light, out the door and in the limo, airport-bound, he wondered if ironic karma was good. Can insolvency look like wealth? It most often does. At least nobody paid the driver, and the limo was more lyrical than ironic.

He wished he'd called JoAnne with flight times. But he planned to call on the way and wouldn't barge in like a college kid, hot and bothered. He hoped he wouldn't look foolish, showing up with a duffel. He laughed at looking foolish—cruising to the future in Central's new ride, a '69 Bonneville with iffy springs, a trade for the hearse, plus four grand that could pay creditors another week or two. He laughed at the hand-to-mouth hustle he'd arrived at and departed, on the lam. Parnelli laughed along, happy to join the fun.

Solomon didn't know if he looked more foolish lately or had grown more aware. She'd urged him on, and he was on his way. It couldn't get clearer than that, and he wondered again at this new anxiety over appearance, after decades of hardly a thought for her and Billy. Had he been so busy or become so desperate? Yes, and yes. No golden time was as good as remembered, but the future, however disappointing, should not preclude a revival. That's what it would be—reaching back does not signal weakness. This was not a turn for the worse. The olden days remained as good as they looked. So, yes again yes, and he stared out the window at first light.

Parnelli turned up the radio. "I cued it up special," he said.

Steve Miller sang, *Goodbye to all my friends at home/*

Goodbye to people I've trusted/ I've got to go out and make my way/ I might get rich, you know I might get busted . . .

Parnelli sang along, synced to each syllable from thousands of sing-alongs. Parnelli's Top 40 was constant. The music of our time did not move on but unfolded infinitum. *Ridin' high I got tears in my eyes/ You know you got to go to hell/ Before you . . . get to heaven . . .*

"Parnelli. It's this exit."

"Yeah, I got it. I been here a million times, man. This time is different. I think something's, you know, coming down. Am I right?"

And I'm goin' with some hesitation/ You know that I can surely see/ That I don't want to get caught up in that/ Funky shit goin' down in the city.

"Something always comes down. You know that. I hope you know that."

"You know what I mean, Solomon. Hey, it's okay. I need to ask you something. Okay? What I mean is, I need your blessing."

"You really don't. I'm not the pope."

"Yeah, you're the king. King Solomon."

"What is it?"

"I been thinking of changing my name. Parnelli is cool, and I'm a driver for all seasons. No doubts. I got no doubts, and you shouldn't too. But what if I want to be . . . I was thinking of, I don't know, something like—Fuck!"

Twenty yards from the curb, Parnelli gripped the wheel, arching his back to strangle the wheel and stomp the brake. Out of gas, they rolled to the curb on fumes. Power loss took hydraulic-assist steering and power brakes to manual. But sounds remained intact. *Oh, Oh big ol' jet airliner/ Cause it's here that I've got to stay . . .*

"Fuck!"

Solomon braced. "What?"

"Empty!" Parnelli fought steering and braking to a controlled landing. Curb feelers scraped, and the front end groaned. A fender skirt popped at the curb, and old Pancho ground to a stop, hubcap clattering down the walkway. Parnelli said, "Piece o' shit. Fuck it. We're here." He turned around, grinning like a chimp but sobering on seeing Solomon's face. "Fuck, man! Are you hit?"

"Why are we empty?"

"It happens when you don't put in more gas. You know that."

"What if we'd run out a mile back?"

Parnelli held firm. "We didn't. You might say I had this one dicked. No. Under control. You'd say I had it under control. You might also say I'm a hell of a driver. You might say, uh, King Solomon needs a ride? Who's he gonna turn to? That's my job. Call me when you need a pickup. Okay? I'll get gas in a can, you know, and get out here to fill it up and drive you home. You know I will."

"They'll tow this car in ten minutes."

"Maybe not. You never can tell."

Solomon sighed, unwilling to assess further prospects for car towing or weeding the turnip patch or bailing water in a sinking ship. The last farewell formed up on regret and longing. He couldn't just walk out, or jump off like Jim from the Patna to the longboat, leaving helpless passengers.

Parnelli looked glum. "You're pissed off. I can tell."

"I'm not. It's okay. It's okay, man. Parnelli." He scooted out, reached back in for his bag and patted Parnelli on the shoulder. He paused. "Parnelli. What's your new name?"

"I was thinking, maybe, Steve Miller?"

Solomon granted the beatific smile. "Perfect, man. Hey, flipside, motherfucker." He backed out and walked away, turning again to call, "I mean Steve!" And he walked away.

"Bless you, Solomon," Steve Miller called, piercing Solomon's heart with a love arrow. Loss and finality hit home. Then again, *Maybe not. You never can tell.* Ah, the spirit, the silly, dipshit spirit of the thing—that's what he loved. That's what tore his heart.

After all that, a guy wants to be called Steve.

Shuffling through the terminal, uncertain, he self-consoled; this visit would be good, a reentry to Earth. Old friends and all that, the karmic flow felt wise and goofy, ordered and chaotic, confusing and precise. And ironic. Why not? What about jumping ship and leaving people in the lurch? That was tough. But without a break, he'd be broken. He'd go back to manage the end, to minimize loss in a losing proposition. After all, greatness cannot emerge from the shadows without the shadows. Greatness? Was that the problem?

Solomon strode forth, burdens crumbling in his wake, new time coming on. But he would not sing "Zip-a-Dee-Doo-Dah."

Reunion came in layers, beginning with the ride from O'Hare. It followed the path not taken, through suburbs of upwardly middle reach and the strip-mall mélange that fed on them. Boutique gingerbreads varied residential to commercial, seeking grandeur in colonial façade and de rigueur shrubbery. Solomon took relief in the arid plain buffering the profane from the mundane. The affluence charade ended a mile or two before the road came to non-descript subdivisions void of glory. But who isn't, behind the show and tell? Harking like a pilgrim to whence he never belonged, he hoped for soul, even if he couldn't sense it on approach. With open mind and heart, he might see what he'd missed, what held people to place, what goodness might reside . . .

Fuck . . .

Soft arrival was quiet, an easy pull to the curb and address confirmation, no rock 'n' roll, no hubcaps, name changes or questions on what was coming down.

What a day. Blinking on a first star, he made a wish. Lo and behold, the Visa card still worked.

On the stoop, bag in hand, he saw from above: still life of self, convergent on the future past. He knocked. It opened. Time warped. Discreetly shaded at the threshold, she waited with him for the years to catch up, to take a moment, to soften the punch. Gravity had levied its tyrannical tax but not too much.

Old acidnauts could handle turbulence by going to protocol in the clutch: grip the sofa, put mind over matter and steer the rocket up, up, up and not down. Let the old familiarity infuse a blessed reunion, until old souls and new selves could level off in joy and life.

Eyeballing up and down, they smiled and stepped into embrace.

JoAnne Keene

Values, priorities and pendulums swing the other way, sooner or later. Split-level suburbs wallowed in highballs, cigarettes and desperation. Simple remedies were affair, divorce and remarriage, until they seemed impractical, passé and comical. Elm Street fell to revolution. But the anarchy of the '60s relapsed to material gain in the '70s, and the pendulum swung shorter after that. Evolution slowed, as schedules accelerated with ambition, anxiety and need.

JoAnne Keene had aged well, posture intact, head high, shoulders open, energy good, smile bright and the old, playful mirth in her eyes. Preened and highlighted, she was what her mother would have called well presented. Happy in her skin, she shone a bit bright, as if all was not as it seemed. But what is? Warm and welcoming as an old friend, she appraised him and vice versa.

Her cushy middle looked normal, and so did a few creases and sags. He marveled at his old crush, intact. Was time the measure of love? She turned like a model on a runway to show why oglers still craned for second looks.

On equal opportunity, he offered a slow turn of his own. She grasped where the spare tire could have been. "Nice. You're just the same, give or take."

Like youths at a trailhead, they ambled into the old comfort with added seasoning, savoring what the years had wrought. He picked up where they'd left off, admiring and brilliant. She went to domestic detail, as he'd feared.

JoAnne had more stage presence than the average hippie. She'd favored drama, entering in T-shirt and shorts or protesting in a sundress. She'd gone against a grain, because she could.

In the future, she stepped aside in a presentation of motherhood, showing an old friend what became of her and her work.

Eloise stood back, held back against interrupting or disappointing. He remembered "the baby," an encumbrance to romance, demanding attention, and he laughed. They reacted as women might. "I'm sorry. I'm not laughing at you. JoAnne called you a beautiful situation. I see why." He sounded apologetic and lame.

JoAnne chatted on, unabashed, by rights. Her child had grown to conscientious, compassionate adulthood. Eloise had lived with JoAnne since the divorce, but that would change, perhaps soon. On that note, they moved to the living room for JoAnne's narrative on life, including Eloise Kessler Keene's identity crises. She brought out photos of the gangly little girl, the stick-thin adolescent in braces, the tall teen, emergent, awkward and aware, blushing in black and white.

As the old folks made nice over snapshots, Eloise Kessler Keene said her name had been another burden. Who needs a last name for a middle name? She'd always thought it affected.

JoAnne informed Solomon that the middle name was after JoAnne's grandfather, Morris Kessler, who loved to pinch her cheek and her *tuchus*—that would be JoAnne's cheeks and tuchus, because Jews name babies for the dead. *Feter* Morris could not have very well pinched Eloise's cheek. Or tuchus. While some women winced at pinches, JoAnne felt affection and flattery. Morris Kessler told her she would always be his saucy tomato. "I was a kid," JoAnne said. "He was psychic. He knew." Morris Kessler died a year before Eloise was born and lived in memory through Eloise's middle name. "He deserved it," JoAnne said.

Solomon spoke to the photo, "You were very tall."

"I am very tall, in case you didn't notice. Jolly Green," Eloise said. "That was my name from sixth grade through high school."

Eloise had suffered a youth of length and gawk. She'd waited for the other kids to catch up and shut up. She'd had a lifetime of it, up to the age of filling out, filling in and gaining stature as a woman who takes no shit. Body follows mind in daily movement, but the converse had held true for Eloise, by necessity. She'd made her way in an unkind world. Mental stature took a few years more.

JoAnne said, "She's a work in progress."

Eloise smiled, "I feel so special, having you two analyze me, like I'm not here. Go ahead and spell words I might not be ready for."

"But you are here," Solomon said. "The child isn't here, but we remember her. A work in progress is the best work of all."

"It's okay," JoAnne said. "I'm the mother."

"If you hit me on the head with a baseball bat, you'd still be the mother," Eloise said.

"I'm not hitting you on the head with anything."

Eloise turned to Solomon, "Yes, apparently, you're in progress too. It's not always good, is it?"

"I think it is. It's not always fun."

"Okay," Eloise allowed. "We never had much perspective, growing up. It was always a competitive volley, rushing the net. That's another story. You're part of Billy. You help with that. He called you the gentlest person. I love that. We've had so little of it."

Solomon returned an easy smile. "I suppose we have some catching up to do."

Eloise asserted herself between the old friends. He'd never thought of towering over JoAnne, but there she was, a lesser peak beside the summits of two tall people at an altitude all their own.

A subtle stoop often afflicts tall people trying to shed an unwanted superiority, but he stood straight, seeing Eloise eye to eye.

She took the challenge and stood straighter. "JoAnne?"

JoAnne reached for the tops of their heads and said, "Sok by an inch. Sorry. Solomon."

"I don't mind playing the child while you catch up," Eloise said. "You can talk about who I used to be and my difficulties. It gives me something to look forward to."

"I'll bite," Solomon said. "What are you looking forward to?"

"After me, we'll analyze you. I heard some humdingers. You don't seem nearly so crazy as the stories. I pictured you in baggy jammies with the open fly—in flagrante delicto. You know?"

He blushed to his hairline.

JoAnne lost a chuckle, and another tableau of the golden age formed in the mind's eye among them. "*You can't always get whatchu wa-ant!*" Eloise crooned, perfectly pitched as her mother.

"You do know me," Solomon said. "I see you got the picture down to the details."

"Not all the details, I'm sure." Eloise smirked.

"You've made your point, Eloise."

"Why, thank you, JoAnne. How nice of you to say so."

Solomon looked from mother to daughter, wondering if JoAnne had stepped out on this production. But as he doubted Billy Keene's participation, the daughter flashed the trademark grin, an uncanny cross between a challenge and sincere happiness to see you.

After what seemed a long time since his arrival, the daughter offered her hand, like opening credits halfway into the opening scene. "I'm Eloise, by the way. You know JoAnne can be so informal; she often neglects the niceties."

Solomon took her hand, putting his big brown eyes on her deep greens for the contact that makes most people fidget. He did not seek ocular intimidation but to enter and see. Her bright eyes, sharp features, high cheeks and long, raven hair identified the mother. Proportionate, physically fit, thin and well-formed felt like the father—like Billy, except for the tall part. Curiosity between tall people is often an attraction. He said, "You seem . . ." But what could he say? Exquisite? Not what he'd expected? Not Billy's spawn?

"Different?" she queried.

"Yes. Okay. Different."

"Which is a polite way of saying I'm not Billy's daughter."

"I didn't say that."

"You thought it. Don't deny it." She smiled again, happily presumptuous as Billy ever was. "I might get a DNA test to put everyone at ease. I'm a little curious myself. You know JoAnne isn't talking, and JoAnne not talking is like needing Alan Dershowitz for the defense. You see Billy's smile, don't you? Besides, I'm way too fair for the other."

The other? He stopped short of asking, surmising the other.

"Eloise," JoAnne said. "You were very cute, in spite of your height, but you're too old for it now. Okay?"

"Too old for my height?"

"No. Too old for being hurtful and thinking it's cute."

"Thanks again for noticing, Mother. But I'm only answering Solomon's questions."

"He didn't ask any questions," JoAnne said.

"Solomon? Didn't you wonder?"

"I did, and I see Billy's smile."

"I'm so glad," Eloise said. "It doesn't matter. Billy was Old Dad to me. Sorry. I didn't mean old. He was never old. He died too young, such an imp. And fun. I really miss that guy. I meant old as a form of endearment. Old Dad. Old Solomon."

"I miss him too. I'm sorry I didn't come sooner."

"Don't be sorry. You did well," Eloise said. "Sooner would have been difficult. It *was* difficult. You can imagine."

The reunion turned to sorrow. Mother and daughter stood by, as Solomon reviewed family photos, coming to the shots of Eloise's wedding he'd seen online. The wedding reached for pomp and ceremony, more like a coronation, as far from JoAnne and Billy's world as a state U from the Ivy League. Solomon held a shot of the wedding gown and cake both frothing with chiffon. “What a photo.”

“Yes,” Eloise said. “More like a scene from Fellini than a wedding. I’m not sure why we saved it.” She took the shot and began to tear it up.

“No!” JoAnne stopped her.

“Why not?”

“Because it is a great shot. Fuck it. You’re right. It’s more Fellini than Fair Oaks. Go ahead,” JoAnne shrugged.

Eloise destroyed the photo. “Billy and JoAnne were such hippies. Duh. And here she is taking Fair Oaks as a personal context.”

“What do you take as a personal context?”

“I’m so glad you asked,” Eloise said. “Check that. We’re so glad you asked. JoAnne?”

JoAnne shot a stink eye but stayed cool, pointing out amusing details, as Solomon flipped photos. He narrated for the daughter, that Billy and JoAnne were a rural strain of hippies. Long hair, marijuana, couch wine and occasional acid were a long way from Haight Ashbury or the Weather Underground, Kent State or the commune. He said a daughter should not think parents corny for playing to type, when reality was so layered. On Fridays, they’d laughed like fools, high on reefer and wine and the loveliest friendship most would ever know. They’d believed the workaday life wouldn’t happen to them—wouldn’t steal their energy and imaginations.

Eloise said she loved that, hearing the new guest share his

memories and insights. She'd heard a bit of it and did admire the idealism and hope of it but couldn't quite grasp the easy sex. "Of all the silly shit JoAnne and Billy couldn't get over, that's the part that killed Billy . . . took him away like a lizard on a bug."

Near the middle of the old photos, Eloise grew tall and taller, got braces and bumps, got no braces and curves. Solomon flipped slower. JoAnne and Eloise shared narrative duty with candor that seemed impressive—or would that be purposeful?

Eloise had been chaste until just before marriage. All her circumspection on regrets made virtue easy, with macho, dull men everywhere she turned. Even the sports fans, business and job guys or the quiet, thoughtful types had nothing original, nary a fresh thought among them. She wasn't good at making nice and wouldn't mate with a dullard. She wanted more.

Men were indifferent for years, save the odd dirt bag or perv. They didn't count. Things changed when she blossomed. Along with the beautiful truth was the hard fact that dirt bags, pervs and dullards weren't unique but common—make that prevalent.

The photo book went from emergent beauty to grim difficulty, to Billy's last shots, grinning like a champ after a rough defense, happy as ever, gaunt down to essence, skin over skull.

And back to Eloise, forlorn and frustrated. Could a woman get more sick and tired of explaining that her father wasn't gay, that he'd enjoyed sexual relations outside the norm because he was a hippie—a fucking hippie who really wanted to fuck this Italian pussycat? Billy didn't know she carried the dreaded disease but should have assumed it. But no, not Billy in need. He didn't know of bisexual boyfriend. "He didn't know. We like to think it would have mattered, but he really wanted to fuck her. He didn't know that women carry the disease more easily." Eloise resented those who asked how or why. Billy's stupid choices led to death. But the world around them deduced that a guy who dies of AIDS was gay, and saying as much was easier than explaining a tragedy. She went along. He wasn't gay.

"Ah," said many knowing people, knowing Billy could have been gay or bi; he was so open-minded in every way.

JoAnne poo pooed Eloise's attempt to defuse nosey people and shared the tack she'd taken on Billy's demise. She'd said it didn't matter what got Billy, because he was Billy to the end.

"Whatever the fuck that means," Eloise said, because it did matter to her. Billy died from an overdose of indiscretion, from weakness and need. Just so, the loss of a parent so young, so vital, took a bit of Eloise too. That bothered her for a year or two until . . . "Never mind. Some other time. It still bothers me. I don't want to think about it." She went to the fridge for water and poured three.

JoAnne recalled the last few decades more generously, displacing Eloise's reverie with a bright side. "Blossomed? She was gorgeous! Just look." JoAnne held a bikini shot of Eloise with her arm around Billy, Old Dad a head shorter.

A woman who carried the dreaded disease was hardly a warm subject for a widow and daughter, but this pair had been candid since the beginning of the hour and time, and the subject was on the table. So, Solomon affirmed, or maybe queried, "At least the afflicted woman wasn't you."

"No," JoAnne said, raising a wry eye. But a one-word answer would not suffice. She lit up, as smokers do on stressful topics, to buy time to arrange thoughts. Exhaling with resignation, she said she'd loved being a wife, Billy's wife. She felt certain she would not be a wife again. No need, and if a man came along, she'd love him. Sex with Billy had been robust, loving and eternal, beginning with a much longer stretch of nonstop than most people could enjoy or endure. "The reality is . . ." She paused on comparative realities and the Universe spanned since the last reality shared with her old friend. "Sok, I suspect reality is something you know little of and more than most people all at once. Things change." She took another breather, as if to infuse her words with meaning. "Monogamy is possible for some people after what, thirty years? We know it's possible because some people live within those rules. Hell, it's a beautiful thing for some people. But they're rare. Other people make it work. But it's a stretch—pun intended." She told the tale.

Billy was mid-fifties when he got sick, still game as a hound on a scent. He lost very little spirit over the years. Old friends loved Billy Keene as they had in the glory days. As a happy person, his joy in life was contagious—make that plain to see and feel. "Mid-fifties, mid-schmifties," JoAnne said. "A man craves some strange pussy to put a little dimension on his life in the suburbs. Married, workaday with bills and a daughter who was chronically embarrassed, busting his hump on a hot-mop business as the whole wide world went to hi-tech shingles and that roll-out shit they got now. Sure, he adapted to new products when he had to. But he clung to the old stuff because heavy attrition in the trade kept him in business. Hell, so many competitors failing was great for him. Sick as he got, he worked as always for as long as he could. He came home sweatin' like a split tomato, happy as a boy after school. Maybe he got laid that day. Not at the end. He couldn't stand up at the end."

"I couldn't relate to any of it," Eloise said. "I wasn't so different from any spoiled kid, but it seemed demeaning and such a waste, not just Billy's casual dismissal of his intellect and education in exchange for hot mops or his juvenile yen for sex or his self-imposed stupidity from smoking dope and drinking beer or any of it. But all of it. I'm sorry now I felt that way. I learned enough to have regrets. I was self-absorbed and would like a do-over."

Eloise was sorry she hadn't given more love and respect. She regretted his view of her wedding as getting even for the hand she'd been dealt. She regretted being Eloise.

Solomon groaned, familiar with the regretful syndrome, knowing the human affliction of inconsequence in life and the world.

"Billy couldn't relate to a three-tier wedding cake," she said.

"Twelve hundred dollars for a fucking cake!" JoAnne said.

"Billy couldn't relate to a diamond tiara," Eloise said. "He tried to fake it. He said, 'No, no! You look terrific! Like the Queen o' fucking Sheba or some shit.' He didn't mean to hurt my feelings. I know it now. I looked silly. I cried. I see the pictures. The tiara was another fifteen hundred. And it was fake!"

"You just tore up a picture," Solomon pressed.

"Do you mind?"

The story unfolded in more loose photos in the bottom of the box.

Eloise said Billy tried relating to Douglas Smythe, his son-in-law, after all. He could not. "He said Douglas was a preppy dipshit who dressed like the guys in Sok's old frat lodge. I hated him when he said that, and now I love him for it. That's coming around from going around, isn't it? Billy compared him to you. I asked why he couldn't adapt to liking Douglas, like he adapted to liking you. You know what he said? He said he didn't like you. He loved you. He said you saw the light, and your ass would make Douglas Smythe a good Sunday face." She turned away.

JoAnne took over, explaining what Solomon knew, that Billy Keene had a chip on his shoulder for anyone who posed as upper crust, who behaved as befitting a man of social positioning with poise and privilege and shit. He didn't even know Sok until that frat crap was long gone—Billy had known *of* Stan Sokolov but only in passing, as another cardboard cutout who postured with a stupid grin, as if to reflect vast potential, family wealth, connections and nothing to say. Young Sok had none of those things and not much else besides. But he had the fortitude to change clothes one day, to ditch that crap and come home, to be one of the family, the salt-o'-the-earth-get-down-nitty-gritty family. Douglas Smythe did not.

"Hey, no biggie," JoAnne said. "We wanted Eloise to be happy, and she said this was it. We had our doubts but minded our own bees' wax. We heard all the gossip and nasty chatter from the Keene and Kessler cousins and aunts and uncles. We saw their eyeballs rolling. Billy said he smelled Jew bait on the breeze."

The nasty chatter required response to the Jew jokes. "These two Jews and a nigger walk into a bar . . ." Ha. What a laugh. What proof of superiority. The Keene/Kessler side of the aisle declined the *goyim* country club for the nuptials—that was the non-Jewish country club in equally unflattering terms. "The Jewish question" lingered at Eagle Crest, where Douglas Smythe's father was president, and no Jews belonged. It could have been birds of a feather and all that natural sort of thing. Or not. The eagle crest seemed oddly similar to the black eagle over an oak wreathe that adorned banners at the Reichstag, but Douglas Smythe's father said somebody was looking for trouble.

JoAnne smiled. "Billy said, 'Old Yiddish saying: *Fuchum*! I drink beer out of a fuckin' bottle, and not with fuckin' Nazi fuckers.'"

Solomon shivered and wished Billy was there for commiseration and bonding anew in modern times—or the times that were not a changin'. He wiped a speck from his eye. "I miss him too."

Douglas told Eloise that Eagle Crest Country Club could not host the rehearsal dinner or the reception because of, you know, prior scheduling and all that administrative nonsense.

Billy had laughed. "Problem solved! Or should we put it off till the schedule clears? We can wait. Maybe next year!"

The nuptials and life got past anti-Semitism and a bad marriage. Eloise's betrothal was a single frame of a movie that played on.

Solomon only just arrived, and already the hours flew by.

"Hey. Go freshen up," JoAnne said. "I'm making brown rice and tuna for dinner."

"I don't eat tuna."

"Okay. Brown rice and broccoli. Okay?"

He nodded. Eloise leaned in for a sniff. "You won't douse up with patchouli, will you?"

"No."

"Thanks. I hate to be demanding so soon, but that stuff gags me."

"I never cared for it either. It was for weirdos. Still is."

"What a close call," she said.

JoAnne prepped the rice precisely, happily nostalgic for the strident rules of the golden days: two to one, water to rice, short grain organic. Let it boil for a minute, lower the flame to tiny, put on the lid and let it be, forty-five minutes. Turn it off and let it set another ten. And do not lift the lid until then!

"I'll be a minute," Solomon said. "I do like to shower off the airplane cooties."

Eloise turned. "You're a clean freak?"

Solomon smiled. "It's mythical. And by nature, ephemeral."

She met his gaze again. "Do you mean you're mythical? Or your compulsions are mythical? What's the difference between mythical and legendary? Are you often accused of speaking in riddles? That's polite for obscurely. I guess that's what a guru does."

"I'm sure it is. I think myth derives from legend. It changes, like youth and beauty. You looked in the mirror with disappointment. Now you see something else. You're aware of your power. It'll also go away in time. But you know that. You should know that."

"Ah, ephemera. I thought you meant that bathing was a waste of time since you'll only soil again before too long. I used to think that about making the bed. Maybe you did too."

"Of course, I did. We bathe every day at the Hima Luja Compound, to be clean. We make the bed or not. As far as gravitational power, I know women who go out of their way to diminish their beauty. They get tired of the pressure. JoAnne is unique. She loved her gift and made the most of it. Still does."

"You mean at her age? I'm confused. We were talking about your hygiene obsession."

"That's where you started. I started on my way to ditch the airplane cooties. That's as straightforward as I can say it."

"I see why Billy loved you. You're the same as him but with a disjunctive route to the truth instead of bearing down the piss-and-vinegar freeway."

He shrugged. "Disjunctive? I've been accused of many things, but never piss and vinegar."

"I might love you too, for Billy and all. Could you be comfortable with that?"

Solomon smirked. "I'd be uncomfortable without it. Presumption can be hazardous, but I presume a bond here and feel safe with it."

Eloise seemed perplexed, or at least reflective, as he took his leave to hit the shower and ditch the cooties.

He wondered if melodrama was intrinsic to life in Hoosierville.

Emerging with damp curls cascading, he felt better, arrived and returned. In the kitchen, he hugged JoAnne again. "You're an elixir."

Eloise watched. "Easy, big fella."

"And you." He smiled at the spawn of his true loves. "What was the attraction, you to Douglas Smythe or him to you?"

The saga continued. Sharing again her distaste for most things hippie or tawdry or squalid, in case Solomon missed it, she cut to the chase. "It was sexual. We thought we were similar in other things too. We weren't. Neither one of us worked, so we had all this free time. We both loved clear weather. Duh. And fresh fruit. How amazing. We stayed shallow. It was a fling, something we outgrew but not soon enough. For me, it was Douglas Smythe, football hero, studly student body whatever. It was weak. A compensation. It was only a few months, really, when he told his parents we were going long-term. They tried to talk some sense into him—social sense. We did it anyway." She shrugged. "Romance is tricky. He hid the nasty side as long as he could. He got worse, meaner and stupider."

"Stupid is tough," Solomon said. "You're over it?"

"Don't fuck with me, Sok. He was truly an asshole, to the core. Everyone saw it but me, till I saw it too. That was a long time after first sex. So? I was young, inexperienced. I thought he was it, and we'd ring the bell every day. He got into a porno website and called it foreplay. It got old, fast, him going like a jackhammer. No love. It hit me. On my elbows, soaking up punches like a sparring partner, watching an old lady on the screen getting it from five guys, trying to remember how I got there."

"No love," Solomon said, not a typical back quote but recalling his explanation of a loveless foray at the frat lodge.

"You're familiar with that sort of thing?" she ventured.

"I'm fairly inexperienced myself. I think I'm old-fashioned. Some people might disagree, but I haven't seen much action."

"Most people haven't seen much action. JoAnne has. Maybe I took a lead from her. The amazing thing was my appetite and the sudden nausea. He got ugly in a flash. I was sick of it, sick of myself for being there. I have to tell you, I bucked him off and went outside and leaned on a wall just to breathe. He coulda bitch-slapped me and put the ammonia under my nose. I woke up. It was over."

"You still regret being with him?"

"I do. You might feel indifferent to . . . romance? Love?"

"I'm not sure what word you're looking for. But I don't think many people are indifferent."

"Numb, maybe?"

"Or atrophied?"

"Yes, atrophied. But less action? If that's the case. For a rock star on the guru circuit?"

He asked, "You mean because of my good looks? Why haven't you seen more action? After the repugnant one."

"You're every bit as good looking as I am," she said. "You know it and may choose to ignore it, but people still look." She drifted to the fridge for a bottle of *Pinot Grigio*, so light, unencumbering and noncommittal. "My dream deflated to something more attainable. I may be traumatized and gun shy. Romance may not be for me." She poured three glasses without asking and served two.

"That sounds tough. You've thought this over."

"I've lived it. You never felt good with someone? Don't you think that's odd? I do. Did you ever have a dog? You must have felt good about your dog. Or cat! That was it! Kitteees!"

Solomon hung his head, "Yes," tipping his hand further, conceding his greatest loves in life were Harry the dog, a bunch of kittens and friends he hadn't seen in decades.

"It's perfect," JoAnne interceded. "I mean, for Sok and me. For Sok and you. Not that our experience is perfect, far from it, but . . . Okay, Solomon. Whatever. It's been, what, almost forty years? We still have friendship and trust. Everything goes away but love." She paused for drama.

He sensed melodrama but smiled benignly.

She laid a foundation. "We change, but we come from the same place. We grew up on the same terms and remember certain phrasing. We can still talk openly and honestly." She looked up, into his eyes.

"I think so," he said. "I hope so. It's only natural that we review in detail. We have comfort and trust. I love full disclosures, but . . . is this a proposal?"

JoAnne laughed. "It's so strange, you here, speaking complete sentences without going off like a fucking tea kettle."

"Gheee!"

"He did," Eloise said. "When he called. I didn't get it at first, but he introduced himself, and it all came home."

"I guess I couldn't help it. I missed you and Billy, and it's been a tough time. The old home stuff just . . . spilled over. Or something. I felt such relief when you answered. I thought it was you," he said to JoAnne. He moved to the sofa to take a load off.

Eloise took the opposite end. JoAnne turned down the flame, put the lid on the rice, set the timer and sat in the adjacent chair. Solomon wondered if such gatherings and discussions were common to the Keene living room, imagining what he'd missed in his decades in the other world. Or is the other side of the fence viewed from the green end of the prism. "Wait a minute," he said. "A prism has no green."

"What?"

"Nothing. I'm mumbling." Most married men would have envied Solomon's access to available women over the years, and he might envy it too, had he not felt the tedium of repetitive introduction, getting to know you, getting to know all about you, the hazards of health, hygiene and emotion for the paltry minutes of flesh. Why couldn't a few minutes lead to more minutes? Because warm, friendly people had surrounded him with little depth or staying power. Why had he stayed? He stayed because. . .

"Sok. Sok. Come in, Sok. Earth to Sok." JoAnne brought him in from the drift.

"Sorry."

"It's okay. I meant Solomon. You prefer Solomon."

"That's my name."

"Okay. You're right. It is. A proposal."

Solomon groaned, sensing more or less than met the eye, knowing yet again why love remained elusive. "We're coming to the beautiful situation?"

"Yes. You've been away, and this is important. The best decision will be informed. That's all. People who didn't know any better thought Billy and I had an open marriage. We didn't. We had an honest marriage. We didn't fuck around indiscriminately. By the way, you never got married, did you?"

"No. I never met anybody. Never came close. I suspect a personal deficiency. I've known some wonderful people."

"It's okay. You have that wise man aura. That intimidates

people. Anyway, an open marriage is not where you fuck anybody you want to. We didn't do that. Everybody fucks when they're young and hot, like Eloise and Douglas. But the heavy passion fades away—hell, then all the passion fades away. Billy and I had a great sex life, and that's saying something after so many years. We figured out that frequency decreases in five-year increments, and it came out to about fourteen thousand fucks. Billy figured we went an average of twelve in-outs for every jizz-bang when he didn't wait for me, and thirty-six when he did—oh, that guy could last. He figured half and half, but I can tell you from the receiving end that he waited damn near every time, so it came to about a million in-outs. You can't imagine that. I can't imagine that. Talk about numbing. And we didn't fuck around. We asked each other if it might be . . . acceptable, you know, if so-and-so . . . you know. For me, it was a friend, a guy we'd known since forever, the same guys who'd been looking down my blouse since college or copping sleeve shots." She stopped for a coy smirk, to make eye contact and take another breather.

"A guy or guys?" he asked.

"Two guys. Four years apart. Okay? I was with four guys total in my life. Okay?"

"Fine. You said a guy, and then you said guys. Okay?"

"Do you mind me sharing like this? It's very personal. Eloise knows or should know, but it'll do her good to hear it." JoAnne leaned to the coffee table for her smokes. She plucked one, butt-lit and inhaled, satisfied with movement and nicotine.

Solomon said, "You mean Randall?"

She nodded. Randall was a woeful slob and whoremonger but

not a bad guy. "He changed after you left. He grew up." She took another hit to better reflect on Randall growing up. "Scratch that. He's still a slob, but not a bad guy. It just happened and seemed weird in the context of an old friendship." She paused, so that the old-friendship-weirdness combo might sink in.

It did. Solomon smiled briefly. Off the hook? Never mind; he'd sort later.

She smoked. "Then it ended. Billy was relieved, but hey, sauce for the gander. I think it made us better. Billy and I stayed on it until a while before he went away. We'd have a little wine, turn the lights low. Sure, Billy'd pop a boner pill. His doctor told him it would probably stop his heart. He said, 'Yeah? So?' He was such an easy guy to love. I never met anybody as unafraid as he was. We used condoms then. I was scared but loved him so much. Anyway, low lights, some vino, just a dab of reefer; it was right back where we started from. Man, he was a one-off. And he loved those guys. He loved you. Too bad you weren't around."

Solomon blushed again at the math and the dots that could have connected JoAnne and himself. "Well . . ." He looked down. Eloise observed, looking beneath his shyness.

"For him, it was two women while we were married, which sounds like tit for tat, and maybe it was. He always said it wasn't fair, that a woman gets laid whenever she wants to—ugly, fat, doesn't matter. But a guy—even a guy as drop-dead handsome as him—had to do the work." She laughed, wiping a tear. "But he'd stay with each one for a long time. He was like that, a great guy, a real man, honest and loving. He kept life alive. I loved the change-up and the fun. You know, fooling around, even just a bit. Who doesn't fantasize about old friends? But I never strayed for long. I'd come around to my senses, over and out for me."

"Or in and out for you," Eloise chirped.

"Very funny, Ms. In-and-out-and-divorced." JoAnne inhaled to prep for the crux: "Except for Stevo. That was odd. I'd never thought about him sexually, much less romantically. He was too hairy for my taste, until, you know, he touched me, and everything changed, and we did it. It was strange, with the multiple orgasms and crazy stuff. I never bothered Billy with the details, but he knew. Stevo was in the picture for a long time. Not that long, really, but a few months, until we both got uncomfortable with it. I guess discomfort is a symptom too. The years don't count for nothing in learning about life."

"No, they don't count for nothing," Solomon said distractedly, imagining JoAnne on top, wondering if that was her objective in so much disclosure.

"I'm going to make iced tea," Eloise announced, excusing herself from the confessional. "It's not so smart to keep drinking wine when you're thirsty."

JoAnne smoked, finding her stride or feeling absolved or on her way. "We had an honest marriage because we could handle it. You know how they have all those dials and lights on a . . . like on a nuclear submarine? We had a system like that to make sure everybody was okay on pressure levels and sensitivity and not getting too horny at home and keeping tabs on mean old Mister Jealousy. Billy got a little touchy near the end of Stevo. I got it. Believe me, I had my doubts about three years into his time with Erica. That was the girlfriend who killed him. She was drop-dead gorgeous from a distance but cheap and made up. She was a whore, really. You think these guns tamed the Wild West?" Joanne hefted her bosom. "Erica had a perfect rack, naturals, but the guys don't seem to care either way. She had the hips, and a flat stomach and Italian features with big, dark eyes and curly black hair kind of like yours. She was smart and sweet, an incredible artist with showings in the best galleries."

"You knew her well?"

"Sure. We hung out, the three of us. Billy loved that, but he wasn't showing off. He loved her and me. He wanted a three way for his last birthday but . . . We tried it once. I don't like to share and, frankly, I was scared of her. I knew where she'd been. Everywhere."

"Why didn't Billy know where she'd been?"

"He did, more or less. Come on, a beautiful woman about forty, single, artist. She had men after her, men from the same mold. That was the thing. She had a few photos with one guy who, I don't know why, and you know I'm open-minded, but he looked gay. What does gay look like? He looked gay. And I asked her, 'Who's that?' She called him a dear, old friend. I asked her, 'You mean like Billy?' She gave me the look, but I gave it right back, so she eased off and rolled her eyes and did a little shoulder number to make her tits bounce. And I said, 'Huh. He looks gay.' And she said, 'Bi.' Down the road, she made a point of telling me that she hadn't had sex with that guy in a long time. I wondered why she told me that. I wondered for about twelve seconds. Then I got scared. But that was way into Billy's time with her. I wondered who else besides the bi guy? But the big question for everybody was why Billy? A hard-working man with tar smudge on his face and shitty clothes, looking freshly beaten by life, hollering fuck or fuckin' this or that or fuckinay on everything, always happy. He was the genuine article. Now you tell me who else fit that profile. Billy never faked it, especially when it came to love and happiness. And he always had a baby face. He got old and didn't look so happy. Man, at the end . . ." She smoked to let it pass.

"How did a fine artist get involved with a hot mopper?"

JoAnne jumped back in, as if happy he'd asked. "She's walking down a sidewalk, fancy neighborhood where Billy's hot mopping the add-on atrium at a mansion. For all I know, she set it up, scoped him out and trolled the bait, wrapping her perfect ass in a skimpy stretch skirt and flopping that rack in a loose silk halter and slinking on by, like honey and molasses. Billy was hot. Women looked. He's up there sweatin' bullets, but he takes a break for what matters, slowing down to smell the beauty, and he whistles low and says, 'No rusty hinge in that gate.' And she calls up, 'Fuck you, asshole.'" JoAnne inhaled.

Solomon sat back, closing his eyes to see what he'd missed in the real world of hot mopping, wolf whistles, an unusual wife and loose women with AIDS. He wondered what he'd had in common with Billy Keene past the common age in a common era, the reefer, acid and Boone's Farm. Well, short shrift can be dismissive and miss the crux of a thing.

"Billy jumps off the roof—the fucking roof—and strides right up and doesn't say a goddamn thing, just bats those baby blues, practically inviting her to slug him or lay down. She laid down, over in the next block where she lived, after they cleaned up in the shower. Three years. Erica and Billy went at it for three years before she got sick. He got sick a few months later."

Solomon groaned like a bull humpback, giving voice to the grief within. He hoped she would not share the hospice segment, and though she seemed ready, she didn't. She put out the cigarette, mashing it in a small ashtray that could not hold the load.

"Don't forget: Billy wasn't your usual labor grunt. He was about a month out from his doctorate in history when he gave it up. Called himself 'Professor Fuckin' Billy.'" She laughed short and reached for the smokes but set them down. "It affects the immune system. The common failure is pulmonary. Hot mop fumes didn't help. You breathe that toxin so long; you get hurt. He had no chance." She looked aside. "He was a goner. He knew it. That's when he started smoking. We both did. He said fuck it—a little nicotine helped ease the stress. What difference could a bad habit make? I went along. I'd have gone along with anything. And I guess it did help. Still does. I don't care. I . . . I . . ."

"I know . . ." They wept.

Eloise wept in the kitchen.

A Fix for Our Need

"Are you really so desperate?" Solomon asked.

"Are you really so blind?" JoAnne rejoined. "We thought of you a long time ago but couldn't find you."

"I think you could."

"Maybe. We thought a dish like Eloise could find a man easy as pie. We factored the age difference too. We were wrong. Sok, Eloise is put together for any man's dream. You're one of the few who knows what happens after the dream. They wake up. I don't blame her for holding back. She's more than physical. She won't work with the wrong man. She met men her age, well-dressed men with good jobs, men who seemed interested, had social skills . . . You ever try to light a cigarette in a breeze? When Eloise said you called, it came clear. And look how it's playing out."

"Get it right, JoAnne," Eloise said. "Finding a man *is* easier than pie. Meeting Sadie's criteria and mine: not so much."

"Is it playing out? I'm old enough to be—"

"—my father? JoAnne? Is *that* where the height comes from?"

"No. Sok and I never did it. I'm not sure he did it with anyone then. He was so out there."

"JoAnne, wake up and smell the incense. I'm still out there! And I'm old! Eloise thinks I'm fit and kind and don't stink and whatever else is on her check list. How do we look in fifteen years? Or twenty?"

"You'll have your stature," Eloise said. "Even if you shrink."

"I am not the only qualified donor out there!" Solomon said. "Sorry. I meant participant."

"Precisely, Mister Smarty Pants," JoAnne agreed. "You preach that aery fairy hocus pocus for a living, all that synchronicity and karmic resolution and no coincidence . . . stuff."

"I live it. I believe it."

"Fucking bingo! And who shows up out of the universe after thirty-seven fucking years on a random phone call? It's you, numb nuts. You! You who we love!"

Solomon eased back to rub his temples, throbbing from a full day, off-road. JoAnne lit a smoke. Eloise pulled up a chair behind Solomon to take over on the temple rub. "It's like this, Uncle Solomon. When Douglas went at me like a pneumatic pogo stick, I had time to do some thinking. After all, if you don't reflect on the downside, what's the point of being there? I didn't think of you, specifically. I thought, *What is wrong with this guy?* I thought, *If I had my druthers, I'd druther be with a gentle man who likes it slow, a good-looking man with brains and wit, a lovable, caring man with a worldview, a reflective man I can love*. You came along by and by." She rubbed his neck and shoulders. "Is this okay?"

"Yes. Don't stop."

"So? I like you. I like what I see. What I feel. You'll get older.

Slower. I like that. We can help each other out."

"You're embarrassing me."

"Sorry about that, but don't you think the candid truth is best?"

"I've had a long day. I'm not certain what the truth might be."

"I can help," JoAnne said. She sat up and laid it out: Billy Keene's mother, Sadie Keene, blamed JoAnne when the hot mop company cooled off and went belly up. She blamed JoAnne again for Billy's passing, and soon blamed JoAnne again and again, as she could, and then she died.

Sadie hadn't been wealthy by modern standards, but she'd be rich in most neighborhoods, her estate at just under a million dollars. That was two years after Billy died—two years of strategizing in her will.

Sadie and her daughter-in-law JoAnne had tolerated each other for years, inasmuch as a Jewish mother can abide that self-absorbed bitch who refuses to wait on her son hand and foot, after tricking him into marriage on the oldest bait in the book. JoAnne had made nice, but the ill will went both ways. Sadie changed her will when Billy died, leaving JoAnne *zipola, bupkis, nada mucho, chub'm 'n tuchus*. That would be nothing, more nothing and nothing again, kiss my ass.

Sadie bequeathed her assets to Eloise, sort of. Sadie knew the tension between JoAnne and Eloise but feared that Eloise would share, as daughters do, even if the mother was a whore who sent her husband out to get AIDS from another whore. Sadie solved that problem with two stipulations: 1) the estate would be held in trust for Eloise's offspring until the birth of said offspring, at which time Eloise would manage the funds prudently, as trustee. And 2) that the offspring must be Jewish, as defined by Jewish law, requiring a Jewish mother. That would be Eloise, whose Jewish mother is JoAnne. Sadie also stipulated a Jewish father, as defined by circumcision and born to a Jewish mother. Sadie did not want some gold-digging *shaygetz* stealing the dough, shaygetz being an unflattering term for a non-Jewish male.

When Billy died, Sadie ceased contact with his wife and daughter. They'd been on life-support since Eloise married Douglas Smythe. "Like a slap in the face!" Sadie said, announcing her plan to cut them out! Out! Out! It didn't matter that Douglas Smythe was no gold digger. She hated the sound and sight of him, hated his Jew-baiting, anti-Semitic, ramrod *goyim* name and reputation. She would leave the money to The Moline Mishpocha Memorial Fund, a cousin klatch that praised Sadie's devotion and good works.

Eloise found redemption in divorce.

Sadie grunted; too late. Eloise was out. The MMMF was in.

Many loved Eloise but agreed that Sadie had a point. Leave the money to Smythes? Then again, The Moline Mishpocha Memorial Fund seemed a waste, a bunch of *kvetching shmegeggies*.

The Moline Fund thanked G-d for the windfall, prematurely but with zeal and hope. Eloise hadn't meet Sadie's terms anyway, and tic, tic, tic went the biological clock. So? Who was to blame?

Sadie Keene fell ill soon after the wedding but held on through Billy's demise, and died three months after the Smythe divorce was final. Eloise used her maiden name by then, but Sadie took no solace and cut no slack beyond a meager nod. Sadie would raise the bar, God willing, Jewish offspring be damned. Eloise would be out! Out! Out! She relished her decision. It felt devoted and good, yet alas.

Sadie Keene passed prior to changing her will the second time. The MMMF lamented, but administrators declined legal remedy, what with the retainer and hourly fees, the expenses and no guarantee, because the *mumbzer* lawyers were all the same.

Nominally lucid in her last days, Sadie's disavowal was nonbinding. The bequeathal to Eloise and stipulations on Jewish spawn remained intact, motivating Eloise to set things right.

Nobody paraphrased intentions or the mother's role. But the family agreed. *Let's face it, a girl her age has fewer prospects. She does have that tush. And those boobies should not go for nothing. So? Maybe she'll find a fella who's a mensch, and that'll do the trick.*

"Our financial stability is not in question," Eloise insisted, pouring tea over ice in goblets.

"It's not?" JoAnne asked.

"It's our laziness. JoAnne is tired. She complains. She doesn't get out. She smokes weed and talks about you and others. That won't put food on the table. Or iced tea." She served tea with lemon wedges, sugar cubes and long-handled teaspoons.

JoAnne said, "Eloise is pressing thirty-nine and unemployed. Plenty of time but not much time to waste. You were always smart, Sok. Solomon. Stanley. Smart; fuck, you were brilliant, connecting dots nobody else could even see." She stared off. "And we saw a few dots. Anyway, you see where we are?"

Solomon took his time, adding a sugar cube, squeezing a wedge, stirring, tasting, for time to see if not for vision. On a second taste, he ventured, "Black tea with . . . mango?"

"Bingo," Eloise said.

"Mm. Nice."

Eloise grew up on talk of Sok, the one-off, shy but wild, a crazy brainy kid from the glory days. She sensed strange glory and small compensation for cigarettes, dope, liquor and hot mop fumes. Yet, after all these years, Sok had lively eyes and a brain to match.

He would credit his fitness to moderation, a little dope at cocktail hour, beer or wine on occasion, no distilled spirits, except for sipping-grade tequila, and eating no animal or byproduct. He got exercise.

He sensed the navigational bearing—he wasn't called Solomon for nothing—and pleaded ignorance. "I don't see where we are. You need a Jewish fella. They have places for that. Sperm banks. You can tailor a donor down to a geographic source, advance degrees, age, interests, hobbies, genetic warnings, anything."

"She won't do that." JoAnne spoke flatly, fatigued from a few laps around the donor block.

Eloise sat up straight as an exclamation mark.

"Might I ask why not?" Solomon asked.

"I won't," Eloise affirmed.

"She has a friend," JoAnne said, "who went through it and spent, what, ten, twelve thousand. It didn't take."

"It often doesn't take," Eloise said.

"Sometimes two people don't take," Solomon said.

"They used a turkey baster," Eloise said. "It was cold."

Solomon shrugged. "A turkey might think that's better than a basting. Sorry, that's a vegan joke. But a baster can be warmed to room temperature on fairly low-tech apparatus."

"I won't," Eloise said.

"Believe me, she won't," JoAnne confirmed.

Solomon looked up. "You could try the *schül*, Friday night, Saturday morning. High holidays, dressed to kill. You'll see a candidate." Schül is Yiddish for school or synagogue, a word common to Jewish households long removed from Yiddish speech.

"A candidate? This isn't a campaign," Eloise said. "It's a commitment! I don't want a turkey baster. I need a man, not a one-time dick. And I don't mean a husband. I mean a father. Yes, it's impractical. I don't care. JoAnne thinks this is all about her for a change. She needs the money for old age. But it's bigger than her."

"You want a father but not a husband?" Solomon asked.

"For the baby, fool! If it happens. I can't raise a kid alone on a few hundred grand. I won't."

"But you'll be . . ." He stopped short of suggesting a job. She wouldn't be working; she'd be at home, working for no pay. Caring for the kid. *With the sleep deprivation and shitty diapers. And for what, another person in a jampacked world? For scrimping and saving because the few hundred grand would go for college? Fuck.*

"Sok?" JoAnne moved in.

"I love you, JoAnne. I don't know Eloise, and I love her too. But I couldn't . . ."

"But you can, and you will. I need it. Billy needs it. Eloise . . ."

"You have cousins. Second cousins, fourth cousins. You could know the genetic stuff."

"Yeah. We know all about them. It's terrific data, really," Eloise said. "The only one halfway sane or stable or socially acceptable is Kevin. He's handsome and bright. He was president of his class in high school. He's not a dimwit. He has epilepsy."

"He does not have epilepsy," JoAnne said. "He had a seizure a long time ago."

"And a CAT scan and all those other tests. Even if I was willing to warm up the turkey baster, I couldn't accept that variable."

"How do you know my variables?" Solomon asked.

"Do you have variables?" Eloise asked back.

"I might. I'm too old. I'm not fit to be a father. My family values might surprise you. Whose family are we talking about? Parental responsibility is not what I crave, and overpopulation strains our world. How's that for variable?"

Eloise clasped hands to chest.

JoAnne intervened. "You are fit to be a father. You've been surrogate father to a cult. You've done your work, and look what you've developed. Now you can bless a child. I love your beliefs. I think I still know you. I think you're a natural at so many things, including things you haven't tried. Sok. We can make this work. By the way, it *was* nine hundred fifty grand. Now it's a million two. We'll go right down the middle. Thirds."

"Down the middle would be halves."

"Okay. Thirds. Fuck it. It's family, like it was ever anything but. We're family. Can you feel it? No shit. You can make a better life. You quit school, and here's a second chance. Your kid could have what you missed. Ivy League. The best connections."

"You're losing me, JoAnne," Solomon said. "Maybe you didn't know me or weren't paying attention. Ivy league?

Connections?"

"Okay. Look. Let's just . . . Let's just say you and Eloise go to dinner. Tomorrow night. No. Go tonight. Espero's." She looked to Eloise for approval or rejection. Eloise shrugged, putting JoAnne a step ahead. "You'll love it. I'll make a reservation for eight. No. Seven thirty. No. Six thirty. Why not get an early start?"

"The Early Bird Special?" he asked.

"No. That's five thirty and depressing."

"I can imagine."

"They have a wonderful menu," Eloise said. "The vegetarian selections are always good. I could eat that stuff exclusively. It's casual. I guess we'll go in what, an hour?"

"No," Solomon said. "I'd rather take you both to dinner tomorrow. Tonight, we have plans: broccoli and rice with nostalgia. Please? I'm tired from travel and emotion. Old guy and all that."

A lull settled like a flat spot on blustery seas.

Eloise turned for her room. Would the living room be his room? Was Eloise in a mood? Did she walk that way all the time, like a cat?

JoAnne slid over to snuggle as she'd done in a former life, when she walked like that all the time.

She said, "Mm . . . Brown rice and broccoli. I love that. The sound of it makes me feel healthier, like you, starting tonight. It's a perfect meal. I'm not sure why I didn't think of it until you got here. I guess that's how it goes. We forget so much."

Solomon sat up. "I don't get it, JoAnne. Eloise seems smart. Frightfully smart. How could she form a liking for me on the spot, much less love and commitment? She never met me."

"It was easy," Eloise said, leaning on the corner of the hallway that led to her bedroom. "I'd heard the stories and found you intriguing. Stories can exaggerate. I know that. And I really don't want to take another hit on a second husband. So, I established plausibility: Could I love this outing, this prospect, this future? I went through the devil's advocacy, my advocacy, pressing a few variables and downsides. You can't think of everything, but it was damn comprehensive. That was before I met you, and the big variables got nailed. Fat, unkempt, smelly, overbearing, stupid, rude, uninformed or dispassionate—any one of those things would have killed it. You're okay so far, and you have a history in-house to support your case."

"Please. I have no case."

"You were a hippie nutter who came to his senses. I feel it. It's like winning the lottery. The lottery is longer odds, but believe me, a man your age dodging so many bullets is a winner. And look at me. Does that help?"

Brown Rice & Broccoli

JoAnne set the four-top on the screened porch with a cloth, plates and glasses, cool water in a pitcher, soy sauce, olive oil and chopsticks. She lit two long candles as a centerpiece and beckoned.

Solomon half snoozed on the couch, easing into snug harbor like a sailor back from rough seas in exotic climes.

"Uncle Stanley."

He blinked.

Eloise gazed down on his meager consciousness. "That's what I would have called you, if life was normal and you'd been around."

"Life isn't normal. You know that."

"I do, and you fit right in."

"Thank you."

"Don't mention it. Did you hear? It's dinner."

"This is what I look like, waking up."

"For brown rice and broccoli? Hup to, Mister."

He rose and followed her to the porch. JoAnne wore a dress with a plunging neckline, a woman unchanged. Did he look foolish, smiling like a kid? JoAnne had survived the old times, middle times and new times. She wasn't flirting or coy; she couldn't help it. He sat, grateful for restoration, what he called comfort food for the spirit. He paused.

"Are we praying?" Eloise asked.

"I'm not," he said. "Are you?"

"It looked like a prayer," she said.

"I like to take a moment."

"You mean the one we're supposed to be in."

"Yes. That one. Or the one just before it. I think of it more as a reflection. Is that the same as a prayer? It's what I do."

"A reflection. I like that."

"Good for us," he concurred, hungry as a traveling man, laying a bed of two scoops.

JoAnne passed the broccoli. "We saw you, Sok. I mean Solomon. On TV. A while ago. You wore orange pantaloons and that blouse, all billowy. You said something about love and understanding."

"The saffron hues are uniquely energetic," he said.

Eloise took one scoop and asked, "So you can run like hell when the bad boys want to beat you up?"

"Eloise, do you mind?" JoAnne asked. "Can you stop?"

"Stop what? Am I bothering you, Uncle Stanley?"

"Not at all. You intrigue me. I hope you don't mind if I stare. I don't mean to stare, but it's been so long, and you are the spawn of my loves of youth, provocative like Billy and a tease like JoAnne."

Eloise blushed: touché.

"You had those finger chimes," JoAnne said.

"Cymbals," he corrected, tapping his thumb and forefinger.

Eloise asked, "Did you play tunes or just prance around like an elf making tingly noises?"

"Eloise," JoAnne asserted. "You married a preppy asshole and have the tastes of a Jewish princess. Okay? Calling foibles is not for you. Not yet. I'll let you know when it feels more suitable."

Solomon said, "You're actually correct, Eloise. We pranced like elves making strange noises, like fools. That was the point. I hope you didn't miss it. I never could get the elfin part down. Too tall. But I was a huge success in the foolish part. Just look." He lay four broccoli spears on top and dribbled soy and olive oil. "What a feast."

"A beggar's banquet?" Eloise asked.

JoAnne and Solomon beamed on cue, remembering a beggar's banquet or two, with pizza, pistachios, ice cream, cheese puffs, pickles, cookies and chips making the rounds to the Rolling Stones album of the same name on the record player.

Solomon ate studiously and harked back to a point he didn't want to lose. "Look, you saw it as foolish, didn't think twice. We knew it was foolish and that you saw it for what it was. We also believed you had no idea that *we* knew it and egged you on to see the foolishness, beginning with ours and ending on yours."

"The monkey chased the weasel . . ."

"Yes, well, some of our charades were more easily interpreted than others. That was our objective. We obviously failed with you."

Eloise dabbled at her rice and a broccoli sprig but stopped to disagree. "You didn't fail with me. I knew it was foolish and wouldn't have thought twice about any part of that silly show. But my parents knew you long ago, and you were coming to visit, so I gave it a second thought. I think you knowing it was the problem. You were superior, fucking with everyone like they were too stupid to get the game, but they got it and thought it was just stupid. I think you failed with you."

"I have that same feeling, especially lately."

JoAnne got up. "I'm having a beer. Sok?"

"Yes, please."

"That's great, Eloise," JoAnne chided on the way to the fridge. "Do you feel better now?"

"Why would I feel better? For helping a man realize his failure? What's to feel good about that? I'll have some wine, please, JoAnne."

"Actually, I do feel better," Solomon said. "Wait a minute: I'm Uncle Stanley, and I'm a failure. How's that for the first meeting of Gurus Anonymous?"

Eloise laughed to a grunt. "That's good! That's what I miss. Miss, hell. What I never had. Well, we did. Billy could out-asshole the best of them. But you, with the self-effacing jokes. You're not afraid to look stupid. That part I love."

"I'm happy for both of us, but self-effacing jokes are not always good," Solomon said. "I'd rather be a success—not a material success. I'd rather be a virtuoso at something than a quick wit."

"But you are a success!" JoAnne insisted, popping two bottles, pouring wine for Eloise. "You're on TV. You speak, and people listen. You can feel what you do. Oh, sure, Billy could feel what he did too, if you count sweat and toxic fumes and tired all the time.

You can feel your soul, for better or worse. And you think about things. You're not numb. You may be the biggest success I know."

"You should run in better circles," Solomon said.

Eloise laughed again. "You're a stitch, Uncle Stan. Really. You crack me up."

"Thanks, I think."

"And you don't look your age. It's because you're thin—or at least not fat. I'm sure you look chunkier naked. That's okay. That's where love takes over. Do you dye your hair?" She sipped her wine.

"Why would I dye my hair gray with white highlights?"

"You might dye it silver," Eloise suggested. "They call it platinum, for added value."

"Maybe I should."

"Or shouldn't. Gray and white is the new thing. You may be a failed guru, but you're still *trés* chic."

"How reassuring."

"Not to change the subject," JoAnne said. "What would you like to do tomorrow?"

Solomon finished his rice and broccoli. "Delicious. I hadn't eaten all day, and you haven't lost your touch on brown rice. Anything is good for tomorrow. I hadn't expected anything and can't think of anything. I'm happy to see you both and looking forward to relaxing time. What a great break. I have to figure out some things too."

"Sounds mysterious," Eloise said. "And elusive. You don't want to be obscure forever, do you?" He said nothing. She took it as a no, he did not want obscurity forever. "The thing is, Uncle Stanley . . ."

"Eloise, stop that. His name is Solomon."

Eloise waited, but Solomon deferred to prevailing currents. "What would you prefer?" Eloise asked.

"What would you prefer?" Solomon rejoined.

"How about a compromise? Uncle Solly? We'll use the money to open a deli."

Solomon shook his head. "No. I got strict instructions. It's not Solly. I had an Uncle Solly. He died of . . ."

"What?"

"We were kids. We called it asshole cancer. It was cruel."

"Strict instruction from whom?" Eloise asked.

"My teacher. Hima Luja. He gave me my name. He often gave new names, sometimes with instruction to avoid obvious nicknames. He told me it's not Sol or Solly."

"How about Solomon?" JoAnne said. "And just let it go. For so much critical bullshit on monkeys and mulberry bushes, you can't let anything go. Can you?"

Eloise blushed to dramatic hues, and Solomon asked, "You are sensitive, aren't you?"

Fingertips to cheek, Eloise said, "You mean my color."

"Gotcha," JoAnne said. "Yes. She's done that forever. Nobody thought much about it, except that it was cute. Now it means she's embarrassed."

"I'm not embarrassed," Eloise said.

"Why deny your sensitivity?" Solomon asked.

"Why won't you open a deli? We'll call it Solomon's."

"Because I don't eat animals or animal by-products. Who ever heard of a vegan deli?"

"What a terrific idea!" Eloise said.

"Great. We'll develop the deli idea tomorrow. Back to your sensitivity and reactions . . ."

"It doesn't mean anything," Eloise said. "Some things make me feel like I'm . . . showing something when I don't want to. I blush."

"And so you are," he said. "Emotion comes to the surface. JoAnne reminded you of bothering a subject to the point of . . . I want to say distraction, but that might be too polite. Maybe it's more like insistence, having it your way, like when you get an itch and scratch till it bleeds."

"I'm sure you're right, Doctor Solomon. You're so smart. How about roller-skating? Tomorrow. JoAnne won't go but not because she's old. She's a klutz. She's afraid to fall and let everybody see what a klutz she is. You know, instead of the vamp she used to be. She's afraid on account of her age too, broken hip and all that."

"I've never known her to be afraid, and I don't think she is now. None of us want to fall," Solomon said. "Look at me. I have farther to fall than either one of you. I'm too tall."

"You appear to plummet softly, and look where you landed," Eloise consoled. "I'm sure you should be concerned, but I think you'll go skating with me. I think you're afraid as anybody anywhere, but it's different with you. That's why you and Billy were friends. You'll go, afraid or not. You might even welcome the fear as validation of something. We roller-skate in the park, on a path, so if you're headed for a fall, you can land in the grass."

"I love roller-skating," he said. "I used to. It's been years."

JoAnne offered more broccoli and rice, happy for a first date on the schedule.

"Why do you look so pleased?" Solomon asked.

"Let's not beat around the bush, Sok," JoAnne chided, touching his hand. "We have something special. You know that. After all these years, you have trouble in life. It happens to everyone, sooner or later. And what did you do? You called home. Didn't you? You've had trials and tribulations, just like we did. Now we converge, like we did before. We have this special love that won't go away. I tried to find you, but not sincerely. Did I think we could make a closer match? Maybe. So what?"

"Do I have a say in this?"

"You're having a say in this," JoAnne allowed. "But your view must not be preconceived. You must be present, Sok. You must see this moment for what it is."

"JoAnne." Solomon sighed. "I am intimately familiar with this moment. My preconception is a work in progress."

"We agree! Look. Eloise is beautiful and smart. Think of the genetic magic. We don't need a conventional father. Just be yourself. That's what you'll do anyway. What else do you have? You're still young at heart and physically fit. You want to spend your years with a bunch of bozos in yellow jammies?"

"That's harsh. And I think you came up with this plan since I called two days ago."

"*That* is harsh, and it makes no difference. I'll tell you something else. Eloise can be nice, once she gets off your case. She has this creepy compulsion to nudge until you think she's obnoxious. She always had the obnoxious agenda. It may be a psychiatric quirk."

"Mother!"

Solomon looked at the daughter. "You called her Mother."

"It happens. So what? Answer the question. Do you want to spend the rest of your life trying to fool people into thinking you don't look foolish, or that you know you're foolish, and they don't know you know it, but they might realize how blind they've been to your wisdom, and at that glorious moment the world will be a better place because you fucked with their rhythm?"

"Fuck, Eloise," said JoAnne. "What makes you so mean?"

Eloise went crimson again and rose like a time-lapse weed, rising, rising, until Solomon said, "Wait. Please. Eloise." She waited. "Is it a date then? Roller-skating?"

"I don't think so," she said. "We'll get all sweaty. And you could fall down. It could be awkward. We don't really want to process awkwardness this early."

"I'd say we're off to a rolling start."

JoAnne stood to clear dishes, again as if on cue. "I got baklava for dessert, for the sweetness. Perfect for a reunion of long-lost friends. Don't you think?

"I don't eat baklava," Solomon said. "Animal by-products. Honey and butter. Not vegan. Most people think nothing of robbing bees of their labors or cows of their calves, but that's what it is."

"Oh, for fuck's sake," sighed Eloise.

"Yes, love is tricky. You said I look healthy," Solomon said, smiling up like a child at the base of the Eiffel Tower.

"Sit down, Eloise. I knew that, Solomon, about honey and butter. I did my research too. I got vegan baklava, with corn syrup, just for you, while you were napping. It tastes like shit, but we'll make you happy. Okay? I have to agree with Eloise on this one. Fuck."

Eloise sat, and Solomon told her, "I want to love you forever, as I've loved your parents. I don't want to offend or insult you. I don't see women in a sexual way."

"Are you gay?"

"No."

"How do you know?"

"I've . . . thought about it."

"Then you're gay."

"No. Every man asks the question. Heterosexual men know the answer. I wonder what it would be like to fly. That doesn't mean I can fly. But you know that. Where was I?"

"You don't see women as sexual objects," JoAnne said, returning with the shitty baklava.

"I don't. Most women want it that way. Others primp for sex, with the lift and spread. A man could be dead and notice some of these babes. The beach scene is dental floss tied to waistbands, down and around. They lay out the beach towel on their knees and elbows for the money shot, and on down to catch rays."

"You're blind to it but see it. Are you asexual?"

"I don't know. Maybe."

"You're not. Listen, buster," JoAnne said. "You can fool some people, like those nimrods in saffron jammies. I know you."

"I think you don't. I see it and laugh. It's like slapstick."

"I think if you tasted some real baklava, you'd love it. You looked at me, Sok. A girl remembers. I'm every bit as sensitive and loving as you are. You're not a tits and ass guy! That doesn't mean you're asexual. You're a lover. Not a fucker."

"Oh, God," Eloise said.

Solomon smiled benignly.

"I'll tell you something else, Mister Smarty Britches. After I talked to you two days ago, I called back. Not your number. I found the cult number. This woman picked up and sounded—sorry—she sounded simple. She says, 'Hi there. I'm Glow.' I said, 'As in Gloria?' She said, 'No. As in Glowing. Call me Glow. It's easier.' Man, Sok. She was . . ."

"She's fine," he said. "She has an unusual way of saying things."

"You mean unusual, like a simpleton?"

"If you say so. She's not simple. She found a niche and came a long way. That's what the place can do."

"What's her niche?" Eloise asked.

"Pastry. She has a following. Her vegan pastries are beautiful and delicious. I should have brought a dozen crullers."

"We had a chat. I like her. I'd try a pastry. I told her I knew you a long time ago, and you were coming here. I asked if you were going to put a move on me? Sorry. I wanted to know. She says, 'I doubt it. I don't know him in that way. I don't know *you* in any way.' She sounded defensive, protecting you. She said, 'He's not like that. If he's coming to see you, he loves you.' Sok, we got your number."

Solomon's head wagged. "I'm not sure what you have, but you're not listening. I don't want to be a father. I don't want to bear a child. And marriage to a woman I just met seems unwise, unstable, ill advised. I have said these things, but you plow on."

Mother and daughter looked at each other, and Eloise said, "Can we start over? On fundamentals. Do you love me?"

Solomon said. "Yes, as the child of my lovely, loving friends."

"I have a place in your heart?"

He nodded, weary from travel fatigue, reunion fatigue, reflection and urgency fatigue. Weary from the world and a hearty meal, he asked, "Do you mind if I lie down on the couch?"

JoAnne and Eloise moved to either side, to rub his tired temples and shoulders, agreeing that a man can suffer sexual objectivity and undue pressure as easily as a woman, especially a sensitive man.

Eloise leaned in. "Don't worry about roller-skating, Solomon. We'll play Par 3 Pitch & Putt. It's fun. I think you'll love it too."

Par 3

The stout woman hadn't looked twice at the tall man waiting but peered at the green from under her sun derby. Tallish herself before turning eighty, she stretched to former altitude for the better view, then strolled toward the rubber pad for teeing off, slowly, for deliberation and lower odds on a fall. She wore a frilly white blouse under a cardigan in champagne yellow, and a calf-length skirt in muted lavender, as if pastels might counterbalance her grim resolve. Par 3 Pitch & Putt is golf in short form, with abbreviated fairways and only two clubs, a pitching wedge and a putter. But she intensified like a sudden death playoff, 19th hole at The Masters.

Grasping her pitching wedge with familiarity, she looked up again to factor slope, breeze and debris. Lowering her eyes to the ball, external variables sorted, she assessed power and aging potential, envisioning the recoil and release in life and golf.

In tectonic shifts under the folds, she rose. Strata gave way. With molten effusion from the core, she pulled back, held briefly and let fly. The ball thwacked to parabolic precision and hit the lip of the green, where it bounced and rolled to spitting distance of the hole.

Turning to fetch her putter, she mumbled that a twenty-yard approach from the tee should actually be a par 2.

Solomon wanted to call: Bravo! But he checked his exuberance to say, "You have very nice form."

The elderly woman glanced his way.

He lifted his chin.

She said, "Yes, it's nice and warm. It's lovely."

"No. I said you have nice form."

"Form?"

Eloise came around the hedge from the previous hole, annoyed and amused at the young German couple close on her heels. "Do they think pressure will move us along?" she asked. They're so serious. But I don't think they're any better than we are."

"No. They're not," Solomon concurred. "They only have better form." Solomon enjoyed being stoned, but he could not remember such potency since the glory days. Eloise called this hash her private reserve and agreed that it felt visible to others—like the elderly woman who stared to the point of obtrusion.

On another nod, the elder headed out for what could well become a birdie 2, and at her age.

"Okay. Your turn," Eloise advised.

"No," Solomon corrected. "It's your turn to go first." She strode forth, set her ball an inch from the edge of the tee pad and scrunched into position. "Eloise. You have to wait until the group ahead of us is off the green," he said.

"Oh!"

"Put your ball in the center and both feet on the pad," he said.

"Oh," she giggled, moving her ball to the center. Looking up the short fairway, they saw the elderly woman and her two younger colleagues stroll off the green to the next tee, a few paces away.

He'd missed it. Did she get the birdie? He wanted to call out again but held back, sensing the futility of counting strokes.

But you can't sense the futility of counting strokes. You either think it's futile, or you don't think.

Never mind; he went with the flow, resigned to any outcome and inconsequence. *No, not inconsequence but . . .*

Eloise recoiled and swung for the bleachers, slicing mightily through thin air. The young Germans stood back, watching forlornly, dismayed at such chaos and no concentration. "That was practice," she said, winding up and giving it the mustard one more time. The pitching wedge hit the ball above the equator, shanking it into the brush. Eloise giggled again and blushed bright pink.

Solomon approached the pad more thoughtfully, eying the tee and setting the ball gently as a lunar module on a soft mogul.

He felt presumptuous but not arrogant. He wanted to teach without words. He was a pro, and that was the point. He stared at the ball, stepped back, spread his feet but narrowed the gap by an inch on the left, three quarters on the right. He spread again to either side and gripped his pitching wedge, linking left forefinger into right pinkie, no choke. A man of stature should take advantage. Any tall person knows the bothers in a life of length. Why not enjoy the benefits too? In final calibration, he took a practice swing, slow motion.

He'd seen the pre-swing on TV in a process that uploaded pre-swing data to the real swing. He breathed deep, raising the club again, this time lingering, eyes glommed on the ball. Leading with his left arm, he visualized a soft, natural flow to the ball to give it life. And flight and balance on perfect delivery to the hole! Then he thwacked the living shit out of it to ensure the one true path. He might not make the hole, but he'd get to spitting distance like the matron of the fairway had done. Why not?

Solid contact felt good for the split second to a second thwack—the ball hit a tree trunk near Eloise's shank to the bushes then ricocheted back at the German couple, who hit the deck.

"Oh, fuck! So sorry," Solomon said, stepping over to offer a hand, glancing down the fräulein's blouse, thinking it odd that so many bare breasts over the years had rendered him indifferent. Yet this harness drew him in. Was it the exquisite German engineering, holding things firmly in place? No, exquisite would be Italian. . .

"*Vas iss los*?" asked Ulrich. What is this? But Ulrich did not specify whether *this* was the wild shot or Solomon ogling Helga's chest. Was Helga the wife? Girlfriend or sister? But their relationship mattered no more than a birdie 2.

"Sorry. One more try. I'll hurry." Solomon fetched his ball, set it on the tee and swung away with no formality, shanking it again but missing the tree to hit the thicket. He and Eloise headed out to search for their balls. The Germans played through.

Solomon called, "Here it is. I found my ball!" He held up two.

"Your ball is yellow," Eloise said.

"Does it matter?" Solomon asked.

"You mean relatively speaking?" she asked.

"Relative, figurative, absolute. Context doesn't matter and neither does the ball. Now we have a spare." He put one in his pocket and threw the other to the green.

"What are you doing?"

"Having a gentle toss. It's what we allowed."

"That wasn't gentle. And it wasn't a toss. It was a throw."

"I had to clear the bushes."

"That's why they call it golf."

"You wanted me to hit it around the bushes?"

"Do what you need. I'll win anyway."

"Win?"

"You know: get there in fewer strokes." She found her ball and threw it to the green.

"Ah. Win. Do you need to win?"

"Yes, win. Or lose, which must be an old familiar for you."

"Yes. You can't really win without losing. But you know that. You wouldn't give me a participation trophy?"

"You wouldn't want one. They're for losers."

"You're harsh. I think you know that too."

"Yes. We're balanced. I'm harsh. You're vague."

He stepped up for the putt, went meditative again and said, "This is why they call it golf." Envisioning a man poised over a ball in mystical haze, the man and putter came to oneness in ebb and flow, as he drew back and . . .

"Solomon." She'd ruined it.

Deflating, he asked, "Must you? Really?"

"That's my ball," she said.

Another couple waiting at the tee chuckled in the liberal good cheer of Par 3. Solomon turned to assess for German origin. But no, they looked Chinese. He said, "I knew that."

"You did not know that. You made a mistake, Solomon."

"A mistake?" He stepped casually to his ball.

She asked, "Do you find me alluring?"

He straightened, interrupting this program for truth and clarity. "I have imagined you. It's what men do. It was purely reflexive, without motive. It was an act of expedience, to get it out of the way. Okay?"

"Please don't condescend. Okay?"

"Condescend?" He hunched again for a tap to the flag, where it lipped the cup and rolled out to the northeast. "That counts," he said.

She shook her head.

"The pole kept it from going in!" he insisted.

She shook again and stepped to her ball. "It counts as two shots."

"The pole was in the way."

She tapped gently into the hole, alongside the pin, and asked, "You're shooting what, five? Six?"

"I shot four," he said.

"Fuck. What's the point?"

"The point?"

"Get your ball. We're holding up traffic."

"I'm getting my ball. I won't condescend if you can cut back on micromanaging. Deal?"

"Fine. Are we done?" She got her ball and turned away.

"Done?"

"Fuck," she said.

"Now?"

He tossed this last question as a joke, but she ignored it, heading up the path to the next tee or the exit farther up. He couldn't tell which and frankly didn't care; moody, competitive and contradictory, she'd turned play into a joust, maybe as Billy would have done, but without the love. "Ha," he laughed aloud.

"Laughing at himself, I'm sure," Eloise said, waiting behind the hedge. Solomon rounded to see the elderly lady. Eloise and he had caught up. "I'm Eloise," she said, friendly again. "This is Solomon. You play very well."

"No. I used to play well. I . . . I'm afraid I'm . . . also Eloise." The elderly woman broke rectitude with a smile, as if chagrined. "Le Compte. I'm Eloise Le Compte."

"Eloise Keene. This is Solomon Kursh."

"Hello," Solomon said.

"We're visiting," younger Eloise said.

"How nice," elder Eloise said.

"Do you live here?" Solomon asked.

"The coincidence intrigues me," the elder said. "Do you realize the odds against two women named Eloise meeting by chance, and one of them has a last name initial K as that of her . . . friend?"

"Does that put me at the vortex?" Eloise asked.

"I daresay," Eloise said. "You're the interstice of a coincidence."

"A coincidental interstice in the golfing matrix." Solomon glanced from one to the other. "The odds are easy, based on the number of people named Eloise, and Eloise here meeting one of them sooner or later. Matching initials on our side would remain variable but with constant potential based on a twenty-four-letter alphabet, so the odds on the subset would be twenty-four to one, but less if you strike the ex and factor the oddball Q. Eloise, surely you've met another Eloise. No?"

Younger Eloise looked perplexed. The elder looked impatient, stepping up the path with, "Shall we?"

Solomon thought two women named Eloise meeting, and one of them having a friend with the same surname initial wasn't long odds at all. He had no more to say. They didn't get it, or the hash had fuzzed him up in lush consolation for stealing his wits. Another man approached, too short to be Eloise's son, striding from the hole, where he'd missed an easy putt and stayed to practice, to get it right. Swaggering like George Bush Junior or Vlad Putin but with irrepressible good will, he came on, his checkered-flag shirt buffeting in the breeze as if signaling the finish line.

Solomon thought to rush past for a victory lap, but no . . .

The short man surged amiably in, grinning like Teddy Roosevelt, shaking his head over the laughable misperception that a short man would lack presence. Anybody could make that mistake and, frankly, he was used to it. Never mind. He inflated the moment, as a man of magnitude will do, a mighty mountain in perfect miniature, striding forth a head shorter than either Eloise and a bit farther than that below Solomon. Thrusting his hand three paces out to ensure world peace, he said, "Pleasure to meet you."

The elder Eloise said, "This is Eloise. Eloise, my son-in-law, Rupert." Rupert shifted course in mid-offer and took Eloise's hand.

"Rupert Gilley. It's a pleasure. Call me Rupe." He shook like a city dweller on a pump and turned to Solomon. "And you are, sir?"

"I'm Solomon Kursh."

"Solomon Kursh! I know that name. You're in a . . . um . . ."

"You're wanting a euphemism. It's most often called a cult."

"Is it a cult?" Eloise the elder asked.

"You might call it that. I think of it as a set of values. In general terms, it's a way of being."

"Are you being in that way now?" This question from the elder seemed fair and open, with a hint of mockery and rapid fire.

"Of course he is," Rupert allowed. "Please, Eloise. If a man follows a way of being, then he'll be that way with regularity. Every time he realizes that he's strayed, he'll jump back on the path. Inadvertent absence becomes less frequent, until the way becomes second nature. In time, it becomes first nature."

Solomon liked this little man of outsized character. "I sense your experience. I think you're being yourself."

"I've dabbled in it," Rupert said.

"I only ask what is the way of that way," Eloise the elder said.

"It's a lovely way," Eloise said. "I'm affiliated too. I'm learning."

Rupert said, "Aren't we all? Well, then. Shall we?"

"Yes. We shall," the elder said, as another woman came from behind the bushes. "And this is my daughter, Jennifer."

"How do you do?" Jennifer stepped up, holding her right hand limply aloft, as if offering it for a kiss. Jennifer stood tall, as her mother once had, head and shoulders over Rupert, her husband, unless he was married to a different daughter.

Solomon stared. Had she just dabbed her nethers after wee-wee with that hand? Jennifer withdrew, but Solomon saved her with an easy reach and polite shake.

"Are you ready, Mummy?" she asked.

"Yes," the elder affirmed. "Won't you join us?"

"I suppose we'll stroll with you," Solomon said. "No rush. This weather is so perfect it gives me wild thoughts. It feels . . . I don't know. Irrational. Like love. I do love it. I suppose that's rational."

Nobody said boo, strolling in loose formation up the path, until Solomon said, "I'm not so wild or irrational most of the time, but this is top-down weather." Rupert glanced up, so Solomon added, "It makes me think of a dashing little sports car, so impractical. This blue sky and brisk air make me want more. I want to go. Go crazy maybe. You feel it too, I'm sure."

"Ah. You want a convertible, and you like blue," Rupert said, closing the gap and falling into step beside Solomon. The women followed a few paces back, chatting over places and people. Solomon thought Rupert compatible in chemistry, cadence and succinct talk, free of cliché and platitude. Rupert thought Solomon reflective and, from time to time, able to shut the fuck up, as a wise man can do. Rupert thought women also capable of the golden sound, some of them. He gravitated to those with something to offer in exchange for something given, be it silence or substance. Silence could be substantial, just as substance could be silent. Both men appreciated a person who could stay on point. "I do feel it," Rupert said. "The air and the sunny blue. It's what we call convertible weather. You nailed it. I'm a specialist."

"You specialize in blue convertibles?"

Angling up, Rupert hummed two notes in the affirmative.

"What kind of cars do you sell?"

"I don't sell cars, if you don't mind. Sorry, it's just my way. I specialize in vehicular placement. I would put you in a Maxi."

"A Maxi. They're cute. And they look like fun, if you can fit into one. I'm too tall. I don't know why they call them Maxi when that name only underscores their . . . deficiency. Pardon me."

"No offense taken. How could you know otherwise? It's a common misperception." Rupert laughed short. "Look at me. But seriously, we have more interior legroom and headroom than many of your leading sport coupes or sedans. And we deliver beautifully on the fun you confine to fantasy. I . . . uh . . . doubt that you suffer such confinement all that often."

"No. I don't. Thank you. But tell me: what are the options?"

"Not so different from the others, really. All the carmakers have gone to option packages, common-sense groupings."

"No, no. I should have said alternatives. What are the alternatives to Maxi?"

"Oh, hell, a fellow could follow any whim that comes along. But if he thinks about automotive fit and satisfaction and fun, as I do every day, he'll make the right choice."

Solomon turned, feeling foolish yet again, engaging a car salesman on the subject of choice, as if a voracious predator might think twice on easy prey. Where else could this conversation go but Maxi as the right choice? Could Solomon say that he'd seen *Fargo*, where the wavy-hair salesman commandeers a country couple, then goes to ask the manager but doesn't ask at all because it's a ruse!

"Please," Rupert admonished. "Don't condescend. You flap in the breeze like pages of a book, and I read you. Car salesman. Right? Am I right?"

"Very good. Yes. You're right, but I'd bet you've been at it for a long time, and your experience makes my thoughts readable. You didn't actually sense condescension on my part because, well…"

"That's true. I'm the brunt of condescension on a regular basis. You don't get comfortable with that. But I did read you. How many mind readers have you met today? I also read test drive. I'm still reading it in the blue sky and sunshine. I feel it in the air. You said you want more of it, and I believe you. Don't you?"

"I do. I wish you had a blue Maxi ragtop waiting here in the parking lot."

"But I do!" With confidence, Rupert led the way up the path.

Solomon hadn't felt this good in a long time. Sure, it was the irrepressible combo: the hash yet again, blue sky and a crazy little man ready to sell him a car out in the parking lot. He flowed along with no assessment on a beautiful feeling too long gone.

"Not really," Rupert said.

"But it is . . . Sorry. What?"

"I don't really have a blue Maxi convertible here. But if I did . . . If I actually had one here . . . Tell me, what are you driving now?"

"I'm walking now."

Rupert looked up. "Yes. What kind of car do you drive now?"

"I don't. Never have."

Rupert hadn't met a new-car prospect who didn't drive. "But you can drive? Have you taken Driver's Ed?"

"That was ages ago. I think I'd do better now. It must be easier now." Both stopped short to second-glance the shrubbery at a bend in the path. A glimmer and rustle seemed aggressively obtrusive.

Two shoddy men with shaved heads came out, seemingly bent on ill will. Jennifer had emerged from similar shrubbery with more discretion after a squat, leaving a tissue that would soon biodegrade. These two came on strong, not strong like Rupert but pungent like ripe cheese or *eau de BO* and #2. Their objective seemed readable as any page flapping among other pages, dog-eared, soaked down and dried out, soiled and beyond normal circulation. Rings and pins pierced their faces and flashed in the sun. Tattoos included daggers, scorpions, barbed wire and teardrops at the corners of their eyes. Anybody surfing past *Lock Up Raw* knew the teardrops meant murder. Teardrop code was unclear. Did each teardrop represent a killing? Or could multiple teardrops be earned in a single, savage murder? Distinction seemed irrelevant in the moment. Solomon said, "I got one of those."

"One of what?" Rupert asked, as a long, curved blade flashed like Ali Baba's in his work with the forty thieves. A thug wielding a swashbuckler knife had its comic aspect. It could have been rubber or spring-loaded but was not. These looked grimy with bad intention.

Solomon stood firm, hoping he wasn't frozen.

"Yer money or yer life, faggots!" The other thug snorted from three paces out, strident as Rupert but with no cordiality.

Rupert stepped up to hold his arms out like a crossing guard.

Jennifer and both Eloises stopped.

Solomon stepped around to regain the lead with proven skill in trauma decompression. Moving massive minions in hearts and minds, he'd freed the birds, broken the shackles and touched troubled souls. "I will give . . ." He held a golf ball up in each hand. ". . . the planets."

The first assailant grunted.

Solomon beamed, step 1 in blessing these hoodlums.

The first thug struck Solomon's left hand. "Now!"

Solomon stood firm, taller than the general population, not frozen but waiting for the precise . . .

But precision went to Rupert, who flowed around, slow motion, into the attacker's arm. Thrusting a palm to the larynx and up, he launched for the slam-dunk. Something snapped. The other thug ran, as the first would have done, had not Rupert swung behind to commandeer the wrist to submission for the easy takedown. The down man whimpered when Rupert took the knife and told him to run, to get a head start on the cops for a change. The man nodded as best he could with a broken jaw, rising and shuffling off.

New friends watched, and Rupert said, "It's for the best. Blue sky, sunshine. We don't want him spending it in jail, do we?"

Eloise the elder said, "I believe Rupert is correct on this one. But we should call it in."

"I'm all over it," Jennifer said, cell phone in hand.

"Rupert," queried younger Eloise. "What was that?"

"Nothing, really," Rupert demurred. "From what I understand, the modern hate groups are grooming up. I'm afraid our fellows are behind the times. That other is something I learned. Efficiency in movement, if I have no doubt. If I can slow things down and don't think, it works, most often. If I can imagine all the time in the world to manage a situation, then I can. But it must stay alive. Always a chance, you know."

"It's something he's obsessed over for years," Jennifer said. "Believe me, Solomon, we are forever indebted to you. You've given purpose to Rupert's obsession . . . Oh, hello. Yes. We've had an assault here at the Par 3 Pitch & Putt. Attempted robbery, actually. I'm afraid the culprits are on the loose, but you might get the collar if you're pronto on the APB. Unkempt fellows, I daresay. Skinheads, I would think. Quite nasty. Two of them. Comprendez?" She listened and answered their questions. "Yes . . . Yes . . . Well, no, actually. We're headed out for a spot of lunch. I think we'll try, uh . . ." Covering the mouthpiece she asked, "Mummy?"

"Cloverdale's, if you change the rezzy to five."

"Five? We're having lunch, Mummy!"

"Persons! Not the time."

"Oh. Yes. Can do. They're really so accommodating." Removing her fingers from the mouthpiece, so police dispatch could hear again, she advised, "We'll be at Cloverdale's. It's only a few blocks up. I believe we'll walk, what with the weather and all. You can't miss us, really. Mummy is grand. Rupert is bold. And persuasive. Everyone else is rather tallish. Otherwise, we'll be at our usual table, snugged in, I'm afraid, with our new friends. Which is okay, really. Friendship is so dear, don't you think?"

So, friendship began on camaraderie, adventure shared and common interests on a memorable day. Everyone among them felt giddy at meeting kindred spirits and surviving a test, as it surely was!

Solomon and Eloise the younger ducked into *Drugs-U-Need* for peroxide, antibiotic ointment, cotton swabs and a bandage. He did not whine but requested a gentler touch.

"Please don't whine," she said, and soon they were on their way to Cloverdale's.

Good weather boosted good feelings. Two marauders had sealed the bond, so the barometer and good cheer were high. A delicious meal at Cloverdale's would culminate a fortuitous walk in the park. Jennifer asked what better for the occasion than a lovely Chablis and luncheon on the terrace. She nearly swooned, "Oh! And the fried eggplant!" Allowing time for visualization, she cooed, "It's gooey in the center, you know."

Strolling to Cloverdale's like old friends on a walk through life, they couldn't know how well they would get to know each other.

Eloise the elder asked about the way of being Solomon had framed as his modus operandi. She'd known people of one ilk or another, but no one so deliberately off as this guy, whoever he was.

Unfamiliar with guru pursuits, the elder assumed a Buddhist context with a tithing base, perhaps communists and/or sexual perverts. Isn't that how it goes? She left it at that, none the wiser and content at that, especially at four under par, equaling her personal best and besting the rest by far.

Solomon didn't mind smug complacence or complacent smuggery either one—ha! Good one. But should he share his inner self? He thought not just yet. He'd seen every play in the book. Most people this elder's age had also seen a thing or two. So, what could they do? Match wits?

She ticked her head as if seeking meaning, looking down her nose at a fool for all seasons. If only she knew—but she did know.

With a curious glance, Jennifer said she loved a good time, especially spontaneous, like this. "To be perfectly honest, fun is my favorite thing of all. It could be my raison d'etrê. And why not?"

Solomon agreed and asked how her afternoon would have shaped up, if not for this random meeting. She said the Par 3 outing and lunch would have been wonderful at any rate, but with this weather and their encounter, it felt divine. He sensed compensation for something less than optimal in Mudville. Or would that be LeCompteville? He looked into her eyes as she peered right back and giggled.

Rupert seemed different, cutting against the grain but fitting in. In the business of liking people or faking it, he likely lit up on any prospect. Stretching his stride to match Solomon's, he could not keep up unless he picked up the pace. Solomon saw and shortened his stride. Rupert looked up, thinking Solomon a decent fellow and a man worth knowing. Beyond that, Solomon Kursh was no mere pedestrian. He'd been a headliner and still enjoyed celebrity. How many people are part of the American playbill? That would be media, where substance defers to recognition. Many lackluster people are famous for being famous. People knew Solomon for what he had to say. Rupert thought him a dynamic thinker who lacked proper management—Rupert loved speculating on someone else's fulfillment for a change. As Rupert recalled, Solomon had run a rough phase on turpitude, denial, the usual media smorgasbord of guilt by association and no comment. But Solomon's words lingered. He had presence, as others merely watched. Rupert, for one, admired a man who could maintain an elevated view with humility.

Rupert appreciated that Solomon had not mentioned fame or fortune in their brief acquaintance. Rupert would value such a friend. Beyond that, the young Eloise seemed equally admirable, poised, well spoken and private. Stable, homey, unimposing and polite. He smiled again for the celebrity thing that gets the girl every time. Solomon seemed fit, but really, he could be her uncle. Or her daddy. Maybe he was. It didn't matter and besides: all would surface, by and by.

Rupert didn't want to scrutinize but he loved the long and lean. Sveltely curvaceous didn't hurt. Jennifer had it, before she forgot the value of silence, and chit chat replaced poise. Jennifer had little worldly experience. It wasn't her fault that she'd risked nothing and faced no fear but core anxiety on the impression she made.

And Rupert was no less a man for automotive placement skills. He could comfort a prospect with variable angulation and the myriad combos available in sixteen-way seats. The irony of sixteen ways was that comfort became fixed! Variation would not be superfluous, until age and shrinkage called for adjustment, time for the trade-in.

He'd thought Jennifer an eyeful, and she'd loved it. He thought Eloise a striking beauty and imagined sixteen ways. Jennifer prattled over fun and menu choices. At what point did she change from grace to gadabout? He couldn't call her graceless; she was too kind and concerned. But the oscillating chatter . . . Would this new Eloise become tedious? How could she, with eyes to melt a heart and curves to make a chest ache? He laughed again at the front-end deception and inevitable transition common to women and men. He thought women ironic for loving bold men and trying to tame them. And men, who crave familiarity until they get it.

"Feeling good?" Solomon asked.

"Just thinking," Rupert said.

Jennifer effused over "baba ghanoush and the most marvelous beach ever on this Greek island, where this perfectly lovely man skewed an entire eggplant and held it over a campfire until the skin turned to ash, and he shmushed it all up and diced an onion into it and added so much garlic and lemon and pepper. I nearly cried, literally! Really! But I loved it! And you know I've tried to get it right so many times, and I can't!"

Younger Eloise suggested another try, on a beach on a Greek island over a campfire. She didn't mean to touch a nerve, but things went mum, until Mummy said, "That may be a stretch. I can't help thinking of the guava tea. At Cloverdale's. Something about it slakes my thirst like nothing else. I know it's not from real, fresh guava, but it does hit the spot. Like now; I'm so parched."

On that note, they entered a soft interlude of padding shoes, as if walking to Cloverdale's on pilgrimage. Solomon felt good nestling in with his familiar self. Productive contemplation could slow the pace, even as the elder stepped it up. That was a rub and a lesson: a contemplative person might convey essence to no avail. Would that be the same as no essence? Contemplate that. Did the one and only Solomon Kursh seem dull as a lump? His pages flapped in the breeze for reading or not, as the quintet strolled in a soft, sibilant breeze and sunbeams to warm the whisper.

On the last bend, another approach, this one in a monk's robe. He stopped to push his hood above his forehead and brightened blissfully but hesitated, as if meeting the pope at Par 3.

Solomon stopped. "Penny for your thoughts."

The young monk blinked. They stared, as if two idiots had met on a sidewalk to watch each other. He held his hand out.

Solomon paid up. They bowed in the Eastern mudra, hands pressed in supplication, and parted ways with no further discourse on the weather or cost benefit of the penny spent and earned, avoiding the volley on a meaning of no meaning.

"My God," elder Eloise said.

"Yes," Eloise said. "Isn't it something?"

"Isn't what something?" the elder asked.

"The way they know each other," the younger said.

"Hmm," the elder pondered

Solomon felt better, sharing essence by example.

The elder led onward, to lunch, noting foliage shimmering in shadows as one of her favorite things. She looked up and again set the pace, such as an old woman could. She really was so damn thirsty.

Lunch at Cloverdale's

"Visiting from where?" Eloise asked.

"I misspoke," Eloise said. "Solomon is visiting. I live here."

"Oh. Then you're not together."

"I'm together," Solomon said. "Eloise is in counseling."

Nobody laughed.

Younger Eloise said, "It's a long story we'll bore you with another time. Solomon and I go back. We may be together again soon, depending."

"I'm not at all clear on your meaning," Eloise the elder said. "Are you rectifying a situation or pondering potential?"

"I'd call that a succinct summary," Eloise said. "Rectifying and pondering about covers it."

Solomon tingled, far from the intellectual tundra, and turning to Eloise, the younger, he said, "I love that."

The elder nodded, short of approval, avoiding further complexity.

"Do you have a family?" the elder asked.

"That's one subject on the table," the younger replied.

"Bit old for that, aren't you?" Rupert asked Solomon. "None of my business. I'd just hate to face that now. The whole baby thing."

The waiter came for orders: two of the fried eggplant, one of the sautéed sage leaves and two of the baby arugula salad, all to share. And a ribeye for Rupert, who returned incredulous gazes all around.

"What? I come here for the ribeye. It's the best thing they do. It's my habit after Par 3, hardly once a month and midday so it won't bother me later."

Nobody replied, as Richard the waiter introduced himself to expound on the virtues of the ribeye, free range and taken directly from there to the slaughterhouse as a Cloverdale Chef's Exclusive, none of that feed-lot monkey business where they test for hormones and antibiotics so they can label it free range, *then* fatten for two weeks at the feed lot with a massive antibiotic chaser to cure the infections rampant in the holding pens. It's inhumane, and it's a lie. "Really, what they do with the cramped conditions and force feeding. I'll remind you that we have veal too, in case you're in the mood." He waited, eventually asking if a lovely white wine might be in order for such a beautiful afternoon.

"In product placement, we call that a solid front end," Rupert said. "A tad dramatic. Drama can help close a deal but carries a risk. You want to minimize that. I'd gain group attention with eye contact here and there, maybe leave out the feedlot bit. The veal may be a tender nerve for this bunch. Wine? I enjoy a burgundy with my ribeye. The weather is also obvious to aware people like us. Sorry. Is everybody okay with the Burgundy? It's quite good here."

But everybody stared at Rupert.

"What? I hope that's okay, a ribeye, because if it's not, I'll order something else." Richard waited. "Solomon? Have I made you uncomfortable?"

"Please, Rupert. This isn't my decision. It's yours."

"Okay, Richard. Bring me a grilled cheese sandwich and some bean soup. Hold the Portuguese sausage—ha! I mean from the soup. You can do that, can't you?"

"I'll see to it. And the Burgundy?"

"No. Bring us whatever looks good. Thank you, Richard." Rupert shook his head. "It's okay. I won't make anyone uncomfortable."

"Too late for that," Eloise the elder said. "We were about to hear your elaboration on . . . I think you called it the whole baby thing."

Rupert thought for a moment and said, "Yes, the baby thing. I said it's none of my business. I think we have enough people, and raising children is not an experience I'll miss."

"You'd also miss a few car sales because of it," Jennifer said. "Spending valuable time with a child and all that. The business term, I believe, is opportunity cost."

"I hadn't thought of that," Solomon said. "But it does apply."

"Those two endeavors are hardly comparable," Rupert said. "I have to work like everybody else. Vehicular placement pays my expenses. And Jennifer's. If I weren't an automotive specialist, I'd be in something else, something other than child rearing, because that doesn't pay anybody's bills. As it is, here we are with new friends, a great restaurant, a free afternoon, blue sky and a warm breeze. You might take this for granted. I don't. This is golden."

"Here, here," Solomon said.

"That's a different subject than what Solomon and I are assessing," Eloise said.

"Please," Eloise said. "Can you clarify what you're assessing? I don't mean to pry. But we've become friends unexpectedly and with such vigor! I'm only curious and ask that you reply only within your comfort zone, of course."

"I want to have a baby. Solomon does not." She chose her next words carefully—too slow.

"I think that is the subject I just referenced," Rupert said.

"No. It's not. I need a father for my baby. Solomon doesn't want the job any more than you do. But I think he'd come around, at least after the hard work of the first few years."

"That's unfair," Solomon said. "That sounds like I'd want the good part while shirking my share of the work."

"That *is* what I mean, technically. But I accept your position. I think you would come around. I also think you'd compensate your deficiencies, even if you're not on hand for the infancy."

"You're a lucky man, Solomon," Rupert said.

"You made reference to a good part that apparently comes after the hard part. What good part would that be?" Jennifer asked.

Solomon responded, defensive and compelled. "I don't know Eloise well enough to commit for such a profound endeavor. From what I sense, she'd likely be good company, intellectually and physically. That's still not the subject on the table."

"So you did notice," asserted the elder.

Solomon continued, "She has an active mind. She thinks about things and stays physically active too. Those two aspects shouldn't be taken for granted any more than this weather. Beyond that, her tolerance for me isn't necessarily my luck. That's easing me in with a shoehorn. Anybody is lucky to get along with anybody else, but push does come to shove. The good part of any romance is the romance. In modern society, we presume romance at the outset. We don't discuss its rapid dissolution in baby care and child rearing. Eighteen years out, romance may return. That would be the good part."

"Touché," Jennifer said. "But naïve. Look: Rupert and I get along because he's always selling cars, at the dealership, in his dreams, or he's planting little seeds—that's what he calls it. I don't mean sexually reproductive seeds, but on the phone, sending emails. Excuse me? It's officially called immersion in automotive placement. Gosh, we keep things fresh easily with such sparse contact. We spend very little time together, so I complain. His work obstructs our romance. I'm amazed we're not done by now. I think we will be done if things get any fresher, pardon my hyperbole, but you all know the exasperation of which I speak." She turned to Rupert. "Love you, Dearie. Always have. But I wish . . ."

"Wait a minute," the elder said to her younger namesake. "He doesn't know you well enough to commit, and you're thinking of a child?"

"Well, yes, kinda sorta. It's a long story," Eloise said. "I'm not being secretive and promise to share, soon."

Rupert said, "If you don't share now, then you are being secretive. *N'est pas?* Further, I do not find your talk of exhilaration acceptable, dear Jennifer—I mean exasperation. Men are perceived as suitable for plug and play on child rearing. That's what happens, suitable or not. Acceptance is also assumed but rarely discussed. Our new friend Solomon is a kind, caring man. If he takes a chance on Eloise, he might make life lovelier for both. But potential should not override scruples and principles. Or his age. No offense, Solomon."

"None taken. I'm not so old. And your point is good. Lovely potential is not a reasonable cross reference on the daily demands of child rearing. I've spent decades fending off additional demands. I endeavor to keep present demands workable. I don't want a child, nor would I desert a child, and that's a different potential. That's the dilemma. Plain logic and common sense are my guidelines. Do I love Eloise? Do I love hanging out with Eloise? Do I find Eloise easy to listen to, to look at and talk to? Is she provocative and engaging? Yes, I said yes, again yes. And here we are, having lunch with new friends after golf. Are we not?"

"Something is missing," Eloise the elder said.

"We're missing the sexual data," Eloise said. "I'm inexperienced by modern standards but willing to take a chance on Solomon. I'm not at all sure he'll agree to practice, for starters."

The group gaze went to the elder, not to measure her response but to brace for indignation. From a pensive moment, she eased into a nod. "She makes a case."

"Mummy!" Jennifer chided, "She makes no case at all! Pardon me, Eloise, but I'm not accustomed to such talk at the table, or to tacit approval from the source of my values."

"Especially at her age and her appearance," the elder added. "If you don't mind my saying so, Solomon, at your age too. No comment on *your* beauty. You're not slovenly, but you should realize her attraction for you and perhaps appreciate it more than you do."

"Mummy! Please. Can we drop this kind of talk?"

"Jennifer, do you really think me outside of fundamental perspective on such a basic subject? I'm afraid of some things. I get hungry twice a day, and I remember connubial conjugation fondly." She dabbed her lips and arranged her napkin on her lap. "In the first of it anyway. Let me just say that if I were Eloise, I'd give this guy about two shakes before taking my pick of the litter in this excellent restaurant. Or anywhere. A woman can, you know."

"That's what Billy said," Eloise said. "He said it was unfair."

The elder asked, "Who is Billy?"

"My father. He had an eye for the ladies."

"I'll bet he did," the elder said. Richard returned with lunch. Eloise asked, "Solomon. Did you know Eloise's father, Billy?"

"Yes. We were best of friends."

"I see. Hmm . . . yes. The plot does thicken."

"You don't see, really," Eloise said. "We haven't seen Solomon in ages. I only met him yesterday. Billy and JoAnne talked about him forever. They'd lost touch. He's visiting from Los Angeles. But we have a purpose here. Solomon would call it karmic, and frankly, I think he's right. For the job."

"A bit presumptuous, I'd say," Eloise said.

"Me?" Solomon asked. "I'm not looking for a job."

"I won't discount you, Solomon," the elder said. "I meant that perfection in a man requires years of development, not one night, not a one-night acquaintance or a one-night stand. You've known him for one night? Eloise?"

"You don't have a job," Eloise interjected, then responded to Eloise, "He has the years of development." She chuckled. "You may see his wisdom by dessert. Can we get dessert? But no baklava, unless they have the shitty corn-syrup kind."

"Such language!" Jennifer said.

"I would agree with your assessment of baklava *sans* honey," the elder said. "They wouldn't do that here."

Richard served the last course and said, "You're Solomon Kursh." Solomon put his hands together and bowed. Richard returned the greeting. "A great honor, Sir."

"Thank you, Richard," Rupert said by way of dismissal. "Eloise, can you back up and fill something in. You say he'd be perfect, but he resists. Isn't that contradictory? If I might use an obvious and tedious analogy, the automotive placement process requires facile application of a few tools. Among them are recognition, isolation and absolution on objections. I can juggle the bunch and give you clear light every time—almost. But if a potential driver looks me in the eye and says, 'I don't want that car,' then I'll take my tool set to where it might better loosen a nut. A true specialist does not take no, until he does."

"Well said, Rupert," Solomon said. "Not only will your potential driver likely come to her senses and be back, but you'll succeed in the most important process of all."

"No, sir. Make no mistake," Rupert corrected. "She will not be back."

"And what is the most important process?" asked elder Eloise.

"Let go. Let go. Let go," Solomon answered.

"Why say it three times if you're so damn glommed onto it?" asked the younger.

"That's a fair question," Solomon allowed. "Letting go is not a singular event but a continuing process, a repetitive exercise against human nature and the wheel of desire."

"Ah, ha!" the elder pounced. "Desire is synonymous with life! Me thinks you do want to jump into the deep end."

"I will concur with caveats," Solomon concurred.

Eloise the elder harrumphed but to no avail, so she spelled it out: "You preach letting go of desire in life, yet you're here having lunch and a fine fusillade to tickle your spoiled brain. You want it both ways. That's obvious to me and, I think, to anyone who's ever felt real physical discomfort in making a living so that others might have shelter and something to eat."

"What would you know about making a living?" Rupert asked. "Really, Eloise . . ."

"She worked at Brannigan's before she met Daddy," Jennifer said. "Lived hand to mouth. It was an egg-sal san and a Coke every day for lunch. Isn't that right, Mummy?"

"Yes, Jennifer. To this day I can't bear the thought of an egg-sal san."

"Oh, gee," Rupert rejoined. "I forgot the hard times, the job and egg salad sandwiches. Except that Brannigan was daddy to her. I feel your pain, Eloise. But let's be real. Old Grand-Dad might be working-gauge bourbon for some girls, but you never drank it, because Old Granddad was Wendell Vanderholt for you! Hand to mouth? How about chafing dish to palate?"

"Um . . ." Eloise the younger began, hoping to put this train back on track. "These points are valid and interesting, but we haven't yet shared the denouement."

Elder Eloise lit up. She put her hand on Eloise's hand. "I'm so happy we met you," she said. "I hope we'll be friends."

Eloise smiled back, "We are friends. The thing is, Solomon and I have a history. We have a context for love, physical, mental and spiritual. And practical. Solomon resists the practical. We stand to gain a million dollars if I have a Jewish baby."

"Is that how you do it?" Jennifer asked.

"A million dollars is not what it used to be," Rupert said.

"It's a million two," Solomon said.

"That's a bit better," Rupert said.

"Compared to what?" asked the elder.

"Mummy, please." Jennifer jumped in. "Rupert has never stopped trying and never slowed down. I wish you could be more generous. At least more patient."

"Every hitter has a slump," Rupert said. "I'll be back on my game. Don't worry about me, but I can't imagine making automotive placements for a lifetime, or two lifetimes for that matter, and having a waiter far from home recognize me. That's got to be worth something."

"Here's to that," Solomon said. "All I ever needed was management. Tell me, Rupert. What's the nature of your slump? I'm not a conventional psychologist, but I have experience in counseling of this nature. That's the gist of psychiatry and psychology on many levels, job counseling. I don't mean to condescend, but sometimes fresh eyes give fresh perspective."

Rupert ruminated. "It stopped." He looked off, at a cloud, going or coming. "The rhythm. The flow. The lyric and the score. The sun and the moon." He looked back, resigned. "It stopped."

"Like you say, every hitter has a slump."

"Not for three seasons," the elder nearly moaned.

"I'll come clean," Rupert said. "We've come so far in such a short time, and you know what they say about luck."

Everyone continued eating and drinking, until Jennifer said, "Tell us, Rupe. What do they say about luck?"

"It favors the receptive mind. What does that mean? In most cases, and this one too, it means the informed mind. I . . . I didn't just recall reading about Solomon or seeing him on TV. I read his biography. I found it interesting. Intriguing, actually. So much so, that I read his other books."

"You have books?" asked both Eloises.

Solomon nodded. "A few. Which have you read, Rupert?"

"*The Invisible Gem* is my favorite, but I enjoyed them all immensely." Solomon smiled; an author fulfilled. "You talk about energy in esoteric terms; such exotic language, you nearly lost me, but a point took hold in regard to luck and receptivity and energy. You enumerated the simple ways that people bring on the negative or positive with no idea of the power they're wielding in the moment."

"Your point?" the elder asked.

"You energize the negative, Eloise," Rupert said. "I'll preface this critique with affirmation of my gratitude to you and my love for you, yes, my love, through Jennifer, to you. Your negative innuendo is chronic. It is not productive and not appreciated. It might be amusing and surely seems convenient, but I doubt you realize your appalling effect. It seems that today might be perfect, since you're recalling—what was it? Connubial conflagration? No. Connubial conjunction: that was it. Today might be the right time for you to ponder your energetic prowess, or, in lay terms, to make like a two-dollar whore and fake it. I mean that you should take the positive side at those times when you're feeling skeptical about immediate family and performance prospects. Capisce?"

"Oh, Rupert!" This from Jennifer again, wiping her chin and dropping her napkin on the table as if to announce *Finito*!

"It was connubial conjugation," the elder corrected.

"Thank you," Rupert allowed. "That's more like it."

Ensuing silence seemed softer still over the crunching of baby arugula. Solomon seemed amused, taking inventory before opening in his deftly daft way, invoking the spirit among them. "Energy is everywhere," he said. "An atomic bomb jams energy to violent compression until it explodes, in conflict with containment. Restraint often destroys. Thank you, Rupert, for reading my books and thanks again for reflecting and, I think, comprehending. Your critique was in my opinion eloquent and articulate, right up to the nuclear bomb you felt motivated to drop on Eloise to get your revenge. Pardon me, Jennifer, for my hyperbole, but it can be a useful tool. I'll remind you, Rupert, to remind yourself in all things. Two-dollar whores work extra hard for their money and should not be bandied about as receptacles for personal points. I don't think you would stab Eloise with a knife, though you did with a cruel comparison."

"Sorry," Rupert said. "I am aware of my deficiencies."

"I am too," Jennifer said. "You're a lovely man who makes the world a better place when you're not being so cold and cruel."

"At least," the elder said, "its drivers are better placed. I regret my insensitivity, Rupert. You see my deficiencies as well."

"I apologize too," Eloise said. "We've dominated with personal needs. I hate to be overbearing, but since the damage is done . . ."

"Quite the contrary, Eloise," Eloise said. "I believe we've pierced a pustule that may now resolve."

"That's what I meant about Solomon. He brings things out. That's why I wish . . . I wish he could . . ." But the younger Eloise lost her way among her wishes and couldn't say what for, sobbing and wiping her eyes, as she stood and excused herself.

Like old hands at fielding awkward moments, the remaining quartet watched her go. Returning to last crusts and crumbs, they soon browsed the dessert menu that Richard had thoughtfully left. Easing things back to composure and calming the space they shared, Eloise the elder asked, "Practicality is best in the social sense. Nobody wants to kneel to convention, but we do. We sacrifice comfort because we always have. What would the world be with no children?"

Solomon ducked under. "Do you have children, Jennifer?"

To which question Jennifer rose, startled, sobbing and rushing off to more private confines, where wits might regroup.

The women did regroup, as they can, when lip gloss and eyeliner get refreshed, when commiseration comes to tacit agreement that only a dab of each would suffice with such vigor on tap. It's so millennial to over-glam, and they counted their lucky stars to have been born prior to *that* malaise. Checking themselves and each other in the mirror, they felt better, ready for the scrimmage out front.

Rupert was about to ask why Solomon wouldn't simply bang her, Eloise, the younger, discreetly and with utmost respect, of course, not to mention courtesy and gentility, to alleviate pressure and expedite his return to the ashram or the compound or whatever cults were calling the Big Top these days. Rupert naturally assumed an extremely lucrative spirituality, based on what he'd seen and read. He hesitated to ask, because Eloise the elder read his thoughts in the worst way, or appeared to do so, her sour puss set in condemnation of men and their vile ways. Anything he said would prove her point: that all males of the species are naughty boys, unable to pass a mud puddle without jumping in.

As a consummate automotive placement specialist, however, fluent in the transactional lingo of circumvention on delicate topics, Rupert said, "She's quite a looker. Easy on the eye, and she keeps up with you. That's no short order, my friend, as you must be aware."

"I can't argue either point or see their relevance. Going against my moral grain would be easier with a comely woman of active intellect. But I won't. I've tried to be clear. I am not formulated by consensus. Our culture is predisposed on the family unit as the hub of civilization. People presume propagation. Political parties compete, with tax credits for more babies, for baby care, education and health. The huggy-baby corollaries are widely refuted these days but get squelched. Many women won't verbalize their preference but live it, free and adventurous. A woman can find gratification outside of childbearing in a rich, full life, like some men."

"Now whose free will are you talking about?" Rupert challenged. "What if a woman wants to have a baby?"

"Listen to you," the elder quipped. "Since when did you want a woman to have a baby?"

"No, it's true," Rupert said. "Solomon here says he wants to follow his moral compass, but he lives adrift, outside of normal shipping lanes." He turned to Solomon. "Do you have a direction?"

"How astute, that you see the difference between free form and the established route. You conform to the vast majority, and I don't. I'm open-minded, Rupert, and share your liberal view. I also assume, Eloise, that your station in life got you here today, in a fine restaurant having leisurely lunch. On a weekday. Did your formidable golfing skills develop before Jennifer's infancy, or after? Did you have a nanny? I sense natural aptitude and professional coaching. I'll cut to the point: Eloise got choked up, and so did Jennifer, on a tender topic. I think Jennifer and Rupert have no children, and it's a bone to pick for her and him and for you and him as well. How endearing for you to want grandchildren. I'm sorry I asked, really, except for peeling another layer of this onion. Marriage is not on the table. It's irrelevant at any rate. I see marriage as a formality, something that might occur after love is secure. I met Eloise yesterday. Repeat: yesterday. Would I marry her? Will I learn to love Eloise, to know that I'd sooner live with her than without her? The point here is happily-ever-after and baby in the equation, as if sleep deprivation, shitty diapers and no travel are incidental to love. We suffer the death of nature. People in the world are starving. Yet baby-makes-three remains unchallenged, unless we challenge it. Nancy Reagan put it best: 'Just say no.' Does that make sense?"

Eloise the elder leaned nearer as Jennifer and Eloise approached. "Could you learn to love me in time?"

Solomon blushed as Eloise the younger might have done.

"Tell us," said the younger, sitting down. "What did we miss?"

"Eloise proposed to Solomon," Rupert said. "For the weekend."

"Mummy!"

Solomon searched for words, wise words befitting—no, not befitting. He wanted words of comfort and something or other, perhaps wisdom, but any distraction would do.

"The point," Eloise the elder said, "is rudimentary, but women through the ages have been kept from making that point. Eloise has tried to make it with you, but you're a hard head. The point is . . ." She took Jennifer's hand for comfort and strength. "The point is the fucking. Sorry, dear. It's an ugly word for an ugly behavior. It's what's become of romance hardly five hundred years since the troubadours. But if you can open your heart and mind, Mister Kursh, you might realize that in the act of love, as in making love with respect to care and . . . repetition and familiarity; well, then, Sir, in *that* free exchange, you may arrive at love. And that is something you might not comprehend."

"Touché, as Jennifer might score the round," Solomon said, happy to return such a formidable forehand. "But I think you're selling a very weak case, that women haven't been able to adequately soften up their men prior to fornication. I will remind you, Eloise: most men will promise anything, will sit, shake, roll over and beg to get the treat. I will also remind you that besides taking a terrible toll on romance, the last five hundred years have taken a worse toll on natural habitat. Your argument ignores the dark fact, that the sexual consequence of a single species is killing Earth as I know and love it."

"Score that round for Solomon," Rupert said, ignoring Eloise, who scowled. "That puts us at a stalemate, pyrrhic victors and sad women coming in for the tie."

Richard appeared. "I know you're full. But I want to share some incredibly yummy choices. I can bring the cart."

Nobody said boo, so Rupert prompted, "Eloise?"

"No, thank you. I've had enough."

And that was the end of lunch, except for the moment of truth in its most awkward form: embarrassment. Rupert and Solomon reached for the check on cue, as men of valor must do, meeting cultural expectation, transcending personal limits. Credit limits were merely obtuse, of no concern, trifles among men, yet each struggled for composure, fearing the card might not fly.

Not to worry!

The elder sprang like a mongoose, no flair or fanfare but quick and neat, to snatch the check by the throat. "Please. This one is for the memory archives, what I treasure most. Rupert, you are an excellent son-in-law, husband and provider. Solomon, it's been an adventure, meeting you. Eloise, you are an excellent woman. Please exchange contacts with Jennifer, so we can gather again to plot against these bums."

"Thank you, Eloise," Rupert said. "We still haven't covered the million two and the Jewish baby."

"No, we haven't," Eloise said. "We'll give Eloise and Solomon the rest of the day and as much of the night as they need to sort things out. We're available, Eloise, for further discussion. I see your point. He's a bit old for you, but he seems flexible. Please, Solomon, don't confuse that with spry."

Eloise Kessler Keene

Silence ruled the ride home. Solomon admired her patient driving and would have said as much but let silence reign, undeterred.

Eloise Keene ruminated on feminine allure or lack thereof. She pondered the time life takes to make up its mind and the learning discrepancies that deliver a girl to forty's front door with regret and urgency. *I mean a woman.*

Wounds inflicted by heartless adolescents had scarred over and faded, but the pain lingered. How did those kids learn such petty meanness? Is nasty behavior instinctive? Some kids need to dominate, to compensate for their own deficiencies. Many kids strive to be average, to fit in. But Jolly Green Eloise Keene had made a juicy target at five feet eight inches by age ten and five-ten by twelve. An inch taller by fourteen, she wanted only to blend in, to get fewer stares and snickers and maybe a bit of common courtesy. She'd given up hope for a boyfriend and would not pick up a basketball for fear of being typecast and a future in the low post.

Douglas Smythe was two years ahead, a jock and a four-letter man: turd. As a preppy bigmouth, Douglas shouted punch lines that triggered toady laughter and rendered him perfect as Prom King. Eloise hated stares, and he granted her wish, blind to her existence.

But a few years later, she turned beautiful in countenance and contour. The boys became young men, and Douglas vaguely remembered her, saying she'd changed. He remained superior, letting it come flooding back, her awkward, gangly past. "Oh! You're Jolly Gree . . ." Predictable and crude, he at least held back on *Queen Bean* or *Stretch Keene.* And he avoided that nerve so unfairly exposed: *Smelloise*. She smelled great or neutral. She performed personal tests, when the name caught on, and remained confident in her scent.

Any doubts lingering in the Prom King quickly faded, as Dougie at twenty-five and Eloise at twenty-two made their way to acceptance and heavy petting. He was Douglas Smythe, after all, the sure antidote to the lonely years, not so long ago. Then came marriage, to the chagrin of both families. The young couple thought it laughable, that anyone could doubt their compatibility or that such lust wouldn't last. Romance took a header in a tender moment when he audibly sniffed and said she was the Smelloise for him. He meant to compliment with his mouth full of her, but it marked the onset of regret.

She further realized, as people might, that the formative years are best for forming and then forgetting. As for safekeeping in the memory trousseau: not so much. Casting out is healthy. Gaining stature in due time, she saw Dougie as mostly average but exceptionally obnoxious, aggressive, biased, assertive, ignorant, superior and rude. She refused to hate him; he was so sincerely stupid. He went from tedious to untenable to unspeakable and inevitably unacceptable. With a potbelly swelling by thirty and interests shrinking, he seemed wrong, a drain on life and prospects. She could not bear him into the future. She gave in to hating him, the sight of him, much less the touch. She knew the hatred would do her in. She'd made a big mistake but could leave it behind, and she did. She felt better still when the divorce was final.

Divorced at twenty-seven, she felt young and alive with plenty of time. She could achieve fulfillment, and a pretty face and figure wouldn't hurt. Finding a good man would be a cakewalk, landing her on gratification with icing on top.

She met men. Men introduced themselves. She felt wise, well qualified to judge on merit and light. She felt reasonable and tempered, ready, willing and patient. She could tough it out.

She'd inherited a wealth of wit and wisdom on JoAnne's kinky compulsion and Billy's quirky views. She wanted good company and quality time. She would have children in time, along with day care and a modest budget for necessities. Her needs included a few entitlements that most of the world lives without, but in a flush society, her goals seemed appropriate. She aspired to privilege and thought it reasonable.

Solomon seemed a tad elderly, chronologically speaking, but he made up in vitality and worldview. He seemed compassionate and, in some things, loving. His baggage with her hippie-fied parents and apparent poverty would sort directly. He would process reversals as people do. He was so damn smart and used his smarts, always thinking. He made her laugh! Dougie Smythe had been so *stoopid*, that she laughed after all at shit and Shinola.

Solomon would be a match with a half-mil for practical needs. This solution was a snap judgment. So what? How long had she waited? How much seasoning had she gained? She knew the market on viable men to fit the criteria, and she knew value when she saw it.

Solomon interrupted at last with a familiar question, "Penny for your thoughts."

"I'm such a disappointment."

"Not so much. Tell me why."

"I want good company, quality time, day care for the kid and some spending money."

"What's disappointing about that?"

"It's hardly the pure white light you prefer."

"No. The pure white light is for dying. Your thoughts are practical. Part of life. Suburban life, but you might grow out of it."

"That's so tolerant. It's discouraging. You were able to ask that guy, that uh . . ."

"Monk. He's a monk. I was showing off. It's an old joke."

"But he knew you."

"He knew of me. Media. It's a small world, often misinformed. I think he understood, but nobody knows, especially him. That's why he's a monk, trying not to think so much. Maybe he'll grow out of it too. Open his eyes and see things."

"It was impressive."

"As intended. He seemed like a good kid. I hit it off with Rupert too. It happens. Not so much with the mother. Did you notice her jaundiced looks in my direction?"

"That happens too."

"It does. I'm also disappointing, trying to gain her favor."

"Yeah. Who cares?"

They got silent again, processing lunch and the post-wine funk, testing silence for comfort between a man and a woman recently met, compared to an old, married couple. Solomon ended the test. "Meeting new friends is a great thing."

She agreed, thinking him gratuitous, thinking he avoided the tough topics of marriage, her relative youth and good looks, her ready wit and enjoyable presence. At a loss in the moment and in life, she felt indefinitely postponed.

"You know, Eloise," he said. "I feel terrible, disappointing you, making you sad in any way. But you baffle me. You said you didn't want a husband, and now you do. Am I missing something?" She pulled in to the driveway and turned off the engine.

"I changed my mind. Okay? I think of a future with no . . ." She got out and went to the door.

"No man? Or no money?"

"Yes."

He followed her in.

She stopped near the sofa to face him. "I see a future that could be happy. We could have that. How terrible could it be, raising a child with intellectual stimulation and a great genetic mix? How many parents get that? The kid will have it both ways on the nurture and nature part of things."

"Nobody can know. We would likely be blessed in some areas, but you overlook a few things too."

"You must mean JoAnne's personality and Billy's instability."

"And the fallibility of certainty. And the cruel mirage of money. And the loss of hope and aspiration that most often comes from need. Do you mind if I lie down for a while?"

"No. I'll do that too. I don't smoke hash in the morning or drink wine for lunch. One little glass, and I'm a goner."

"Yeah. Me too. What were we thinking?"

"Smoked the shit outa that rock."

He smiled. "You have a lyrical sense. Where do you get it?"

"Same place I got my height."

Solomon pondered mysterious essence as she read aloud a note on the table, saying JoAnne had gone to a farmer's market way out near Bonnie, an old friend she hadn't seen in ages. She might be back tomorrow, and don't mess with dinner. She'd made them a reservation at Espero's for six thirty.

Eloise looked up with a shrug.

Solomon eased inexorably into the sofa and JoAnne's neat fix.

"I guess we better hurry," Eloise said.

"It's not yet three."

"Yeah. All the time in the world."

"It's like a honeymoon," he said. "Two restaurants in one day."

"That's not like a honeymoon," she said, shuffling up the hall.

Nobody slept.

He drifted fitfully.

From the same semi-daze, she rose in an hour to shower and change, leaving the door open to tease or taunt.

He thought of Billy and JoAnne and knew what Eloise looked like naked: like a naked woman but taller. He felt blessedly French, free of the giddy, squeamish pubescence ingrained in many men—or did he feel lifelessly French? His forehead wrinkled when she stood in the hallway. "It's not good, you know, you repelling me this way."

"How am I repelling you?"

"I'm naked. You won't even look at me."

"That's not very fair," he said.

"To whom?" she asked

"To me, for starters. I'm your Uncle Stanley. What would be the point of seeing you naked?"

"You might see the practical side of the issue on the table."

"I've seen it many times. I live near women who go naked as often as not." He sat up and turned to her. "Just as I thought. You're fit and trim."

"So?"

He lay back down. "Very nice. Do you feel better now? More romantic?"

She did not feel better, turning back down the hall to clothe herself. He fell asleep, as old guys will, relieved of pressure.

"This puts me in an awkward position," Solomon said after settling in at Espero's.

"Awkward?"

"I'm sitting across from the personification of love in my life. I've loved very little, and you feel like family to me."

"I would hope so. But I think you must feel like family with many people."

"I know many people. If nearly any of them walked in here, I'd say hey and give them a hug, and we'd embrace. It's fanciful and self-perpetuating, based on bliss and contact. It's also layered and circular and rarely like family. I feel pressure to sire a child here and be a father and marry. Yes, I think awkward fairly describes it."

"Solomon, it's not pressure. It's a situation." She reached for a touch. "Life is awkward. You built a life with people who don't fit."

"A few don't fit by choice. The others can't fit. Misfits. We put them out as beggars—I mean missionaries. We used the money for food and shelter, so the work could proceed. When that stopped working, we went to good works. I didn't build a career. I'm another misfit who put one foot in front of the other with no destination in mind, no objective but making do, like you. Look where it got us."

"Not too shabby. We have a baby, change a few diapers, walk the dog and bingo: a million bucks! You know it could be worse. It is worse for many people. For most people."

"Oh, now we're getting a dog?"

"I should think so. Don't you want to? We must, with your silly sense of humor and . . . love. A dog would be wonderful. Who could understand you better? It would be a marriage of greater convenience with a dog."

"I had a dog. I never got another. I'm not sure convenience and a dog would suit you. I have no idea, really, what might suit you."

"You don't think much of me."

"I don't know much of you. I knew your parents to be energetic and imaginative, so I assume you are too. And look what happened to them. No offense. Look what happened to me. I'd simply rather be broke than stuck."

"Yeah, Billy got stuck in a hot mop bucket, sloshing hot tar. But everybody works at something. It's not drudgery, if you love. Okay, let's say I could get the money without the baby. Would I rather? I don't know. I don't think love can be persuaded. Not verbally."

"You don't love me. You can't. We only just . . ."

"But I can and do," she said. "Yes, it was on first sight only yesterday. But the stories took years and came home, even though you don't fit them anymore. You're resistant to potential, to an act of faith. We wouldn't stay in a suburb if we didn't want to. Do you know how awkward I feel, throwing myself at you?"

"Do you?"

"You think I do this easily?"

"Don't you?"

"Solomon. Please don't do that. I'm pointing out a practical, workable solution to a bunch of problems, and I admit that I wouldn't mind having sex with you. Do you honestly believe I'd offer myself so indiscriminately?"

"Well, I don't know much about discretion in love." He paused to reflect on the puzzle. "Love is not rational. It's a radical emotion. I don't know that I've been in love. Have you? Do you know?"

Her eyes moistened. Her face drooped in sadness.

He leaned in. "I'll tell you something else that I make no secret of: I'm broke. Flat broke."

"Fuck, duh. What was my first clue? You show up with a change of skivvies, a few shirts and a toothbrush in a cheap cloth bag. Were we supposed to think you left your portfolio and Louie

Vuittons back at the clubhouse?"

"I would prefer cloth with a million dollars or a hundred million. You should know that."

"Yeah, fine. Your cloth bag works out for the best. But your economic status also makes you a witness for the prosecution. You must see the synchronous convergence here."

"You could call it that. But bearing a child is no remedy for having no money or destination. I can't tell where I'm headed or what you want. You said you didn't want the American plan."

She'd ordered a Pinot Blanc for the lightness after too much wine at lunch. The sommelier poured a taste for the gentleman, who deferred to the lady, who said, "Come on. Come on."

Raising her goblet for a toast, she plucked another heartstring.

He took over and said, "Here's to friendship and love and health." The tinkling goblets loosened another tear. He drank, looking through his wine at her, wondering why golden hues seemed cruel.

She said, "Yes. I don't know what I want. It changes. I made a mistake in marriage. Now I'm alone. I have JoAnne, but you know what I mean."

"I don't know what you mean. You're alone. I'm alone. JoAnne is alone. Those people over there are alone. Don't tell me you don't want to grow old alone. Nobody wants that, but you must find comfort in your own skin or everybody around you shares the discomfort. Do you know what solitary comfort is worth?"

"You're so smart."

"Sorry."

"Are you? What little girl ever imagines she'll fall in love with an old guy? I'm sorry too. I mean older guy. Let's just have this wine and a nice time. I'm done. Is that okay?"

Solomon thought of the old guy who kept rolling out of his hospital bed until the nurse gave him a boner pill. A joke might lighten things up, but he felt better in restraint, and he smiled.

She took it as affirmation of what he surely could see.

He wouldn't have thought her so needy, and he asked, "Are you so lonely? Depression often comes from a certain failure—I don't mean to lecture. I speak freely. The point is important because everyone experiences depression in varying potency and duration. Yours seems manageable but persistent. I think the failure may apply to you. You're too exacting on yourself."

She blushed. "I don't know what failure I'm suffering. I need stimulation. JoAnne is not in the world. Not like you."

He sipped and laughed. "I got a ride to the airport with a fifty-five-year-old man, calls himself Parnelli because he's a driver. You remember Parnelli Jones?"

"No."

"See? We're not playing on a level court. Never mind. Parnelli Jones. Indianapolis 500. You know that one, don't you?"

"Yes! I know about the Indianapolis 500."

"Okay. Parnelli Jones won it a bunch of times. We ran out of gas and coasted to the curb, rubbing tires, popping hubcaps. The guy is a fuckup. He said don't worry; he'd get some gas in a can for when I needed a ride back. And he changed his name to Steve Miller there at the curb. He'd set it up, playing some old Steve Miller tunes on the way. He said he'd feel best if I gave him my approval. Is that the world you imagine me in? Because that is the world I'm in."

She said, "Yeah. It's the world of your making, but you are part of it. JoAnne watches TV, smokes dope, goes to the mall."

"JoAnne appears to have grown into her world and her life. My world is not of my making. It's the world of my default. It's my failure at free will. Do you have any idea what a nutter I was when I hung out with your parents? I forfeited free will to chase a non-idea. That's what cults are. A cult provides thoughts for the group. I'm not in the world of self-made women and men. I let a certain world envelop my days. From the suburban angle, I look exotic and adventurous. From the shabby house and soft world I live in, my life looks futile and failing."

"What a bullshit assessment."

"It's accurate. The point in regard to your depression is that I give of myself to others all the time. I live close to needy people, so the give is nonstop. Sometimes, I give to critters and feel best about that, and I'm not alone in my preference. Energy flows as second nature in the direction of need. It rarely flows in, sometimes for months on end."

"The women there love you."

"They admire me. They help me find my happiness, but their energy is not the love I need."

"Do you know what you need?" she asked.

"I'm frankly exhausted, and I'll admit that I'm also depressed. I'm anxious but not like you. You have very little give. That's harsh, but I see you give when it's comfortable. Look: I'm not in the world. I'm in a fix. Like you and everyone, I'm stressed, perplexed and a few bucks short. But I'm not depressed. Not overly depressed at any rate."

They drank like sparring partners between rounds. She asked, "What should we do?"

"What should we do?" he asked back, peering through the wine. "I'm not sure we should do anything. We could go swimming so I could check out your body, but we already got that out of the way."

"I don't mean to make you uncomfortable."

"But you do. You go out of your way to make me uncomfortable. How's this: I promise to love you forever. Okay? You and JoAnne. I love seeing you both. I'm sorry about Billy and wish he was here. I cried when you told me."

"I know."

"This isn't what I expected."

"How could it be?"

"I guess it couldn't. I just wanted . . .some comfort."

"Do you think I'm pretty?" He looked up. She blushed, and he blushed too. "We blush together," she said.

"Don't get started," he said. "Yes, you're pretty. You know that. Why wouldn't I think it?"

"Could you see me . . . romantically without thinking of Billy and JoAnne?"

"I don't think so."

"You're not related."

"Hmm. Yes, we are."

"Maybe in the heart. Not by blood. You love them."

"What are you getting at?"

"I don't mean to put you on the spot. I think it could work. I like being with you."

"Good. Let's enjoy this. What can we talk about if we don't flog the phantom?"

She poured. "Do you have any clue how different you are?"

"You mean from other people?"

"From other men."

"Most people live conventional lives, if that's what you mean. An active mind and some pizzazz are different. Your personal experience with men is a different subject."

"Yes, it is. You're different. You know that." Their eyes met but couldn't hold. "And the other part, your approach to the world. You're not aloof or indifferent. What is it?"

"It's nothing. I don't make light of it. I've maintained guidelines for years. That's all. Maybe they've made me different, I hope for the best. Anyone can be different. Religious people follow guidelines too, but they're rote and rigid with hellfire consequence for natural things. Seekers are formative, on a never-ending path of trial and error, ideally with less error as they get farther up the path."

"What will you do now?"

"I don't know. Clean up the mess."

"You could get a job. JoAnne hates it when I say that. She'd hate any job she could get because she's only qualified for shitty jobs. It's the same with most people. Look at every Powerball winner; not one shows up for work the next day. But you could be special."

"You see this potential between us as winning Powerball?"

"Money can buy peace of mind. And you could get a job you

wouldn't hate. You're famous—okay, you're a minor celebrity."

"Minor celebrity?"

"You could lecture. You have credentials. You could teach people how to approach life as adventure. You could sell shoes. I could imagine you feeling my feet. And think of the beaver shots." He looked up. "Hey, I'm just fuckin' witcha."

"That's what Billy said."

"I know." The waiter came. She ordered braised brussels sprouts and tofu and suggested the fried green tomatoes, and they'd share. He said yes and chose curry soba noodles with cashews. "Yuck. Curry."

"See, we might not work out after all?"

Silence settled again to a rhythm, fluidly mutable on romance, practicality, money, lust, humility and need. A seasoned seeker of light and a woman who happened to be the svelte daughter of old friends had reached an impasse, until they spoke at once.

"I think we're evenly matched," she said.

"Did you have a career when you got married?" he asked at the same time.

"My career before Douglas? Speaking of menial and mundane?"

"Yes. That one."

"I helped with Billy's business. I'm not sure what was worse, getting bored or working in that smelly office with that stupid crew."

"What's your daily routine now?"

"I'm not lazy, if that's what you think. I didn't make a killing on the divorce. Douglas was filthy. He had money too. They're not rich; they're wealthy. I could have struck gold, God knows; JoAnne was all over it, as usual. I didn't look back. His parents loved me for that. I didn't make a case because it was personal."

"But you thought about the case and the money."

"I should have. But I hated him in so many ways, I wanted out like a prisoner wants out."

"You called him filthy. You're a hygiene stickler too, huh?"

"That was a joke. But yes, I don't like stink. He was bad. I thought he stunk more when it became a stinky situation. I read this article on how to know when your marriage should end. Every spouse imagines how life would be if the other spouse died or got killed. If that thought occurs regular, it's time to move on. I thought about it every day. Isn't that crazy, to marry somebody and then hate them?"

"Some people will tell you marriage is crazy."

"I mean the proximity of love and hate—extreme emotions forced to turn on each other."

"What did you learn? Why couldn't it happen again?"

"It could but would be far less likely. I had issues long before Douglas. He represented those issues and seemed like a remedy. I was wrong. He was a creepy guy from way back."

"And you were a fool?"

"Yes, I was. Do you find that satisfying?"

"I think so. Self-admittance is most often a prerequisite of personal development. Thanks, by the way, for showing me around. What would you be doing if I hadn't shown up?"

"I'd be sitting on the sofa with JoAnne, thinking up Jews who can still make a baby."

"You're okay with that?"

"No, and I resent your presumption. We have engaged in a difficult but practical process. I won't jump into marriage again without assessing many things."

"Like age difference? Or genetic history? You don't know mine. Or net worth? You do know mine. Or compatibility beyond a brief recreational range?"

"I also read that the optimal age of a wife for a husband your age is one half plus seven. I did the math. It's a match. Your genetic history derives from Morris Sokolov and Pearl Epstein. Morris's parents both came from Galicia around 1880. Pearl's side came about 1910 from Austria. It's all Jews with the same bad diet, too much salt and *schmaltz* and lack of exercise leading to the same ailments for centuries. Your net worth is *nada mucho*. And we've already done more prep work on compatibility than your average young'uns, who'd be humping like rabbits by now. Not us. We're taking it slooow . . ."

"You've done your homework. I was never good at that."

"You're surprised?"

"Maybe. You seem so practical; it's made you cynical."

Eyes puffy at the mention of her cynical nature, she said, "I didn't mind showing you around. A fun day reminded me of life. That's better than what I've thought lately."

He wanted to squeeze her hand but held back.

She said, "I know a gelato place a few blocks down. They make their own spumoni. Have you ever?"

"I don't think so."

"We can walk. Are you okay with that?"

"Yes, dear. I'm okay with that."

They enjoyed espresso on the way, served correctly. She asked, "Can you imagine this in a paper cup? I've seen it. Really."

"The horror."

"Yes. Demitasse and saucer with cubed raw sugar and a little spoon will ruin you for the cheap shit. Oh, and the little sprig of lemon peel. Am I foolish for loving that so much?"

"I love it too," he said. "I often feel foolish. It's vital to my work. You may have noticed."

They shared a sweet, foolish smile. She took his arm to stroll in cadence, as tall people do, to avoid the tangle. She turned wistfully on arrival at the car.

He got in. The ride home was brief.

She unlocked the door, walked in and turned again near the sofa. "Is it uncomfortable?" she asked.

"Not at all," he said.

"Well then . . ."

He stepped up. "Don't fuck this up. Okay?"

She breathed short, a sob or a laugh. They turned away and turned in.

The Morning After

She set a latte within sniffing distance and said, "Hope I didn't wake you. It's six thirty. Time for work."

"Work?"

"Yeah. You remember Dobie Gillis, don't you? Billy sent in for the whole collection. Maynard G. Krebs? Www . . . Ww . . . Work!"

She wore a long t-shirt and he suspected nothing else, either in the devilish innocence of beautiful women or the playful dare of her mother's daughter.

"I didn't know Billy was a fan."

"The playing field isn't so slanted. I know all about Parnelli Jones and Maynard G. Krebs. What was the other one?"

"Steve Miller."

"Yeah. Who is Steve Miller?"

"He had a band."

"Ah. I'll bet JoAnne knows him."

"She does."

"Anyway, you got me thinking. I love that about you. Sorry. I appreciate that about you. We never decided what to do today, so I came up with a fun thing that might be productive. And giving. We can go to the dog pound. My friend Angie volunteers there to meet guys, but she is a bona fide dog nut, so it works out either way. She goes weekends and walks the doggies and gives them a bath and says it's her best thing all week."

"Has she met a guy there?"

"Yes and no. She's weak, but I get it."

"You mean the guy wasn't perfect. She wants a prince to sweep her off her feet? A guy in a tailored suit with no-limit credit cards?"

"Yes. A prince would be perfect."

"And she judges by appearance."

"Not entirely. A handsome, rich prince would be best. Short of that, it could be an above-average prince. She's been around enough to lower the bar, but not by much. She really liked one guy as a friend. He made her laugh all the time."

"Isn't that a sure way to a woman's heart?"

"Sometimes. He could say it's cold, and she'd howl. Strange, but it worked. He was sweet and smart, a lawyer in this great firm where they love him. But he was tall, so she didn't see his bald spot much until . . . he was eating her and she knew it couldn't work."

Solomon squinted as if to see the crux. "She was looking down at his bald head between her legs and called it off?" Eloise shrugged. "I hope we don't run into her."

"We won't. She goes weekends. Would you hate her that much?"

"No. But I think she's a waste of space. I think the guy was eating her wrong. The problem was remedial."

"I agree. I thought less of her. Why would she let the guy eat her in the first place if she didn't think it through?"

"People get excited and make mistakes. Maybe she'll miss him and give him another shot with some pointers. Or a wig." Eloise smiled like a child. "Do you think things through?"

She blushed apoplectic but realized his question framed a bigger picture than cunnilingus. "I do. But I have to feel it too."

"That would be ideal and easier for a woman. I knew a woman, just out of a marriage to a doctor. I'd met him when they visited, a mean, pudgy little guy. He played a small part in her drama—her melodrama. She came back after they split up, ready for a makeover but uncertain on direction. She made a show of her sweetness and light but was distracted, nervous, like failing in a marriage with a rich guy meant that she was a failure."

Eloise blushed.

"Not like you. She had a Mercedes and a mansion. She dropped names. I only saw her rut after getting my relief. I like to call it an honest mistake, but . . . She was up on current events and pop art and wore very few precious gems, to be discreet. She needed a refresh. She'd parked next to a van that looked like a Demolition Derby refugee with a bumper sticker that said: *Don't postpone your joy*. She said, 'My God, I love that!' We laughed and talked and so on."

"The classic cult retreat. I thought it wasn't that way with you."

"It wasn't, but I tried it. This was a long time ago. I was younger, about your age. She was older, good looking. It didn't work. I knew it wouldn't. I was weak."

"It obviously worked."

"It didn't work. I should have known it couldn't go anywhere meaningful or have any meaning for that matter."

"You are so full o' shit. You're sitting here pontificating that a fellow should deny a woman who makes herself available because it might not lead to a relationship? That's rich."

"You're right. I wanted it one way or another. I'm not sure what she wanted, but it was more than sex. Affirmation? Affection? A place in the organization? She went down like that guy from the animal shelter. I should have loved it."

"But she had a bald spot on top?"

"No, but . . . I told her to slow down, so she came up, all frazzled and famished. We slowed down, but I got her scent. You do that too." He shrugged. "Some things take a while to know. She'd had sardines in olive oil. That's what I smelled. It stopped. The manly part."

"It happens."

"Usually for a reason."

"The smell was on her neck?"

"I don't eat animals but did as a child. My mother ate sardines every week or so. It was a different world. I remember the smell."

"A bad smell."

"No. I'm not saying it was a fishy smell. That's bacteria some women get, and others don't, and men make jokes . . ."

"Like the blind guy who thought he'd found a tuna boat?"

"This wasn't that. It was in her skin on her neck." He rolled his eyes: end of story. He sat up to sip his latte.

She smiled from the end of the sofa, "Yes. The scented part

around the collar bone."

He nodded. "Maybe I was shallow like your girlfriend."

"No. In her case the view from above was no surprise. Your case sounds like a mistake, an honest one for a young man. Pheromones are critical. Love won't work if the scent is wrong. People don't realize how scent rules romance, and romance rules history. You're sensitive to it. I can believe it shut you down."

"What's to believe? It happened."

"I never told this to anybody else, not even JoAnne. Douglas smelled wrong. I don't mean BO from not bathing. I mean wrong. I mean like one time in a Thai place they added that fish sauce, and I thought it was rot and sent it back, and the waiter said, 'No, no. It good. Good.' That's not fair, because rot is worse than stink. Douglas didn't stink in the conventional sense, but people expect a sardine smell on sardines. Do sardines come from Sardinia? I have to check it out. Don't let me forget."

"He smelled like what, peat moss? He could be unwell. Scent is more than a linchpin for romance. Stink indicates malfunction."

"Yes! That was it. He was sick." She scooted down to put her nose on his neck. "Nice," she said. "I don't care if you go bald. I mean for the top view."

"She assumed it was her fault, but it wasn't," he said.

"Because you should have known that she smelled like sardines before everyone took their pants off?"

"No. Fault usually relates to motive. I think she tried to absolve doubts, so we could relax and chat like the extraordinary people we were. That didn't happen. She got things going again and came back topside, and I held my breath for a minute, but that won't work. It fizzled, and down and up and down . . ."

"It didn't end well."

"No, it didn't. It ended on efficiency and regret. No absolution. She cut her visit short. What could I say? Don't worry, it's only your smell that makes my dick limp?"

Eloise laughed, baring her neck. "Check me out."

"I did. I wanted to see if you smell like JoAnne and Billy."

"How can you remember Billy's scent?"

"Call me unusual. Or a good dog."

"Unusual is easier. She was needy, but I think your story goes a bit further."

"She didn't want to be alone. She wanted identity, and a little revenge with a younger guy would also help her catch up on what she'd missed. She felt rejected. She was lonely. She thought I was important. HL was in the news. They talked about millions. You can't have your cake and eat it too, but she wanted to eat me in order to have me. I smelled sardines, and nobody got some cake."

"It was a bad blow job?"

"Eloise, must you?"

"Answer the question."

"She did not get a boost in self-esteem. She thought I could change her feelings of inadequacy. I made it worse."

"Touché. But tell me something . . ." He looked up. "You think about these things. Do you realize how few men would remember anything but the blow job?"

"That's also based in compensation. Don't you think?"

"Do you have that problem often, with your dingdong?"

"JoAnne smells the same as she used to with that added aging thing. Most people get it. Me too."

"You smell good."

"I want you to be clear. You must be clear. I'm not the prize package of perfection you might think."

"Why would anyone think that?"

"No reason at all, but they do."

"This is a pattern with you and me. You try to make a point on one thing and another, and I don't get it."

"You did get it. I'm a normal person, maybe not normal but as culpable as the next guy."

"That's not a point. That's like saying the grass is green. You point out obvious stuff and then do an oblique loop-de-loop, like you're the Wizard of Oz. You have this male fantasy that an elegant woman smelled like sardines, so you couldn't keep it up, so she blew you for mercy, because she was drawn to your power."

"That's too simple. It's abrasive and cruel."

"I get that from Billy. And it's what you said."

"Give Billy a break. You get that from you."

"Fine. Am I wrong?"

"No. You're not wrong. That's my point."

"Sorry, Dude, but you are pointless."

"I hate that."

"Dude?"

"Yeah. I'm pointless there too. It seems millennial and stupid. Are you millennial?"

"No. I'm too old. You must feel relieved about that."

"Why would I feel relieved about that?"

"You know: that I'm too old for something. Fuck. You're so

inspiring at times and such a pain in the ass otherwise. Can we go in thirty minutes?"

"I can't say I'm inspired. But I'm willing."

"That's good for a guy your age. Willingness and a latte ought to get us going. By the way, you should shower."

He heard the phone ring from the shower and knew it was JoAnne, checking to see if her daughter had achieved penetration with a Jewish sperm donor, one she wanted for his smarts and bill of health. In minutes, he was ready, shorts, flops and T. "JoAnne?"

"Yes. She may stay another day."

"I wish she wouldn't."

"I know. She doesn't get it—doesn't get you."

"Like you do?"

"Like I do. And she's motivated more than you might think."

"That's too bad. We're all in need. Most needs are excessive. I'm sorry she's oppressed with it, but that's usually the case."

Eloise leaned on a jamb, waiting, puzzled, in a pose with an objective, measuring male response to a sultry slink in a clingy shirt, perhaps. "What do you need, Solomon?"

"Oh, don't you worry." He fussed with his T-shirt, tucking it in, pulling it out, looking up to assure, "I have my needs."

"You stay blissful and get nothing. You call nothing what you need, and that makes it a charmed life for you. Correct? And now we're on our way to play with puppy dogs."

"It's peachy, if you can manage it," he said, regretting his gaze, turning out the door and away from the taunt. He nearly asked that she cease and desist but sensed futility. She seemed naturally seductive, so what could she do, cover it up? He tried a mantra: bad idea, bad idea, bad idea . . . Mantras can be affirmations, indicating stress in need of dissipation.

Every path comes to hazard, but what was this, a cul-de-sac? A just return? And for what? Did karmic resolution thrust him back to base need? Did they conspire to lead him astray? He waited by the car to visit the dog pound on another beautiful day.

She steered with her knees to light the joint, by no means impulsive like JoAnne but more practical. He laughed.

"What?"

"I don't think so." She accepted cursory response as dopey shorthand on a great day unfolding. He'd missed JoAnne for her fun and beauty. If he'd been in love with her, they could have scratched that itch on his way to the cult. People could love each other in passing back then. Except that they couldn't.

Forty years later, JoAnne was down to modest comfort: rent, groceries and casual entertainments, not so bad. What if they'd mated, and Billy split? Who'd be driving then? Would she quack over his failure to provide? Would they feel contempt?

How could he fare any better with a younger woman? She could be happy with a younger man, especially with cash on hand. She could find him in in the yellow pages or online. Nobody would believe her photo, but she could deliver as represented.

What's the point?

He'd carried the torch too long. He needed a torch valet.

Eloise laughed, passing the joint.

Going to the Dogs

A shelter resounds in woe, oddly uniting kindred spirits.

"They're in jail," she said.

"They must think so," he agreed, taking it in, one to the next, pausing for the timid faces in back. "This is tough."

"So are you." She pressed on. "Come. They'll feel our calmness and strength. We'll make them happy for a while."

The front desk clerk had sent them back to the volunteer coordinator, a young woman who said there wasn't much to do beyond walking and bathing. New volunteers could work their way up to kennel cleaning, but that takes time. Eloise said, "That's okay. We're here for bathing and walking. We'll give a little comfort. Help them look their best for the interview."

"Are you planning to adopt?"

"Not right now," Eloise said. "Maybe soon."

The coordinator led them to a galvanized tub on a pallet with an overhead spray. "You need to lift the dogs into the tub. Okay?"

Solomon nodded.

She instructed: wash until the water got dirty, drain and refill.

Towels and a blow dryer sat on the counter by the clothes dryer. The walk, after, would help them dry. A blow dry after that should do it. The dogs must be dry before returning to the kennel. Moisture increases bacterial risk. Wet towels go to the clothes dryer for a continuing supply of dry towels.

Eloise set the flow, as Solomon relapsed, verging on bonkers at the first pooch, consoling in fluent squeal. The others tilted an ear, taking heed. Encouraging each dog to enjoy the shampoo, the scrub and rinse, they moaned and groaned in harmonic relief. It felt simpler than golf, with greater return. They didn't argue. She said few golfers would give up a round to wash dogs.

"How about tennis players?" he asked.

"Or gurus? This is like cult work, I think, but better."

He smiled at the sting of it, ignoring the soak. Crooning and crowing, they also howled. The dogs loved the play. Those as yet unwashed feared they would get none, that care would cease again.

All got washed and walked, down to the last sullen pup, a lab mix with a rash on her face. Just old enough for estrus, she came alive to speak and be heard. Eloise pressed her flanks. "This dog is preggers."

"Is she glowing?"

She put Solomon's hand on the womb. "Pups." He shrugged in stock response to overpopulation of one species or another. The dog whined, telling where she'd been, asking what came next. He said they were also uncertain, like everybody.

After bathing, she pranced. She ran around them, binding them with the leash. Released, she ran ahead and back between them. She cried in her kennel, watching these two who came and would go.

The volunteer coordinator said they'd made a difference.

"The lab mix on the end is pregnant," Eloise said.

"No, she's not," The coordinator said. "We would know."

"You should know. That's why I'm telling you."

The coordinator smiled curtly and went for the vet tech. The day was warm but the dog shivered for the exam and what she sensed. The coordinator said the rash was abrasions from falling out of a truck. The driver kept going. Somebody brought her in. Last week. "We gave her extra days, thinking he'd come in, but. . ."

Solomon and Eloise squinted at *extra days*.

The vet tech ended on a nod, pulling the info card from its plastic sleeve on the kennel, putting a leash on the dog and leading her out and down a side corridor. The dog looked back.

"What are you doing?" Eloise called.

"We have so many," the coordinator called back. "We can't adopt a pregnant dog. It's against the law." At a set of swinging doors to the side, she said, "She's inoculated. That compromised the pups. We didn't know. We didn't feed her enough for a litter. The litter can be big, and these pups would likely have deformities. And we'd have that many more pups to . . . process. It's for the . . ."

Faint and wobbly after a rigorous session on nothing but latte and marijuana, Solomon ran after. "Wai wai wai wait!

She went through the doors.

"Wait a minute! That's my dog!"

"We can't . . ." She called back.

Bounding on adrenaline, he yelled, "Waaiit!" Into the difficult place, he sensed failure on two levels: attachment and discourtesy. He would sort both later. In the moment, he shuddered to match the dog on the table, who looked up, tail wagging, still shivering. The vet tech filled a syringe.

"No, no! No, no, no, no, no!" he yelled. "That's my dog!"

"Sir. You can't be in here. You cannot adopt this dog."

"I am in here. I obey the laws of physics and God! And you're wrong! I can and will adopt that dog. You will spay! And abort!"

"For a hundred eighty dollars?"

"Make it . . . Make it two hundred dollars for all I care!" He pondered two-twenty, but the vet tech set the syringe down, shaking her head, lifting the dog off the table.

"No. It's a hundred eighty, if you're sure."

The dog leaped for a tongue lash on the alpha male who wept, who would later call it fatigue and hunger and that damn reefer. The dog jumped next on the woman, alpha bitch after all.

The outing ended on instructions for pick-up the next day and care and feeding, post-op. The two volunteers walked to the parking lot, mussed and soiled as hobos, shocked and tired on a tough morning.

"I guess we shouldn't come here too often," he said.

Bumping her hip on his, she wrapped an arm around him and turned him. "I'll always love you for doing that."

"I won't forget this." He leaned back for the eye-to-eye. "You are truly someone I will always love as well."

"Thanks for seeing me."

"I see you. And I do love you. Can we can adopt and be done?"

"Sh . . ."

He deferred briefly but asked, "Can I borrow a hundred eighty?"

"How would you pay it back?"

"I've decided to get a job selling shoes."

He suggested avocado sandwiches for lunch. Eloise had a twenty in her shorts, so they stopped for bread, tomatoes, mustard, mayo, avo and onion. "No, wait. We have mayo. No, better get some new."

"And a cuke. They dissolve kidney stones."

"Do you have kidney stones?"

"I don't think so. But why fuck around? And I don't eat mayo."

Grocery shopping and late lunch at last wound things down. They ate at the kitchen counter, reviewing the day's work and the dog on the way. "That was impractical," he said.

"Our first child," she said. "Could it count?"

"Oh, it counts. Just think, with discretionary cash, we could do that all the time."

"Hallelujah, you moron!"

"Pardon me?"

"Sorry," she said. "I must be confused. I thought you just came to your senses on an easy endowment for the cause. How about The Spirit of Solomon Doggie Refuge? We had an eye-opener. Are you paying attention?"

"I do miss the kitties," he muttered. "But I can't take on an animal refuge. Not now."

"Because you're too old?" Eloise asked.

JoAnne came in.

"JoAnne," he said.

"Not JoAnne," Eloise said. "I like Sylvie. She was Billy's aunt,

Sadie's sister."

"Sylvie was a saint next to Sadie," JoAnne said.

"Oh, Mother!" Eloise turned. "It was incredible! We washed dogs. At the pound. We got a dog."

"No. We're not getting a dog. Mm . . . Avo sandwich. I haven't had one in years. You two look a bit worse for wear."

"We already got the dog," he said. "You're gonna love her."

"It was so great," Eloise said. "Solomon saved her!"

He made her sandwich and told the story.

She listened with practiced indifference. Had need displaced her compassion? People change. But JoAnne?

"Solomon is so good," Eloise said. "He could be a psychologist. He thinks I don't give enough. That's why I have anxiety depression. I don't think I'm so different. But I thought he might like a shelter session, and we went, and it was . . ." She got stuck on what it was. "He saved her." She held her face and cried.

"My God," JoAnne said, splaying her sandwich for a bit more *picante*. "I thought I'd walk in on whip cream and vitamins by now."

"JoAnne." Eloise caught her breath. "Your dear friend and I had a milestone experience."

"That's what I'd hoped for," JoAnne said.

"We got back a little while ago," Eloise said, "with a beautiful life to show for our effort."

"You mean the dog?" JoAnne asked.

"Yes. The dog. I'll take care of it when Solomon leaves. We'll work that out."

"You mean like a pre-pup? Pretty good, huh, Sok?"

"Yes, JoAnne. You do have a sense of humor."

"It's a hundred eighty" Eloise said. "A loan. I'll pay you back."

"You want me to pay for the dog?"

"He's broke," Eloise said. "You didn't know that?"

"I suspected," JoAnne said. "We'll fix that. I have to look at the will again. I can't remember if we have to wait nine months? We can borrow on the inheritance. They do that, you know. I read about it."

"You mean a loan factored on future proceeds," Solomon said.

"Yes, that's it," JoAnne confirmed through a mouthful of avo shmush with hot sauce. "God, this is good. I forgot. I'm such a fool."

"A factored loan is a bad idea," Solomon said. "They nail you on points and fees. And interest. It's like a payday loan. And they won't bet on a pregnancy coming to term. Sorry."

"Fuck," JoAnne said.

"JoAnne. We didn't screw. He won't sire a child."

JoAnne held up a finger, for time to clear her gob. Finally shaking her head, she said again, "God," on a bigger bite that could not pass for ladylike.

"We can name her Sylvie," Solomon said. "The dog."

JoAnne garbled, "You'll call her Sylvie out back." She looked negative, tired and tiresome.

Solomon looked glum, seeing JoAnne squeeze the old magic to a grimace. Twinkles and comets slumped to sludge. An avo glob oozed out the sammy, as hot sauce ran to her wrist. Not to worry; she slurped everything back to the hopper.

Eloise said, "We need dog food and a bed. A water bowl and a food dish. And a toy. She's a pup."

"And flea powder," JoAnne said. "And pills for the worms. And carpet cleaner for the puke and piss and shit. Get extra newspaper . . . Sylvie. Fuck." Another glob plopped to JoAnne's cleavage and stained her blouse. "Fuck!" She peeled it for a rinse and stain remover and threw it into the washing machine.

Finishing the sandwich in a lace brassiere, she shrugged.

Eloise blushed, as a daughter might.

Solomon said, "Sylvie. I like it."

JoAnne shoved the last of it down her eat hole and garbled, "What the fuck," on her way to chips and celery sodas from the pantry. Talk of payday loans and a new dog went to sinful snacks.

Eloise said she read that people who hang with older people tend to look older.

"That's right," JoAnne said. "Me and Sok'll bleed you dry."

Solomon said he hadn't eaten potato chips in decades.

JoAnne assured him they were toxic and addictive.

And it was time for a lie down, each to her own and him to the sofa for a break in a long day of emergence, discovery and bonding.

JoAnne thought: *Didn't fuck. Fuck* . . . Soon she snored.

Driver's Ed

Coffee in go-mugs helped cut the nap funk. Eloise and Solomon drove to the market in late afternoon. "Will you learn to drive?"

"I think so," he said. "You know, JoAnne had a big heart."

"Yeah. That's youth for you. I think you changed too."

Gazing out the window, he inventoried no money, a duffel, a couch to lie on. "Yes. I sometimes wonder . . ."

She reached to tussle his hair. "A co-ed you used to know got old, and you didn't. Solomon. Uncle Sol, I'm counting on you to boost our spirits with dinner. You worked wonders on brown rice and broccoli. Just think what you'll do on a grocery run."

He said, "I'm thinking brown and wild rice with wok-braised snap peas, water chestnuts, bean sprouts, mushrooms and cashews in sesame oil and cayenne."

"Don't stop," she whimpered.

Groceries went thirty bucks and dog stuff another thirty. She paid. He smiled weakly, as if money had no meaning, knowing he had no meaning.

"It's a phase. You have resources," she said, hoisting a bag.

He took the other. "You speculate."

"Don't you?" she asked.

"I think tomorrow will be another day for progress."

"That's a start. I didn't think you dealt with progress."

"Spiritual progress."

"That sounds like bullshit from a man with no job or home." They proceeded to the door.

"It could be bullshit. But I have a job and a home. I'm gainfully employed on the ethereal plane. My place is meditative. I sit for an outing that goes nowhere and everywhere."

"You're a nut, but you know that. Sitting any old where can get you arrested. And your outing is called the LSD experience."

He smiled. "That's what it was, and it was a stepping-stone."

"To ethereal progress?"

"I think so. One form of meditation is zazen. You sit forty-five minutes and walk fifteen. Ten hours a day. Light meals, no talking, a day or three days or ten."

"Not the romantic getaway a girl dreams of."

"You might be surprised."

"When it's over, you have ethereal productivity?"

"Yes. It's like money in the bank, currency you can take along when you die. You could do it. It's not easy. But you're old enough and qualified, I think. Meditation becomes familiar and fertile."

"I see your point about us," she said. "Ethereal productivity is an oxymoron. You should know that. Money is spendable before you croak, or it's play money."

"You're a nut too, a tough one," he said. "Most people can't see ethereal productivity. They see new carpet or a TV. I'll tell you what else, Miss Priss, you can spend it beforehand."

"You mean like you're spending it now?"

"Now I'm overspending. Can you make change?"

"What do you produce, ethereally?"

"Happiness."

"You can be happy with meditative skills, but you eat on other people's money. You give me doubts."

"I can do that. If you love me in doubt, I'm grateful."

"I'm sure you are. I still doubt your plan for getting by."

"You're not alone in doubting me. I share happiness. I sometimes give it to others who have none. What's that worth? You compel me to make a point rather than share an insight, but compel me you have done. Sylvie. Where's the monetary value on that one?"

"That's a good point. Okay. Solomon: Where was the money to pay for that one?" She turned at the market doors, to see Jennifer and Rupert Gilley.

"Hello," Rupert said. "We were just talking about you."

"We were just talking about me too," Solomon said. "I hope your talk was more promising."

"Actually," Eloise said, "we hope your talk is more productive."

"It must have been," Jennifer said. "We were trying to decide on a good night to have you over for dinner. Isn't it marvelous that you two do your groceries together? We don't. I mean, we are, but this is different." Jennifer waited for polite curiosity to congeal. "We had a, shall we say, disagreement. We're reconciling. We try to do that when we can, so we don't . . . grow too far apart. Anyway, we're shopping. We think it would be lovely if you could come for din."

"Sounds great," Eloise said. "I love it when other people cook. We're cooking tonight for JoAnne. And we had a very long day, a great day, actually. Solomon saved an amazing dog, and now she's coming to live with us."

"JoAnne. What an original name for a dog."

"No. JoAnne is my mother. We just sort of, I guess, eased into a first-name basis. It started casually, you know, part of that transition from parent-child to friendship."

"That's nice that you're friends," Jennifer said. "It makes all the difference, really."

"Yes. Like you and Eloise," Eloise said.

"Some days are better than others," Jennifer said. "I love my mum all right, but she gets more demanding. I suppose we all do."

"She's in the game though," Solomon said like a gamesman. "Observant and competitive."

"That's good?" Rupert asked.

"It's better than boring," Solomon said.

"It's great running into you again," Jennifer said. "We do groceries together about once every few years. That's far less frequent than our spats. And here you are. It makes me wonder if we've passed before and didn't know it. Okay, how about . . . Tuesday next week?"

Solomon suddenly saw the future as just around the corner. It seemed a thing to reckon, not complicated but calling for attention. *Okay, I'll stay till then and go back Wednesday to sort and wrap up. Plenty of time to sort possibilities, if I don't get stuck.*

Eloise waited; he seemed about to speak but didn't. She made a note of another bad habit and said, "Perfect."

Jennifer asked if JoAnne might like to join them. For din. She'd asked as a courtesy, but it made sense for Eloise the elder and JoAnne to enliven the exchange. Thoughts mingled on JoAnne's rough take and the elder's curmudgeonly way, but all deferred to tact. A mood in either matron could be a drag, with parochial views, condescension, snide snippets, petty quips and so on down the drain. Solomon assessed in a blink, and Eloise said, "That's so sweet. Let me check with her. I'll call you."

Walking to the car, she asked if he thought the elder would join them for dinner.

"We can assume that she will. Do you think they'd feed her in the garage? Besides, she's not so bad." He set the bags in back.

"I thought you didn't like her."

"No. She doubts me too. That doesn't mean I don't like her."

"You do like her?" she asked.

"No. But I won't waste time not liking her. You'd be amazed, how many things I've seen turn around."

"Would you like to have dinner with her?"

"I had lunch with her. Might even be fun to see Eloise and JoAnne in a volley." They got in.

"I doubt it. You're talking winner and loser on that one. I'd rather get to know Rupert and Jennifer."

"Whatever you think, dear. Shall I drive?" he asked.

Smiling halfway, she said, "Soon. Soon."

Rupe

Car salesman sounds blunt and diminishes Rupert Gilley's nuance, expertise and service orientation. Worse yet, car salesmen are often aggressive, inattentive and ruthless, which couldn't be further from Rupe Gilley's approach. He sought to elevate his calling to the nobler heights. Honing his skill in matching driver to vehicle for optimal satisfaction, he hoped to meet needs with a bit of the unexpected for good measure.

Rupert Gilley is a vehicular placement purist of surgical precision. His archival knowledge evolves apace with upgrades—and downgrades the manufacturer might ease under the radar, if not for him. Focused on practicality and open-road exhilaration as a motoring enthusiast, he is also versed in basic transportation and the efficiencies of the entry model. Known for honesty and fair play, Rupert Gilley stands out in automotive counseling.

Rupert G is a Maxi man. People the world over see Maxi as a dynamic combo of durability, performance and fun, in town or cross-country. Anybody calling it cute should be prepared for Rupe Gilley's correction: Maxi is a bona fide mountain rally car, first in class and outside its class too, on four pistons balanced and turbo charged for heart-thumping, asphalt-eating power. Mountain rally car? How about a frozen tundra car or a Death Valley car too?

Only Rupert Gilley, of all Maxi consultants, globally speaking, crunches stats on the ratio of individual sales to total sales per month—has done for twenty years. He computes a moving average, even with average life on the sales floor at only forty months. The stats show: nobody knows Maxi placement like a twenty-year man.

Why does he hone on excruciating detail? In virtuosity, he shows that no Maxi woman or man has exceeded .01 percent of total sales worldwide in any month, except for Rupert Gilley, who topped the one one-hundredth benchmark in seventy-four of his two hundred forty months.

With solid renown and referral business, gratitude from customers and respect from colleagues, envy notwithstanding, he thrives. The ultimate Maxi man sounds as redundant as some Maxi features, like sport-mode shifting on the floor *and* on steering wheel paddles. But is dynamic performance ever redundant?

Rupe Gilley defaults to cross-checks and back-up contingency. A prospect might enter the showroom, not knowing Rupe Gilley from Jack Sprat. Should he reveal his remarkable record? Hmm . . . Who else would hit these numbers and stay mum?

As top producer of the month worldwide for nine of the prior fourteen months, Rupe earned another interview in *Maxi & Me*. Shrugging off the praise, he reminded readers that something done right looks easy and is easy if done right. He suffered anxiety on his first interview, but the second go felt like one more test drive. He advised: "Every prospect is a laydown, and a sure buyer can look like a rag picker, so don't judge. Share yourself." That is, a laydown can look homeless instead of flush. Sizing up is human nature, so size up if you must, quickly and be done! A specialist takes care on each answer. "It's not easy, accepting a slob for potential. And you cannot script. Nature is a series of phenomena, unpredictable and fluid at the point of sale. A placement pro is part of that flow.

"Closing questions? Even worse. Any buyer will sense stock answers and tense up on a salesclerk. That's a sad downgrade from a placement pro. We all had to start somewhere, without timing, without hope. Now move on."

Rupert caught the interviewer's eye and asked, "Just for fun, what color would you choose?" As she fancied choices, he blurted, "No!" And he softly asked, "Would you prefer the *Cosmo*? Or the *Vitál*? Been in town for long? What is your line of work? No! No! No! And horrors, no! What might I do to earn your business today? Oh, God, no!"

Hanging his head like a humble man, Rupe Gilley, #1 in the world, explained his lesser performance for five of the prior fourteen months. He had the flu in one of those months, so he stayed home to spare others. In another month, Jennifer the wife had visited her mother, and her absence affected his game. He did not mention that the mother-in-law had lived two miles away before moving in, because performance comes down to stats and insight, not psychiatric analysis of a man's stress.

His third month below the top tier included vacation time, as required but unnecessary. The fourth lesser month had him finishing second, two units back, not too shabby. In the fifth month off the top, he deferred to sportsmanship: the better woman won.

To what single aspect did Rupert Gilley attribute success?

That was easy; success on the floor comes from presence, which sounds vague, possibly obscure, but Rupert G wasn't about to tip his hand. Obviously, he meant a greater presence. He would not expound, would not say that he stayed hungry or it all comes down to jugular instinct and no slack, ever. No, he would not. Why jump into a ditch with a perfectly good sidewalk beneath him? He wouldn't.

On reflection, he said, "Listen. I don't mean listen to me. Listen to your prospect. Let your prospect close the deal. *You* answer the questions. Every buyer is there to buy. Just stay out of the way, so the show can get down the road. Facilitate, don't press. Your prospect should feel your indifference." He called vehicular placement a study in technique, wherein friction is minimized, so the effort never shows. His stupendous placement record also showed commitment, another shortfall for many Maxi consultants. Platitudes mean nothing without application. He did not fall short but went long, and there you had it. He would not approach an idle browser who happened to be his up, because he didn't need to, because any prospect will buy or not. Rupert Gilley learned early the difference between allowing a placement to arrive and forcing that placement to stall in traffic. It was just that simple: success was available to closers who could step back, then step inside with a feathery touch on a soft stroke.

"But no closing questions?"

"I don't use them. Ever. They're ham-handed. No matter how gentle, they add pressure every time. I might suggest a color if I see a match on accessories or make-up, but I take things into the tall weeds as soon I can, where product knowledge is key. I share mechanical fundamentals quickly, to establish trust. You may see one preference or another, if you pay attention. From there, it's a small step to a trim package or a power or convenience package, safety package or lighting and security package. They go along. The sooner you write the contract, the less chance of hitting the guardrail."

"Into the tall weeds but not into the guardrail?"

Rupe smiled. "I'm trying a change of pace, dropping to a downgrade, like eighteen-inch wheels when the nineteens are stock—Stock! And twenties are all the rage. I'll tell you why. It's because the roads in this city and county are shit, if you know what I mean. County? How about the whole damn country? Oh, they know, the prospects, and how, and a smoother ride on solid insight builds trust!"

The interviewer gazed upon a man willing to down-sell. "Just curious. Does a buyer need to pay for a downgrade?"

"Of course, that depends. You do what you can and fall back when you must. Common sense. Get the deal!" If Rupe Gilley still smoked, he would have fired up just then, to inhale another hit of confidence. But he'd quit, and such an interlude reaffirmed where confidence comes from: within and not from smoke. "A top-tier Maxi man freely exchanges merchandise for moolah on the basis of expert recommendation and otherworldly wizardry. Or woman. I do not sell; I suit product to consumer to make the world a better place."

Then it was the interviewer's turn to smile sanguinely, with another great interview in the bag or the can, or on the disc or the bluetooth, on the way to wherever synapses went in tech times.

Rupe Gilley could feel momentum. "I live as I counsel, with ebb and flow or, if you will, like a revolving door on moolah and motor vehicles, in and out. In come recognition, appreciation, trust and repeat or referral. Out goes maximum automotive gratification. And if that ain't love, then what?"

What? Oh, Rupe liked to throw a solid punch at the bell to make them think about what (the fuck, pardon me) was going down, because a little doubt and wonder make a closing surer still.

Maxi Man captured the long and short of it. Some people dismissed such focus on a single automotive brand, called it parochial or obsessive, limited or passé. But what line of work achieves excellence without focus? The building blocks don't change; Rupe Gilley built a career on those blocks. A product placement person has tunnel vision, blind spots, performance flux and depression anxiety and so on, but that's life. A single product might seem simple, but simplicity is deceptive by nature. Who knows this better than a single-product expert delving into the layers of nuance? Could any consumer remember a major purchase from a consultant who lacked product knowledge or service orientation? An automotive brand has more moving parts than meet the eye. From the base Maxi comes the Maxi X in hardtop or convertible, the Up Towner and Gentry Squire, the Jimmy Crack Corn hop-up and, as the incredibly clever configurator could demonstrate, millions of personal mods, if a prospect could take the time to shape the dream. Most do and then seek expert counsel.

Models change yearly, down to the look and feel of the thing.

Materials and color options race headlong to a better world as mere plastic gives way to space-age polymers, elastomers and new customers. A car can evolve in design and engineering in one model year! Rupe Gilley knew these changes. When he bemoaned bad ideas, the factory listened. "A carmaker puts a new drive train in its hottest model, it's time for a new brochure. Ya think?" Acid-etched honesty got their attention. The tranny was new, but the brochure was old! The new tranny was online, for sale, downloadable in schematic detail from wiring to positronic ESP shifting mode. And Rupe let 'um know it: "Brochures might be passé. But if a transmission can respond to a driver's thoughts, then the brochure oughta say so! Read that thought! Capisce?"

Rupe recalled an elderly buyer who walked in wanting the Jimmy Crack Corn engine hop-up, until Rupert counseled: "No. The X has plenty of power for you." Rupe sold him the X in forty minutes, a record with yet again nobody paying attention. A few years later, at trade time, that elderly buyer had grown older and called to say he'd be trading for more power, probably to the Boxster. The old man said he still loved Maxi, especially the jump seat for the dog, but he wanted more power.

"Boxster is a hell of a unit, and such a trade would obviously not be with me. So? Why did the old guy call? Just to say what he might love next? Not likely." The consummate consultant let it all hang out on what the crowd craved. "I said, 'Bertie. I made a mistake. It doesn't happen often, but it happens. You're not a gear head. I got that part right. I failed to see that, from time to time, you like to get it on. You love your dog. I would ask a brief moment of your time to show you the new Jimmy Crack Corn. It screams.

Bertie. It screams. I was wrong. But this is right! *And* you can get it with an automatic transmission that reads your mind! Okay, maybe not *your* mind, but it can read most minds. Jimmy Crack Corn went automatic! And listen to this: it still has a jump seat. For the dog! The Boxster does not!'"

The line went silent but more like a fertile crescent than dead. So what? What was to lose? And into that awkward stillness loped the inveterate Maxi whisperer. "Bertie, this new tranny factors bladder pressure as a cosign tangent from lumbar transmitters and blends that data with alpha waves coming in to the side-impact system. You wanna tickle the redline? She knows!"

The Maxi master let another pall settle, let the great whirligig grind cogs in Bertie Bertram's skull, before emitting a low rumble that rose to laughter. "Not really, Bertie. I'm fuckin' witcha. That bladder pressure and alpha wave stuff. It's bullshit. Oversell. If you were here, I could ask you to wait in the showroom while I check on something and leave you sitting a half hour. We don't do that here. We do have the ESP tranny, and she does know. How she knows, I don't know, but we have the schematic to show it."

Yet again, silence was more than met the ear. Into that precise pause for reckoning the tranny, the schematic and knowing, came the wager, a friendly one, just for fun. "What say ye to a bet, Bertie? I pay ten grand if I lose. You buy a Jimmy Crack Maxi ragtop if I'm right."

"If I don't like the Jimmy Crack Maxi, you'll pay me ten grand?"

"I will."

"And if I do like it, I buy it?"

"By golly, Bertie. You got it."

"Okay. Get out your checkbook. I'm coming down. It's a bet. But I want you to know, full disclosure and all that rigamarole, I just came from the Porsche dealer. I ordered my new Boxster."

Rupe Gilley let the loss sink in, but not too deep. "Well, futz. I did not see that coming. I should have, but I get crazy. What nimrod nincompoop old duffer with time to kill, calls to say he doesn't want what I'm selling, because he already ordered something else?

"Okay. I had to calm down. No use worrying about timing at that point. I used to worry all the time. It doesn't help. Besides, what could Bertram Bellingham Belcampe III do, sue for payment on a foolish bet? I'm being candid here. Not likely—that he'd sue. And what's the measure of heroic placement without heroic odds? Bertie already ordered the Boxster! He'd settled on colors and packages and the endless frills Porsche gets them on every time! A la carte!"

Rupe declined to flog the competition for taking a car from sixty grand to a hundred ten thou on popcorn and candy that's invisible to the naked eye! Most of it! Never mind! Chin up! "Let's just say my client and I knew he was taking a beating up the road, and I was holding an inside flush to the heart. He had the money but didn't want to get took! I said, 'Great! I love a challenge, and one more thing, Bertie!'

"'Oh, now comes the catch,' he says.

"'Of course, Bertie,' say I, keeping it lively. 'Always a catch. Bring Binky.'"

Binky Belcampe was the dog. Rupe Gilley understood family needs with specific regard to love and devotion, loyalty and respect, till death do us part. Bertram Belcampe III had just survived Mrs. Bertie Belcampe IV. Rupe Gilley felt these things. The crusty buzzard would have croaked long ago, if not for that dog. That was the pulse of the situation. The Porsche salesman probably sold around the dog, lying through his teeth, that most dogs prefer to ride shotgun.

They don't!

Bertie was down in a jiff to learn, among other truths: inventory on hand happened to include a Jimmy Crack Maxi ragtop in Pumpkin Cayenne Spice with an Emerald Sea Mist top and Blanched Pineapple Buff interior. Rupe presented with casual confidence, knowing Bertie Belcampe would love it because Bertie was colorblind. Rupe confided that it was the most outrageously beautiful thing he'd ever seen. Bertie saw it in black and white, as Rupe pointed out the triple mid-body racing stripe, a seven-hundred-dollar line item on the window sticker. The closing stroke would be to *throw it in!* And softly verbalize, "That's a freebie, Bertie. On me. It's like found money, seven hundred smackeroos, served on a platter."

Alas and alack, Bertram Belcampe's face twisted in disgust.

Rupe saw and asked, to be sure, "Is it the greatest, or what?"

"That stripe is bloody fu . . ."

"Oh, that! It's a decal, Bertie. A decal. Not under the clear coat but over it. You're right. They separate and curl on the edges in a few years anyway. I'll have it removed at my cost."

"And you say the colors are good?"

"I say they're perfect."

Bertie Belcampe shook his head. "You don't play fair, Rupe.

How's a Boxster guy going to compete with Binky?"

"Well, the Boxster guy could have shifted to the 911 and a jump seat big enough for two dogs. But he didn't. And a few beautiful miles from disgust for that stupid racing stripe, Bertie grinned. 'Binky loves it. He rode shotgun in the Boxster, but we were only fooling ourselves to think he could go for long without a lie down in back. You win, Rupe. Wrap it up.'"

"Yes, sir. Give us ten minutes to get the stripe off?" Bertie Belcampe III squinted at ten minutes, but Rupe pulled a dog chew from his pocket. "You know, Bertie. I hate to be presumptuous, but it happens. We already detailed your brand-new Jimmy Crack Corn with a hand wax and filled the tank. The docs are on the way."

"You . . . factored the dog on a win before we got here?"

"Yes. So did you. God bless you both." The ten minutes went to thirty because triple racing stripes get peeled gently, inch by inch, pre-warming with a blow dryer. Residual stick-um takes a soft cloth and acetone. The area gets gently waxed and blended. That's artistic integrity. Correct removal takes time, in which, Rupe worried, Bertie might demand the seven-hundred-dollar icing elsewhere on the cake.

He did. "Uh, Rupe. About that seven hundred smackeroos . . ."

Rupe winced but would forfeit the seven hundred and raise another seven if he could get this thing signed and off the lot before Bertie B realized that the 911 has a jump seat, and money means nada to a newly single geriatric with a shaggy chick magnet in back. "Bertie, you should call the Porsche place to cancel, to play it safe."

"Yes," Bertie said. "Common courtesy and all that."

"Excellent, but first!" From a drawer, Rupe pulled a bottle of Suprema Ortega Viejo Santiago and two crystal sippers. He poured for the next compelling presentation. "Suprema Viejo. Have you?"

Bertie stared, then sniffed. "Hmm. Well . . ." Then he tasted, absorbing the meaning of . . . what? He tasted again and again. By the time the docs came, Rupert had only to point here, here and here, as he dialed the Porsche place and asked for sales. Bertie signed off, as he'd signed off there too and written a check, but Porsche USA had standards to keep and would surely allow a gentleman to cancel. "Hold please for Mr. Belcampe." With his palm over the phone he said, "Don't mention it, Bertie. The seven hundred. It still goes. No charge *and* no charge for removal."

A bit flustered, Bertie took the phone. "Yes. Look. I'm going to cancel on the Boxster."

Rupert called, "Binky!" Binky jumped for another chew, this one a pig's ear with cheese flavoring.

"Woof!"

"Ha!" whooped Rupe.

"Woof!" barked Binky again.

"Yes. Cancel. Sorry!" Bertie said, handing the phone back and taking another taste, already poured.

"You know, Bertie, you have a good eye. It looks better. Why booger a line with gewgaws?" Rupe recalled the classics with leather straps to hold the hood in place, like the Morgan. Damn if the car didn't look better without. Too bad the hood could fly off, unstrapped. Some vintage Jags had leather straps, XK 120s or 140s, not bad but still a distraction on some beautiful curvature. "It's a bit like spoiler fins . . ." Rupe could go on. But the gentle wax and blending guy snapped his alpaca rag like a shoeshine man: all set.

Bertie and Binky Belcampe drove away on a plan, down to the strip to try their luck. Triple racing stripes would have gone unnoticed if Rupert could have kept his pie hole shut, but no. He unwittingly gave Bertie a shot on another seven hun *and* put time on the clock. What a bonehead move. As it was, the sales manager might eat seven, but fourteen? Uh uh. No way.

Bonehead moves aside, placing a Blanched Pineapple Buff in Pumpkin Cayenne Spice under Emerald Sea Mist Jimmy Crack Maxi the same day it rolled off the transport was a benchmark. The match occurred on lunch break, after Rupe Gilley's three-sale morning, prior to his three-sale afternoon. Seven Maxis in one day? The *sales* force—Rupe sounded derisive—could aspire to seven in one just as teens could get air at the foul line and fly to a slam dunk for the replays: in their dreams. It would not happen.

Rupe Gilley had glowed, entering The Rainforest at happy hour.

Word was out.

A hush fell on jam-packed patrons, until it broke on a chant: *Rupe! Rupe! Rupe! Rupe!* Every woman and man among them whooped that single syllable to cap a grueling week.

He laughed. They cheered.

He raised a fist. "Can do, goddammit. Set 'um up!" They romped. Seven in one day? Success was the osmotic force among them, displacing contagion with hope in such a lusty place and time.

Praise gushed. Rafters trembled. The crowd shouted out for the little colonel: "Rupe, the giant killer!" Exultation lingered . . .

Time rolled through sleet and snow, cold and hot, as Fridays bunched into fours with diagonal slashes for easy tally and remembering, until forgetting. "I don't know what happened," Rupert said. "Something happened. Beyond my control. I still have my skillset, I think, and I've experimented somewhat."

"Why don't you try something else?" Solomon asked.

"I did. I changed it up. You don't mean throw it out whole hog, the dealership, the works, do you? I tried that right off the bat, actually. Just quit. For a week. What hit me was the love. The love makes it work. I learned to love it on product knowledge, from the heart. I knew from the first time I laid eyes on Maxi . . . That sort of thing. I could place that car on love. People felt it. Okay. What other work could I love? Uh . . . How about . . . Uh . . . Nothing! I stayed with Maxi to see if the love comes back."

Solomon listened and delivered the news. "Rupert, my friend. You must relinquish everything, to see if anything will return. Your love may not love you back for now or ever. You must let go completely to find out. If your loved one isn't free to leave, then it can't come back. People get lost in one-sided love. They cling, so love will return. It doesn't work. The point is to give breathing room, allow perspective. Either let your love go, or it may never return."

"What could a car want more than a proud owner driving it?"

"You could put it that way."

"You're a smart man, Solomon, clarifying in simple terms. You have perspective. It's not complex. Car salesman falls into a hole. Can't get out. I cannot fathom the speed or depth of my fall. *I* changed nothing."

"Better a quick fall than a long tumble. That's what I did. The fact is: old rock stars live on when the crowd thins."

"Ah, yes. We live till we die. That is cold."

"I'm down from millions of fans to hundreds. Maybe Maxi lost its niche, or the niche went away with downsizing."

"Maxi is the epitome of downsizing! Maxi came alive on downsizing! Are you kidding?"

"Okay. You fell like a dictator's statue in a coup d'état. The world changes at a faster pace now. Only yesterday, we were on top of the heap, and here we sit, wondering what."

"Your heap may be passé. I'm automotive. If I thought the brand had lost its appeal, I'd find a new brand. But it hasn't. I have."

"Maybe. You've heard that some people make things happen. Some people watch things happen. And some wonder what happened. Take solace, my friend, you and I have been all three people."

"Yes. And here we sit."

"Yes."

A Drought in The Rain Forest

Talk fizzled.

People drinking in silence seem forlorn, meandering a maze in low light.

Bartender sees. Bartender feels. Bartender knows.

Rain forest sounds redirect on dew drip, bird call, monkey howl, cat growl and waterfall. Soothing sibilance displaces silence.

"He wasn't here when I sold seven in one day. He doesn't even know me. And it wasn't that long ago."

"He's a bartender, and he's new. He likely heard of you," Solomon said. They shored each other up, shoulder to shoulder, sorting things from then to now, and the beer was excellent. "The world ain't what it was. The kids are dull, staring at their phones, the lost and lonely getting loster and lonelier. They still drop out but can't tune in. They shut in. They forfeit curiosity. They do as they're told and take refuge in apps. They're walking into walls."

"Stepping into traffic."

"Staring. Staring. We sang and danced."

"I leave my phone in the car," Rupert said. "Incommunicado is the new revolution. I'm hard to get."

“Yes,” Solomon said. “Refreshing.”

“Staring at a phone is jerking off on real life,” Rupert said.

“Have you tried social media?” Solomon asked.

“Have you?”

“No.”

“Me either.”

They drank. A low-lit bar with jungle sounds and great beer was also refreshing, what they’d come to.

“The tough part is,” Rupert began but began again. “The tough part of it was . . .” The tough part of it was that no marriage should suffer with numbers like that. But it did. Jennifer did not comprehend. She could obsess on an idea she heard on the radio, or a gadget she saw on TV, or a new craze or fabulous fad. Automotive units sold, however, had no relevance. She drove a Mercedes, for the sheer logic of the thing. She couldn’t see his skill or his place at the top or his decline. She begrudged him no happiness. She asked why the long face. Outings were meant to cheer him up, like Par 3 and Cloverdale’s. Like a good sport, he went along, cheerful in his way.

And there he sat, sharing what his wife had missed.

“She feels it,” Solomon said. “And a little fun never hurts. Who knows what might come along, out in the world?”

“That’s Jennifer’s prescription. A little fun,” Rupe said.

“She’s smarter than you think,” Solomon said. “Fun won’t always work, but the side effects are nil, and look what came your way. We met! Believe me: she’s much better than a sourpuss.”

“Yes, but what a sourpuss she may grow to be.”

“The mother seems difficult. Not my cuppa tea. But she’s your safety net. Nobody wants a mother-in-law caretaker, but necessity is another mother, as you surmise."

"Let me put it this way," Rupert said. "A practical player keeps his eye on the ball. He senses variables and ignores distractions. He won't end a slump on a round of Par 3 Pitch & Putt and lunch. A bit of fun is nice, breaks up the rigors. We unwind and refresh." He drank his beer. "Or, I could wish upon a star. Same odds, I think. The constellations grant epiphany on the rise and fall. Or what changed. I think you understand. Yes, the mother and the money bother me."

"You're too hard on yourself. You didn't solve your problem on a casual outing. You made new friends. You're sitting with one, airing things out. You cannot know when the light might shine, or if the first step of the next phase is already behind you."

Rupe conceded his intensity and futility. Stuck on success everlasting, he'd ransacked his peace of mind but stayed in the dark. He'd walked the showroom floor. "It was crazy. Obsessive. You'd call it attachment."

Solomon nodded. "That it was, even as you preached indifference on a cool approach. It's classic: crowding the issue on bad returns."

Rupe hailed another round.

Solomon didn't like parsing values with a car salesman; the world needed no more cars. But he liked Rupert.

"I'm automotive. Engineering, tech marvels, performance wonders. It's in my blood. Who gives a fuck? It's a car!"

"Not just any car. You told me that. It's the vehicle for fun, and you're the man for the job."

Rupert insisted further: as a top-tier guy, he knew what was good, what bad. "I could call it up or down and close a deal on specs! I told them: pure-air filtration is vital to health. Do I wanna stash my dope in this clever secret compartment and breathe seven years of bad air? They bought it! The purifier was five hundred bucks where the dope stash used to be for nothing. Hell, I could go to starburst wheels in satin black and ratchet a bottom line four grand more. Four grand! For wheels! On my say-so!" He guzzled for the glory days. "Steering-column shifters went optional. You can get them, but why? Another five hundred dollars for redundant clutter? I never used mine. Nobody did, really. A nuisance. Get it? I cleaned up the product and boosted value!" He called for another round. "Till the wheels fell off." He went bottoms up. "You don't drive."

"I tried," Solomon said. "Sideswiped a car in Driver's Ed. Long time ago."

"Pedestrians are rare. This town is working grunts who drive to work. I don't talk like that where I work."

"But you think like that at work."

"You thought like that before I did. You influenced me."

"I had a driver. I rode in back."

"That's rich. You had a driver, so you could meditate going down the road? You didn't like things either. Then came the off-ramp."

"I was busy. The driver was available."

"And you failed Driver's Ed?"

"It was a stop sign. The teacher said, 'Signal right and turn right.' I signaled and turned into a parked car. But he never said go to the corner. First and last lesson."

"Fuck, man."

"But freshmen had no cars on campus then, and I was changing anyway. I had no interest in worldly things."

"Cars are in the world, and you weren't."

"I couldn't relate. That day in the park, the weather got to me. Ions or barometric pressure or neutrinos. It got to you too. Good for us. Isn't driving like riding a bicycle? You don't forget?"

"How can you forget what you never learned? Hey," Rupert perked. "We have a loaner. I can teach you."

"Would you?"

"Has anyone tried since Driver's Ed?"

"Nobody offered."

"And you didn't ask? Why is that?"

"I'll tell you what," Solomon said. "I'll buy the blue convertible, and you teach me in that."

"You sound like a discretionary spender. Would you lease or finance or pay cash?"

"I don't know, Rupert. You tell me."

"Fun fact: It's cheaper and easier to buy a new car in the USA than a used car. You might get a rebate. But I'll teach you in the loaner. Then we'll order yours the way you want it. It'll take a few weeks, and you'll learn to drive."

"Thank you, Rupert. That's very generous."

"You're welcome." Rupert raised a toast, glugged for gusto and dove back in. "Marriage is no walk in the park. You know that."

"Never married," Solomon said. "But I know many who are. I

think avoiding the park is the solution to what ails them."

"Avoiding the park? The fuck are you talking? Is this a riddle?"

"You compared marriage to a walk in the park."

"Oh. Yeah. I get it. Never married. Never drove. You are rare. I could say that I don't know what gets into people, but I do know. If I ever split up with Jennifer, I might meet a woman soon enough and think well of her and imagine fun times forever and get married again and live happily ever after for a few years and wonder why I did that."

"I can only imagine. Take Eloise's mother, JoAnne, for example. I knew her decades ago. We were best friends—her husband too. He was her boyfriend back then. They were very bright lights then, and I idealized them. I had a crush on her. It was easy. She changed. Me too. It's long odds, thinking you'll stay on a path with someone."

"Did you long for her? Eloise's mother?"

"She was beautiful smart. And sassy. Once, in a group gathering, she . . . Well, it was many years ago. She's matured, the sass fermented. I liked being around her. I thought of her lately, when I was lonely."

"Your Eloise is an incredible beauty," Rupe said. "Also sassy. Do I sense . . . emotions?"

"Eloise is a beauty. And whip smart. I can't be certain what you sense. The family connection goes way back. Yes, it has emotion."

Rupert said, "And you think I'm tough on myself. You know, Solomon, Jennifer and I worked things out for a long time. She loved my moustache, called it a feather in my cap, if you know what I mean. Her wealth got us a house—no fixer upper for us. An estate. I enjoy it. A man can get lost in a place that big. You can imagine: Eloise poo-poohed the match. She called me a car salesman. I ignored her. She hates that. I was on my game then, oh, brother. I had a mention in *Newsweek* for my approach and stats. Eloise lived a few miles over then, so Jennifer and I had a great life. It's not bad now but not like it was." He gazed off, at the great old days. "Who knows why things go badly? I won't give up. What would I do? You know what she suggested? Eloise? She said I might shave that thing off for starters." He stroked his moustache. "For starters! Shave that thing off."

"She must mean well."

Rupert scoffed.

"Maybe she meant well at some point in life."

"You're catching on."

"But she has a point. If you get in a bind, you tweak a few things. A moustache is perfect. You won't feel it, but you pass a mirror and wonder, 'Who's that?' You're all new."

Rupert said his moustache was a force of nature. It made him the little colonel. "This hamster on my lip attracted my first girlfriend. She swore, from the moment she saw it, she wanted . . . Solomon, I'm confiding here. This moustache has tickled more taint than a gynecologist. I treasure those memories. This 'stache defines me and I think of . . . Melanie McGrew. That was her name. You think I should shave it?"

"Probably. It's something to give up. Shift things around. You can't tell what might work."

"Why would I give up something that identifies me and I like it? How could that be good?"

"It's the giving up that's good, not the loss. Surrender puts you on top of the struggle."

"Struggle? I don't struggle."

"You don't? A moustache will come back."

Rupert watched his beer, as if for clarity.

"Zen teachers say that investing in loss leads to strength. Immovable mind."

"You mean intransigent mind. Inflexible mind."

"Not quite, grasshopper," Solomon smiled. "The Zen guys have heard clever retort for ages. Youthful banter. Immovability comes in two forms. One is flowing. The other is physical."

"That sounds thick. And convenient. Flowing immovability?"

Solomon turned. "Move me, Rupert."

Rupert turned. "You know I've had some training in this sort of thing." Solomon waited. Rupert touched Solomon's shoulder and pushed. Solomon held. Rupert pushed harder.

"It's more than convenient. It's part of the gem. It's a gift, especially in an oddball life."

"But that's physical."

"We live," Solomon said. "We shouldn't live outside the body, so physicality is essential to life in the body. The lesson, my friend, is that body follows mind."

Rupert asked, "Can I learn that?"

"You're learning it now. You felt it. Most lessons are available but overlooked. When you tweak an angle of perception, things open up. It's like the difference between thinking *so what* on the one hand, and on the other hand thinking *ah, fuck it*."

"You and your hands. I think if a house of mirrors could talk, it would sound like you."

"That's clever too. But you do see the difference."

"I don't. So what? Ah, fuck it feels more precise."

"Perhaps it is, for you, these days."

Rupert looked up at his new friend. "I thought you understood, Solomon. I'm disjunctive. Contrary. Society would put me in the asshole column. But society is wrong. Surely you know that. That doesn't mean my glass is half-empty. It means fuck you and the glass you rode in on. Capisce? Can you learn that?"

"I can't imagine why anybody would think that way of you?"

"That's who I am. I see things for what they are. It's not bad. Let's say, for example, I loved Jennifer's genteel, goofy way. Now I see it as affectation. She didn't change. My lens got smudged."

"Or it came clear. But a man with your natural skill should not suffer from clarity."

"That, my gifted friend, is the challenge on the table. People spend years looking for answers, but it's the right question that's hard to find. I question my disjunction, as it leads to my dysfunction. The question may be immovable. Am I an asshole? It's the big question, but the follow-up is bigger. Am I comfortable with it?"

A fern bar in late afternoon filled with early birds, Happy Hour coming on. The two earliest birds took solace in commiseration and sundry jousts. When the barkeep looked, they nodded. When two more frosty drafts sat before them, Rupert plumbed further depths of his dilemma. "She finds it boring. She calls it car sales, like her mother. Lately, she calls it car no-sales. She's exasperated. Can't say I blame her. I'm bored. Don't get me wrong. I meet a viable driver like you, and I want to make the placement. I imagine gratification, fun and fuel efficiency. I feel good about what I do."

"I don't drive yet. Don't count your chickens."

"Yeah. Maybe we'll get stinko and go for a lesson."

Immersed in jungle audio with a jazz overlay, they shared a good feeling. Sound effects, climate control, excellent hydration and jazz softened their dilemmas and their outlook. Solomon recalled a college friend who had a moustache for years and shaved off half.

"That would look goofy."

"Exactly. He had fun with it. He'd go sideways talking to someone, and when they looked away, he'd turn to the other side."

Rupert laughed. "That's the stupidest thing I've heard all day."

Solomon agreed. "Yeah. He shaved the other half a day later, but like I say, he let go for an outing. His 'stache was back in two weeks."

Rupert looked up. "Eloise is something. Your Eloise."

"I'd hardly call her my Eloise."

"She's the type of woman you could imagine. The physical part is plain to see. Many women have that. Jennifer has that. I see men looking. But she's loud. Eloise has presence. She doesn't condescend or yak away. She's reflective and smart."

"Yes. All of that."

Rupert waited before asking, "What is she to you?"

Solomon shrugged. "She's my friend. She's actually the daughter. Her parents were close friends in college. I dropped out."

"You're her uncle, so to speak."

Solomon laughed short. "She makes that joke. You're a car salesman. I'm Uncle Solomon." They drank.

Rupert asked, "What gives? I see a spark?"

They drank more, dousing the non-response, until Solomon asked back, "Do you see it in me? The spark?"

"For better or worse, Solomon. I think I do. Not a strong spark but a struggling spark. I think you're resisting some crazy love and can't do anything about it, and nobody can figure why you'd want to. Do anything about it."

"I should fall madly in love because she's beautiful and smart?"

Rupert slowly turned. "Do I hear test drive?"

Solomon slowly opened. The situation was no secret, really, but wasn't for show and tell either. Rupert seemed too curious, but they'd begun a friendship, and relief resides in confidence shared. Solomon said he had few friends and fewer close friends. He felt it the nature of leadership. He'd risen to it, all expenses paid, insolvent and trying to sort a future. The ethereal currency business had him broke at street level. Still loving life for the joy therein, he felt tired and tired of it. "I'm not ready for the challenge, mother and daughter," he said. "I thought I knew JoAnne. I have few clues on the daughter. They want my help, so the money can set them free." On a sigh, he went to detail on terms and conditions.

"It doesn't sound like a scheme," Rupert said. "The money is in the family and should go to them as rightful heirs. The only plausible objection might come from the daughter. But Eloise is game. I saw her. She sees you as a man, not an uncle. I hope you don't mind me saying so; she has a sparkle in her eye."

"All that and more. She has JoAnne's and Billy's spirit, and she's her own woman, worldly wise as JoAnne never was."

"Not very nice to say about a close friend."

"I don't mean to criticize. JoAnne was rough in a lively way. It played better on a young woman in brilliant antics. Billy was hugely alive. All of us young and stoned, tripping on love. Bad grades were the ultimate hazard, and we didn't care, except for flunking out to Viet Nam." Solomon paused. "We didn't give a flat flying fuck. We thought pain was physical." They drank to the olden days. "I don't know where Eloise learned poise and a soft touch. You haven't met JoAnne but . . . You see my dilemma."

Rupert listened, assessing cost and benefit, risk and reward. He said, "I don't. I'd do it. If I were you."

"Do what?"

"Solomon. Give her the goods. Do you really need a corner man for something so simple?"

"I won't take advantage. It's not my nature. Did you hear what I said? And I won't commit to parenting. Do you really think that sexual thrill is fair trade for skipping out on a child?"

"I do not. I think any sexual contact could be called exploitation on one side or the other. More likely both sides. I also think baby and Daddy are not required."

"But that's her motive."

"Okay. She's what, thirty-two? Thirty-five?"

"Eloise is thirty-nine."

"Okay. Believe me, I've had a crash course in biological clocks. At thirty-nine, many women aren't so fertile as they used to be. You might not get her pregnant. You'll definitely get in some solid practice rounds—that sounds harsh. You'll call it exploitation, but she likes you! Hell, man, she's about a six-inch putt from love. And you're holding out on principle? Look at the odds, man."

Solomon stopped the bartender for a change-up: tequila neat, two shots, top drawer. Rupert kept pace on a sip and went down the hatch. Solomon shook his head but downed his too, turned and said, "I'm tied off. I can't get anyone pregnant."

"She doesn't know?"

"Yes, she doesn't know."

Rupert shook his head, unable to comprehend a man's hesitation on the verge of Paradise. "Solomon. She's a classic. Steady sex will likely lead to love. You can marry her or go away. But sitting here like Bubba Hotep or whoever you take a cue from, is . . . very strange!" He called for another round. "If you don't mind me saying that too."

"She's Billy and JoAnne's daughter. I can't agree to sexual relations or love or whatever under false pretense."

"Tell her you're tied off and then do it?"

"Are you daft? Why would they chase this crazy scheme for one point two and jump in the sack with me for no baby?"

"I think she loves you."

Two more shots arrived and met with quick dispatch.

"She thinks she loves me," Solomon allowed. "It's practicality with an infatuation back. Many women love the idea of finding love. And she wants the money."

"Oh, man, you're explaining away the magic."

"I think she admires me in a way she can't admire her parents. I'm guessing. It doesn't matter."

"Now who's daft? It obviously matters."

"What'll we live on? Honesty and love? I'm coming off a thirty-five-year binge. It didn't pay out."

Silent again, they struggled on impasse. The bartender brought two more shots, "On the house, fellas." On a synchronized half-nod, they drank to fortune's bounty, however meager.

In a minute, Rupert said, "Talk about too hard on yourself; it paid out. You're Solomon Kursh."

Solomon said, "*You could* do it."

Rupert had imagined *doing it* already: top, bottom, sideways, rearview, upside down. He had not imagined it strategically, for the betterment of all, as Solomon seemed to suggest.

"You said the baby has to be Jewish."

"Technically, it would be, if the mother is Jewish. But you're right; the bequeathal stipulates a Jewish father. But all rules are up for review. We break them for a better outcome."

"You're saying that I take up with Eloise, your Eloise, in a love cycle, incognito? Not romantic love but clinical lovemaking, until she pukes and misses her period? Then what? You take over?"

"I haven't thought it through."

Poor Rupert, beside himself with enthusiasm and doubt. It seemed worrisome and provocative. He didn't air hazards so much as he weighed prospects for success, with rationale as rigorous as cold, hard steel. "Jennifer would go along, I think. They're practically girlfriends."

"It wouldn't be incognito. It would be discreet. I don't fault your willingness, and I can't help your anxiety. It's a bad idea."

"It could happen at her mother's house. Or should we mount up at my place? Jennifer can make baba ghanoush on a campfire in the yard, and Eloise can pass judgment. Gee, it keeps getting better." Rupert laughed to keep things light.

"All I'm saying is that the money on the table would liberate JoAnne and Eloise for life, if they don't squander it. I don't think they would. As for reasonable impregnation efforts, that would apparently be acceptable. I would caution any sponsor against enthusiasm. I shouldn't need to explain that."

"No, no. Not at all. And you'd be okay with that?"

"No, Rupert. I would not be okay with that. I'm not certain I could accept that. I feel pain at the thought of that. Does that mean I'm in love? I think Eloise would not be okay but would love a baby. I think JoAnne would be way okay with avoiding poverty in old age. She may be fuckinay okay. Motherfucker."

"Yes. Old age and poverty; the dirty combo. Unless you're a high-class Hindu. The old Brahmins leave home with a begging bowl. You could do that. But have you thought of . . . ? This is getting gothic, but what about a donor? You know, retail?"

"That would leave a record. Wouldn't it?" Solomon asked.

"It could leave a record of a Jewish donor. A PhD with banking connections and literary credits, an academy award nomination, even for best color correction in post editing on a short subject in a foreign language. How about a heart surgeon who practices law on weekends? A Jewish mother's fantasy."

Solomon tolerated his new friend's humor based on stereotype. "That's good, Rupert. But Billy Keene got his piss and vinegar naturally. This family is not conventional in regard to credentials. They'd think that Ivy League stuff insulting to Billy's memory. He sloshed tar on roofs. We could try a Jewish donor, and get Eloise knocked up with no husband to show for it. Years of court. I looked into it. One guy fathered a hundred forty babies as a donor number. They filed a class-action suit against the sperm bank to get his identity. I think needs are clear here. We deviate at our peril. We stay lost in the maze."

"You make a compelling case for yourself."

"If only I could."

"You would?"

"I don't know. I doubt it. I can't even make a case for you."

"Yes. It would be awkward, unless everyone was gung ho. Not too likely. How about a turkey baster? I'd be happy to pony up."

"That wouldn't be for me to say, but Eloise said she won't, won't, won't. I think a natural deposit is best."

"Yes. More precise," Rupert agreed. "I would think."

They thought and drank. In deeper shadow and rising din from the growing crowd, Rupert said, "I like them tall."

"Yes. Me too," Solomon said.

"Why is that?" Rupert asked.

"Why is what?"

"I'm short. You know?"

"Yes." They drank. Solomon said, "You can take cold comfort, my friend. I've loved them short as well."

"Hmm. Yes."

"Fuck!" Solomon said.

"What?"

"We forgot to pick up the dog."

Rupert checked his watch. "Come on. We have time."

They flipped credit cards onto the bar in another hazardous venture, nodding when the bartender asked, "Half on each?" Waiting for approval, they bonded yet again, when the little terminal rang affirmative.

Jennifer Le Compte Gilley

Jennifer LeCompte Gilley achieved her station as a woman of grace by nature and nurture and the best education connected money could buy. She learned why some people warrant deference and others need help. Tender mercy came naturally, and she loved helping out on any little thing. Nobody actually measured social altitude, but hers was pleasantly aloft, at the top.

Jennifer believed that doubts challenge the very best people, sooner or later. Skilled in social poise, she often made additional effort on the optimism thing. She preferred sincerity but could finesse a sunny outlook. Feeling dismay, she reminded herself that anxiety is common to everyone. Hotchkiss, her pussy, throws a hissy if his kibbles are late.

Jennifer felt her self-doubt as a case of nerves, mostly, and hoped to balance with good cheer. Just the other day, she'd said, "Hey?" She should have said, "What?" Hey? So what? Little things lingered a bit much, *les petite choses en passant*, things that a person should forget, but she did not. She regretted cliché. She longed to be freer in spirit, not inappropriate but a smidge more loosey-goosey. That sounded crazy and felt crazy too, crazy and good.

As to neurotic self-doubt, she chalked it up to genetics, at least partly. Nobody avoids the parental blueprint, and Mummy seemed a more certain source with each passing season. That didn't mean that she, Jennifer, would come to see the world severely, as Mummy did. Then again, Mummy's contrarian view was mostly habit, a family quirk, a winning combo of superiority and sensibility. What else could a blue bloodline lead to? Humility? Not likely.

Would Mummy sit this one out, so the younger set might enjoy unencumbered engagement? Again, not likely. What? She should eat in the garage? She needs the gossipy innuendo of an effervescent dinner fête. Who doesn't?

Jennifer envisioned memories in the making, aglow in candlelight. Solomon wasn't young, and neither was Rupert, really. But the age span from Solomon to Eloise was less than Mummy to Rupert, and Mummy could be stimulating, if she chose to pass on easy prey.

People knew the Brannigan Empire for the single malt whiskey wars that put Brannigan on top. The LeCompte side had no such celebrity but didn't miss it, all the while sipping premium scotch. Factor the Vanderholt imprimatur on Mummy's mum's side, and you got life's perfect storm. That would be money, power and scads more of each. *Oh, gosh, it seemed so in oodles.*

Mummy should join for dinner. She'll be okay; she's adept at the parry and thrust best suited for the likes of Solomon and Rupert.

They're both so . . . hornery? No: ornery. That's it, but they seem hornery too. What a hoot. Gosh, naughty can be fun.

As a woman of means by any measure, she anticipated

glittering pleasantries. Elegant and exquisitely delicious in every morsel, the evening would tingle in warm recollection for a long time to come. Planning the fête down to detail and flow, Jennifer tingled already.

It began well, innocuously droll, with arrival and reception at the porte cochere, as if the LeCompte-Gilley place would entertain anything less than marble steps to an archway over an entry corridor. Jennifer waited to meet and greet with a laugh over absolutely nothing but the great good fortune upon us, on the way to a shimmering soiree. *Oh, look, they brought the mother. How odd. She must have insisted, a familiar idiosyncrasy at chez nous. But the dog? Might it have fleas?*

Jennifer effused, leading up the marble steps. Under the archway, through the corridor, across the courtyard and through the formal sitting garden to the entry foyer, the guests followed, silent but for clopping heels, ogling what great fortunes had wrought. Jennifer glanced back at a lovely gingko to see if the dog would pee on it, but the dog only returned her gaze.

Sculptured busts waited in the entry foyer, cooler hosts. Jennifer said the décor would be "a bit much for some," but for others, it made for giddy recollection of a bygone world. "These accoutrements are part of my essence. They feel like . . . like a homecoming." She laughed again, a bit more nervously than she might have hoped for, explaining that the LeCompte-Gilleys called it "the place" to understate the grandeur. She'd come to loathe the starter mansions so prevalent these days, peppering the countryside with embarrassing effort, and she paused to share the challenges of finding suitable abode. Oh, dear, she'd combed the region for a proper twelve-acre estate. She wanted a real mansion. If it was crumbling, then crumbles be damned. She had a smallish castle in mind, tucked lushly in a forest, above a gently sloping greensward, up at the end of a curving drive. *Et voila!*

"I do not begrudge some people's need for gilded houses sitting cheek by jowl with fake columns in front. But, lordy, what a girl had to go through to get her point across to the real estate agent, that a mansion is beyond earshot of the neighbors. I told her: We don't want to hear their fights or their flatulence! Oh, dear!"

The guests chortled appreciation, as hoped. When the dog barked, they laughed again, cuing Jennifer quite nicely on her adventure. "The real estate woman showed one place, from which I could actually hear the neighbors at table, dinnerware clinking on plates. No, no, no, no, no, I told her. I got exasperated and went on my own, you know, in the car. I do that. I got lost and stopped here. This old man was doing up some shrubs in front, so I stopped and asked if he knew of any places like this one that might be for sale. He said this one might be for sale. Now you know the rest of the story. I suppose any lengthy pursuit can jade a view. I loved it right off. It has no columns. My gosh, have you ever seen so many columns? Who do they think they're kidding? They don't support much, except for hollow claims on affluence. Really, why would anyone want everyone to think they're wealthy when they're not? Can you imagine buying a home built for artifice at two million dollars on an 80 percent loan?"

"You'd be surprised," the elder said, easing in from a shadowy chamber off the main study, pausing between Romulus and Remus to note the presence of another woman, presumably the mother.

"Oh, look. You brought a dog." Letting the imposition sink in, she said, "This place would be a bit much for some. Not us."

"I already told them that, Mummy."

"We were born to it, once upon a time. And I'll tell you something else. Jennifer made it look easy, and her perseverance is a tribute to *noblesse oblige*."

As if on another cue Rupert strolled in from another adjunct, presumably the minor study, with a warm welcome. "Eloise, noblesse oblige is a virtue by which wealthy people care for the less fortunate. It's not the process of wealthy people spending vastly on castles." He strolled to the pooch, stooped for a tongue-lashing and said, "Hello, Sylvie! Welcome to our humble home." Up like a busy man with a schedule to keep, he ducked out like a perfect husband and son-in-law to set another place at the table and arrange a throw rug for the dog.

The elder said, "I'd call the others very fortunate: the grounds staff, housekeeping staff and kitchen staff, thanks to Jennifer. They're still employed! Tell me," She spoke to Solomon and Eloise. "Do you like it? Be honest? Is it the most fun place you've ever seen?"

Eloise said, "I do, actually."

Solomon concurred on a polite smile. Not to worry: Eloise the elder had grown accustomed to tongue-tied admirers, in view of such opulence. He said, "I know a few dozen people who would move in tomorrow. If they could."

"Okay," Jennifer said. "It's very nearly din, so we'll all move into the parlor for hors d'oeuvres et les cocktails." And they did.

Jennifer served Brie in filo, baked to perfection, oozing onto cocktail napkins. She tsk-tsked the debris. "Let the crumbles fall. Ground sparrows have to eat too!" She meant the rodents whose forebears predated the aristocracy on the scene. She didn't mind any original species and loved the place. "Did you see Rupe's Maxi out front? Isn't it perfect, noble beast and all that?"

Solomon asked, "Rupert or the car?" Among stifled chuckles, he lowered his baked Brie to Sylvie, who accepted with aplomb.

Jennifer giggled, appreciative of glib refrain and Rupert's good nature. Up next: mushroom caps stuffed with rice. She noticed that Solomon hadn't eaten the baked Brie, in spite of moans all around for its scrumptious taste. She thought she comprehended this *vegan* thing on the rules, more or less, but couldn't quite get the reason for it or how it could possibly exclude cheese.

Never mind. Nature would take its course, and the evening shaped up as great fun. She couldn't grasp Solomon and Eloise, but getting to know them would clear the air. Had they become an item? They hinted as much, but she didn't think so. He seemed removed. And odd. Men usually get distant once they taste the sweet meat. But had he received? At least a man his age should require conjugation less frequently than a man like Rupert. Then again, Rupert at fifty-three wasn't the young buck he used to be. Had he dissipated from age, or was it familiarity? Tedious repetition sounded harsh, but show Jennifer LeCompte-Gilley a man who took care down the road like he did back at the intersection, and she'd show you a unicorn. A dinner party could be fun, if it could stay a tad above the wicked truth.

At any rate, romance with a man seemed much more elusive than the you-know-what. Solomon was about as handsome and fit as a man his age could be but still seemed a tad out there for Eloise, especially with her leg up on that half of the general population known as women. What a looker! She could have her pick. Men don't care anymore about pedigree; they want youth and beauty. She's present and smart and not too chatty, like some people. Why would she chase him? He's tall and well-spoken, but his salt and pepper curls seem an ill fit for anyone, him too. Why would a man need such flamboyance? And he's what, a guru? That's hardly a CEO of a Forbes 500 or a professional or celebrity. Rupert had known of him, so he does have that. But still, it seems curiouser and curiouser that they have these beer-drinking sessions and call it nothing but friends having a beer. Is that all? Rupe seems secretive and frankly rather devious, like sharing with his one-and-only would betray a confidence.

Rupert knows his wife's needs and has given it his best. A man can't keep the same pace over the years, in spite of her urgency. His sperm count analysis proved viability. And he was sweet, whispering that she should be checking him in for the sample, instead of that nurse with the eye-popping rack. Twenty-something and stunning, with a two-button reveal on a set of thirty-sixes to make a wife wary, she seemed an appropriate fantasy for the occasion. Jennifer noted, "Modern medicine is so specialized these days." She assumed clinical facilitation. Unspoken was Jennifer's viability, or lack thereof. But with an admirable pair of six-shooters herself, no tummy fat, a *très jolie derriere*, pretty green eyes and hips a man could hang onto, she could not believe herself barren.

Ah, well, a girl knows love when she feels it. She felt as well that it was Rupe's slump in sales that had him down. Most importantly, she believed them viable in marriage. They could opt for travel and fun. Wouldn't that be a loss, with wealth enabling mobility to coexist with a growing family. An au pair can manage the children while Mummy and Daddy are dancing the night away with amusing friends, stolen glances, whispered nothings to the wee hours. With affluence, romance can endure. It's no wonder so many others end up in divorce.

An au pair could care for offspring originating elsewhere. But the children would be of different blood. She'd still have all that nurture side of things, but if a woman is indeed infertile . . .

Well, it's a terribly changing world, and an open mind seems best, with all that "new thinking" going around. She simply doesn't take to unorthodox and heretofore unacceptable approaches.

But enough of somber analysis. Jennifer LeCompte-Gilley was feeling good, moving into phase two of a grand dinner fête. What a fun expression of self it was shaping up to be.

Eloise Brannigan LeCompte
or
Elder El

Eloise the elder called Jennifer's dismissal of the kitchen staff unwise. "It makes no sense, giving them the night off, leaving you all the work."

"But Mummy! They prepped! I love to serve!"

The lively repartee began on irony and warmth. Things flowed in the grand manner, until an uninvited guest asserted her gross, personal need. Rudeness seemed easy to avoid, but there it was, soiling polite society in base form. A question plopped onto the table, obsequious as a scraggly cat, grabbing the entrée and dragging it to the floor.

JoAnne said, "I planned to wait, but I might as well jump in." She had an idea that Rupert might be the man for the job.

Rupert blushed deeper than a man of fortitude wants to do. Emotionless, like a rock—or a boiled beet—he regrouped on life's variables and vicissitudes. "I don't know how this . . ." He turned to Solomon. "How could you?"

"What are you talking about, Rupert. Spit it out, man!" demanded the elder.

Rupert laid it out in naked boldness, expounding on awkward circumstance and impropriety. Yet he segued disingenuously to the children as our future and for whom we do it. He shut their mouths. The banquet before them went from steamy to tepid. Grinding like grit in the soufflé, Rupert slogged through.

Sylvie stood to yawn, turn and lie down on the other side.

Ignoring this outlandish interruption, elder El resumed her dining pleasure, to spare Jennifer's labor from room-temp oblivion. She looked around, one to the next, until they ate again, and she proceeded to cross-examination: "The question unresolved: where will the money go if Eloise cannot find a Jewish sire for her child? Has anyone looked into this?"

Rupert spoke, as if for the defense. "We don't know, but . . ."

The elder overruled. "Rupert. Please." Redirecting to JoAnne, who might best pluck this turd from the punchbowl, she pressed, "To whom does the money accrue, if we see no Semitic issue from Eloise? That is the question."

"In that event, the inheritance goes to Manny Rizovsky and Minnie and Julius Silverberg," JoAnne said. "Minnie and Manny are brother and sister. They're Sadie's siblings."

"Will they claim the prize prior to conception?"

"Good luck with that," JoAnne said. "What's to claim? That Eloise hasn't conceived? So what? She has all the time in the world."

"Not all the time," the elder said, referencing the clock tic, tic, ticking away with thunderous resonance in a few ears nearby.

"When you're eighty-five or ninety-two," JoAnne asserted, "and they are, six or seven years is all the time in the world. You must have considered time, relative to old age." JoAnne smiled sweetly to the bone, as family and new friends winced, and the wound drip, drip, dripped.

"You mean the six or seven years Eloise has left for ovulation?" the elder asked.

"Yes. That's what I mean," JoAnne allowed. "She could have more years than that. I didn't hot flash until forty-eight."

"Have you leveled?" asked Elder El, moving on. "You think Eloise could have another decade or more, but you, Joan, need to pay for basics in the meantime. Don't those basics drive this exercise? Isn't this outing meant to cover your needs?"

"Do you have a point?" JoAnne asked.

"I believe my point is succinctly stated," elder El replied.

"I believe your point is succinctly barbed."

"I believe acerbic defense is best on a limited budget."

"Is this part of your point?"

"I'm afraid it is. Life is expensive, a fact you have comprehended, and bitterness can be more costly. A person is better off living within her means. We've managed it for generations. I won't dilly dally on your needs, but I will guarantee that the LeCompte family trust will not be exposed in any way, shape or form to a bastard claim. Rupert is not Jewish but he is legal kin, which details seem to elude you. And I assure you, Joan, that we're not concerned with . . ."

Eloise the elder erred with intention on a bastard abbreviation from JoAnne to Joan. Just as Winston Churchill had called the bad guys nazzies, she meant disrespect. Joan or JoAnne, the hippie mother, might not get the gist historically, but she'd feel slighted, as she should. Elder Eloise puffed her lips dismissively as she uttered the paltry sum "with which we cannot be concerned. I believe it's one point two that you're after."

Jennifer perked, as a woman of the Brannigan-LeCompte clan might do. Jennifer valued freedom for fortunes to rule the world. With Vanderholt exclusivity and the Gilley component as a bonus, as seen in automotive trade journals around the world, Mummy's perspective put that trailer trash hussy in her place. Elder El did not condescend; the Brannigan-LeCompte heritage was founded on democratic principles with regard to liberty and social parity for all who could afford it. A loud woman of no means, however, was unconscionable, uninvited and a poor fit. Who ever heard of the mother-in-law tagging along to a dinner party? She's not even the mother-in-law but an old friend of Solomon's, a former paramour for all anybody knew, and now he courted the daughter in a peculiar way. Who could tell?

And this notion that Rupert might stand in, or lie down such as it might be . . .

"It's disgusting. And stupid. Can anybody say, DNA test? Did you presuppose freedom from proof?" Elder El asked.

JoAnne said, "That won't happen. They would never invite the *nahoras* with open arms, which is what any challenge would do. They'd be cursing themselves."

"The nahoras? Are they part of the FBI? Because no probate court will grant this bequeathal without proof, easy as a cotton swab." The elder practically banged the gong. "Fools." They sat and stewed.

Rupert hung his head. He'd gone along! Damn.

Solomon looked glum as a cooling spud. He'd declined the roast and the baby leeks and shallots alongside. Why? Because the leeks and shallots had touched the roast? Jennifer's best effort was boiled down to salad, relish tray, broccoli, bread and olive oil. Young Eloise followed Solomon's lead, as if Jennifer's roast was a comeuppance.

Jennifer knew of the vegan thing, but this was a dinner party!

Rupert seemed beside himself, a leg man after all, bushmaster exposed, not that Eloise was a slut, but still.

In fact, she seemed more distraught.

Elder El had called it a dire need of the sadly disposed and mumbled over desperados who'll grab anyone on the way down. Such is the prospect of aging, underfunded, but that didn't justify jeopardy for a happy home or a family of fabulous wealth.

Jennifer faulted Rupert for going along. Goodwill is one thing, but this proposition, this so-called helping hand, would require her husband to hump another woman! Require, hell! He had no compunction! Regret? Ha! He'd explained fertility cycles and optimal timing, like Bill Nye the Science Guy! To women! His helping hand was pleasure-bent. Oh, sure, he'd bag a beauty for the good of all, twitchy as a kid in a candy shop.

Grounded in substance, attempting absolution on lust, Rupert began again, humble as a man caught out unjustly, restating his premise—his squirming rationale. So began his drivel on the missing tribe of Israel, the thirteenth tribe, or the fourteenth if a purist insists on counting Ephraim and Manasseh as separate tribes instead of counting them both as the tribe of Joseph, their father, after all. "This is not an erudite detour on a ticklish subject, except for Judah Maccabee—bear with me now. Judah led the Maccabean Revolt against oppressors who sullied the temple. Judah and his sons routed the bastards in a battle of reclamation, well and good. But they found oil for the Everlasting Light for only one more day. More oil was eight days away, round trip. In the balance: their covenant with God to keep the Light shining. The sons mounted up and rode with Godspeed, you might say, and made it back in eight days to find the Light still shining. And that's why we have Chanukah, the Festival of Lights. And the Maccabean Games to this day in Israel."

"Now we have Chanukah?" Jennifer asked. "The gall!"

"I lay this background as context to a literary truth too long overlooked. The hero of the most important book ever out of Ireland is a Jew. Leopold Bloom."

"Wait a minute," JoAnne said. "I'm still holding my breath for Elder El's point. I can't handle so many loose ends."

"You lay this background?" Jennifer asked.

"Leopold Bloom, the most venerated character in Irish literature, is a Jew!"

"Gesundheit," Solomon said. Nobody laughed.

Rupert bore on. "His countrymen are often named McCabe, from the root derivative Maccabee. Don't you see?"

JoAnne moaned, "Give it a rest."

"Here, here," Elder El concurred. "Really, Rupert. You can do better. I've believed that for a while now, and you should know it. The point is . . ." The elder paused as her train of thought jumped the track, as elder trains can do. But she hadn't jumped. She'd only pulled into a way station to quench a curiosity. Looking at the younger, more confused Eloise, she asked, "You would go along with this?"

Eloise blushed severely, in shame.

The elder honed in. "You're okay with sexual liaison with another woman's husband, a man you don't know, much less love, repetitively, to secure funding for your mother's retirement?"

Eloise looked up. Tears rolled, and she sobbed. "It wasn't my idea. I feel pressured. I thought I loved Solomon, or could learn to love him. No, I did love him. I was on my way to loving him. In all this . . . crazy shit, pardon me, he said he's had a vasectomy. He can't impregnate. I feel terrible, coming to a lovely dinner and ruining it, my mother bringing this up, like love and babies are part of a strategy. It's the most awful thing I've ever . . . Excuse me, I'll wait outside." With that, she rose to smile sadly at Jennifer and shuffle out.

Looking back, in years to come, she and Jennifer would agree that their friendship formed when Eloise walked away from lunch, and Jennifer followed suit. It sealed at the dinner party, when Jennifer stood, dropped her napkin and in the spirit of girlfriends who don't give up, followed Eloise out.

"Down to the hard core," JoAnne said, topping her wine glass one more time with a 2012 Pommard Clos des Epeneaux, second bottle. Elder El frankly didn't care about cost but had forewarned her daughter that four-hundred-dollar wine might intimidate the guests. Little had she known the hunger and thirst on its way to dinner at the place.

"Oh, Mummy. You are practical," Jennifer had replied. "But you serve wines by the case, at twenty-five hun a bottle. I mean, really!"

The elder had clarified, "We pour those wines for people who can tell what they're drinking."

"I'm sure. And these folk won't know the diff between exotic vintage and couch red, will they?"

"You've been tasting with Rupert again. I can tell."

"Is that a problem? Try to get into one of your generous frames of mind. Okay? Our guests won't know the price, will they? They'll just think it tastes good."

"And what'll you say if they want some of their own?

"I'll tell them: Pommard Clos des Epeneaux. Some years are more amusing than others. We prefer the 2012. It's a few bucks more, but hey. What else would I say?"

"Have it your way. You are a sweet girl."

Intimidate the guests? How about irrigating the lush, needy mother-in-law? Worse yet, Solomon brought two bottles that got Jennifer cooing over their absolutely campy character, as she set them discreetly on a side table, in back.

"Boone's Farm Apple Wine. It's a private joke," JoAnne had explained. "It's mostly for shits and giggles. And nostalgia. We drank it years ago, so cheap. We could take that punch back then."

"Of course, you could," the elder had affirmed. She affirmed again when a bracer seemed propitious, and JoAnne offered a top-off all around. Solomon and Rupert declined. They'd had enough. The elder gave the half nod any barmaid deserves on an offer. The women drank with no toast, eyeing each other over the rims.

"No need to belabor impracticality." The elder leaned on her elbows. "No secret ever survived the confidence of six people. Few things remain secret in the best of conditions, and all is revealed on emotional strain. We're talking about a human life here."

"Or not," Solomon interjected.

"A human whose parentage could never be contained as a secret." The elder sipped and pondered, letting implausibility sink in. Or maybe she'd derailed again.

"You had a point to make," JoAnne said. "I can't remember the context or imagine the relevance, but you seemed intent."

"Yes. My point. I used to question my daughter's affection for Rupert. I got over it. I won't say she could have done better. She brought home some real fools, upper-crusters, blue bloods and inbreds, preppy mutants who give folks like us an iffy reputation. For all I know, she brought home those aristocratic dullards to show me up and make a point. She trusted her instincts, and Rupert proved to be a fine fellow. But he made a severe error on this one. I hope it won't be a debilitating error. It's an error in judgment, and I hope we can let it rest. The odious idea brought to this table will not materialize. I hope everyone is clear on that. I will hear no further discussion."

And that would have been that, until JoAnne said, "I can see Rupert. I mean, what she saw in him."

"You mean you could see doing Rupert," the elder clarified.

"Yes. That's what I mean," JoAnne affirmed. "I always liked the feisty little guys."

"Billy wasn't little," Solomon said.

"He wasn't big. He wasn't like you."

"If I may," Rupert began tentatively, gathering thoughts, mustering courage for a long shot on salvation. "The idea, such as it is, on a practical solution, was never on this table. Since meeting in the park, we've begun to know each other. Solomon and I are friends. I value that. I think he does too. We talk. We discussed the problem. That's all. Please, Eloise, rest assured: I did not make an error in judgment. If I had a doubt on this situation, I would say it's his feeling for younger Eloise. It's not clear. I believe she loves him and would marry him to satisfy pecuniary requirements. I'm disappointed in anyone who thought me capable of . . ."

"I apologize, Rupert," Solomon said. "It was idle thought, insensitive and ill-conceived. I meant no tarnish on your character."

"Nor I," said the elder. "Forgive me again. I trust you know my position on this sort of thing. I'm sorry I doubted you."

Once more, the matter appeared settled, the gun sounding the end of the scrum. On booming silence, nothing remained for the dwindled circle of friends but to savor the end of the day.

It began a few days prior on sunbeams and sky blue, startling and spontaneous, on hazard and fun. It went to way past dark and the dregs. They drained into JoAnne's glass. The elder winced at the dark specks flowing to the goblet.

JoAnne said, "Fuck it" on a different family's tradition, pouring it down the hatch. Resigned to her luck, she said, "Dollar to a donut, this wine was a buck and a half. It's good!"

"Did you bring donuts?" asked the elder. "Or a dollar?"

"You're right. I didn't bring either," JoAnne said. "But that's good too, Elder El. Very good."

"I suppose one woman's good is another's relief."

"I know this wine," Solomon said. "It's not a buck and a half. It's more. Well, we got it by the case for a bit under five grand, as I recall. It's an old favorite." He held the bottle at arm's length. "Pommard Clos des Epeneaux. Brings back memories."

"I'm sure I'd feel the same way if I were you, one day in the lap of luxury, the next day exiled to the land of sofa sleepers."

"That's cruel, Eloise. I'm on break, a sabbatical if you will, to visit old friends."

"Of course. I hope you don't mind, but I took a look. It's easy these days. You were the Grand Poohbah, taking the baton from your predecessor and mentor who founded the, uh, movement."

"Yes."

"Pardon me, Solomon," she went on, "you don't appear to be nearly as stupid as this outfit's demise might indicate."

Solomon could not refute.

She rose and steadied, turning to the buffet for another bottle, already corked, in a bucket. "We drink the good stuff first."

"Yes," Solomon said. "Your palate is never so fresh as in the beginning. Like life."

"Yes, well, some of us are so far past beginnings; old rules get reshaped." She moved slowly to his chair and turned the label up. "Tell me, please, that you know this wine."

"Pomerol. Château Le Pin. I do. Not so well as the Pommard. I only had the Pomerol twice."

"Only had it twice," she back-quoted, setting the bottle on the table and wiping his glass with his napkin. "How good of you to put it that way. You were riding high." She poured a dribble.

He lifted and looked through it, tilted and watched its legs. He swirled and sniffed it. "Oh . . . God."

"So, you do believe?" She poured three fingers.

"I believe that a power greater than that of humanity made this wine possible."

"You are a wise man, Solomon, named for a wise king."

"I'm not a king, nor will I be. Riding high is a frame of mind, Eloise. I think you know this. If we're wise from time to time, our foibles balance the scales. Thank you."

"Yes. Like now. You could not split this baby."

"That's a bad analogy," he said. "We have no baby. Both women here are sensitive to that. But you shouldn't forget . . ."

"You're also sensitive on the baby issue."

"If you mean my feelings on human population, then yes. I think we're adequately dense for now. But you know this too."

"Yes. You may be surprised to learn that I agree with you. But you must be aware that the notion gets skewed when it's applied to one's own family line."

"I don't begrudge sensitivity."

"I would ask if you . . . Have you imagined a child between Eloise and yourself? I think you haven't. I think you're a man of principle and set some things aside a long time ago."

Solomon smiled politely; no need for a gratuitous exchange.

"I have a proposition," the elder said. All eyes turned. "I want to do something. I love Jennifer, obviously, and I love Rupert, mostly for loving her as well. I want happiness for them. True friendship is rare. We can't foresee it, but it may happen here. In any event, I'd like to establish a business. I'll underwrite you and Rupert as equal partners." She poured a few fingers of the good stuff for herself, to look through it, tilt it, sniff it and murmur.

"I'm not a businessman," Rupert said. "Not really."

"A car business. Three makes." She sipped and savored.

"I'm not a businessman either," Solomon said. "I can't drive."

"I have one stipulation—well, I'm sure I'll have more than one, but for now we'll call it one. I want you to . . . convert . . ."

"Oh, brother," JoAnne said. "Let me tell you something, Miss Hoi Polloi, money can't buy love, and it can't buy souls—not some souls. I think I speak for my dearest old friend in telling you . . ."

Solomon interjected to save the day, to soften the point for no more bloodshed. "In telling you that I can change my noses, but I can't change my Moses."

"I want you to change back. I want Stanley Sokolov."

"That's funny," Solomon said.

"I daresay," the elder challenged.

"Jews get a new name right before they die. It's kind of like last rights but different. I got my new name, Solomon, early in life and ventured forth, as we must, sooner or later. I'm back. So . . . Okay. Call me Sok. Or Stan. Your choice."

"Just that easily?" the elder asked.

"Letting go is a developed skill and, I'm sorry to say," Sok said, "one of my vanities. Yes, just that easy. Much easier than running a car dealership I know nothing about. Easier than understanding your proposition. You want Rupert and me to open a car dealership so we can remain friends, and so Eloise and Jennifer can be friends too?"

"No. It's more than that. Okay. Let's forget the proposition. Let's just say that I looked into your story."

"You already said that," Sok said.

"I did. But I came to a dead end on the bankruptcy, so I called my accounting staff. They're quite good. You know what they say about artists: those who can't, teach. They say the same thing about numbers people: those who can't, work for the government. The government could not find Henry Lawrence's money, just as you could not find Henry Lawrence's money."

Sok's brow bunched in rows. "You found Hima's money?"

The elder shrugged smugly. "Who's to say? We tracked the Barranquilla deposits. That amount alone seems excessive. Was Mr. Lawrence involved in the drug trade?"

"Colombia! I knew it but didn't think . . ." Sok's head lolled with rolling numbers and odds. "No, it wasn't drugs. I don't think it was drugs. I don't know. I would have seen symptoms. The drug trade and Barranquilla mean cocaine. Marijuana and psychedelics are different, though some excellent marijuana came up from Colombia a long time ago. It wouldn't pay anymore."

"But cocaine would?"

"I don't know. It must be lucrative because people still do it, but I doubt that Hima was involved. From my experience, you could count all the people in the cocaine business who declined a little sniff on no fingers. I'm speculating, but I think I'm right."

"It doesn't matter. Upward of four million dollars is sitting in a numbered account, as we speak. The question is retrieval and disbursement."

Sok or Solomon lifted his goblet to gaze through the Pomerol Château Le Pin before pouring it down the pie hole. No wince nor recoil rippled the pond. Coming to his senses, he saw things anew.

Retrieval and disbursement would have been possible last month, but this month, the elder's accountants were watching. He ventured, "That's obviously not my money."

"Obviously? Whose money is it?"

"It would belong to the people of Hima Luja."

"Not to the organization?"

"The organization is bankrupt. The court appointed no receiver because of no assets and no receivables. We had the buildings but liened them to gain time. I think if we could . . . expedite."

"And just how many people of Hima Luja?"

"Thirty-two."

"That's it?"

"More hang on but without tenure or commitment. The other compounds are closed and foreclosed. Central is basic shelter. Subsistence. But not for long."

"That would be an equal divvy on the thirty-two?"

"Yes. A hundred twenty-five thousand each on four million."

"Yes. You shouldn't need government work any time soon. I'm advised of good prospects to retrieve and disburse anonymously, if we expedite. Do you follow?"

"Yes, but. Is it worth the risk?"

"What risk?" JoAnne sat up, rising from resignation to anticipation—from a loss of one point two to a payout of point one two five, or so she presumed, that the booby prize would be hers to share.

The elder asked, "Is it a safe bet that none of them will spill the beans?" Elder El spoke over JoAnne in the heat of the hunt.

"Most of them, all but four or five, could handle cash

discreetly, especially if it came anonymously with urgent counsel to live and be happy, as a wise person might do, or lose it all. If they fail, there's no trail, I would think."

"Why couldn't that work for the other four or five?"

"They'll fail because that's what they do. They're driven to messing things up, to prove they were right all along or some silly shit. That was the beauty of Hima Luja."

"You have an odd aesthetic sense. I'll try later to see the beauty of failure more clearly."

"The people are flawed, not worldly but stuck on beauty and kindness. They're losers in a practical world. They fit in a cult, not bad people, not average."

"Solomon. Stanley, you amaze me more every minute. Can we proceed? Are you happy, letting them eat failure?"

"I'm not. Let me think. The problem cases would need a buffer or safety net. I'm not sure what."

"A blind trust to dole a monthly stipend, say a thousand dollars?"

Sok thought, pouring another inch. Suddenly feeling foolish, he turned to JoAnne, who lifted her goblet, and to Rupert.

Holding the bottle to the light, Sok saw it half full, an optimal view on which Eloise and Jennifer reentered, arm in arm. Rupert sensed a romance, unanticipated but perhaps workable in a brave new season. He mumbled, "Oh, brother," couldn't help it but was easily ignored. "You really must try this," Sok advised, holding the bottle for two more pours.

"Oh!" Jennifer chirped. "Mummy! You've corked the Pomerol! Eloise! If this doesn't cheer you up, you might as well be dead!"

"Which brings us," the elder proceeded, "to the deposits at Bucaramanga, Barrancabermeja and Medellin. Do the dots connect? I suspect our friend Henry was not in drugs but in finance."

Sok sipped and savored. "The cartel had billions to launder. Why would they bother with Hima Luja?"

"They didn't need the cash," the elder said. "They needed the optics. Henry Lawrence left a numbered trail with no names, except for one, and he got stuck. The cash got booked as donations to the cartel mission from a legitimate donor. That would technically be you. The cartel mission gained legitimacy and doled money in return to Mr. Lawrence's heirs, the *Hitlerjugend* of the Third Reich. But the jugend got old and died off, and what's left ain't so young anymore. The cartel doled millions, more than a pittance to them, but not by much."

"What is a cartel mission?" Rupert asked.

"Hallefuckin' and Hima Luja," Sok said, clearing the smoke on cold review. It was easier with fine wine.

Manny Rizofsky
and
Minnie & Julius Silverberg

"I don't know," Uncle Manny said, "but if I had to make a bet, I would bet that she won't. What, with the *vacocta* parents and the *shaygetz* husband? What? Now she's supposed to rebound like a basketball on the perfect *shayna punim*? Get real! If you think that deal has a chance, then Vegas you should not consider."

"The shaygetz husband is long gone. She's a beautiful, beautiful girl. So why not?" Minnie corrected.

"And the . . . whatchacallit, the biometric watch," Manny said.

"The biologic clock," Julius said. "Not yet. She's not too old, and I got news for you: not every boy is such an *alta cocker* like you, stiff in the back more than the front. She's still a looker. A looker! She can get a man, a husband, and have the baby and get the money, and good for her! That's what I say."

"Maybe," Minnie said. "But where? At the *Yeshiva*? You want she should hang out with the fellows who don't bathe until they smell like goats and won't sit next to her because she's a woman and expect her to do all the work while they read their books on Saturday? You'll get about fifty to one in Vegas on that bet too. Nah! She can get a man, a real man and a Jew, no doubt about it! What, with those legs? *Oy.* Up to the neck with those legs. But where? At the mall? She has no job. The mother is, pardon me, crazy and common. If the daughter just so happened to meet a mensch, the mother would scare him away. Away! If you know what I mean. So? What? She can get a man easy enough. But any man won't do. I don't know too."

"Let me ask you something," Julius said. "Have you decided what you'll do with the money? With your share?"

"What kind of question is that?" Minnie replied. "We'll keep the money. Next thing you know, you're living another ten years. Or twenty! You know what they want now? Three hundred, three hundred twenty a night! Three hundred twenty a night, I'm telling you. Ginette Kornblatt had to pass a test. Three tests. They made her walk a hundred yards. No, fifty yards. No, maybe it was a hundred. I can't remember. But in her condition!"

"They all do that," Julius said. "They let her use her walker."

"What, walker? It's like a football field. A football field, and she had to walk the whole thing."

"Like a kickoff return from the end zone?" Julius asked. "She should make the highlights. I'd like to see Ginette Kornblatt dodging the defense. It wasn't so dramatic as you'd like to imagine. It's a safety thing. Safety, in case of a fire or whatever they got going on that you want to leave in a hurry."

"And make a BM," Minnie said, refusing consolation. "Start to finish on her own! Start to finish! From the bed with her pants on!

With the approach, the getting ready, the business and the other. Start to finish!"

Julius clicked his tongue and shook his head at what the world had come to. "Everybody wants more money," he said. "We live too long. Now we pay for room service if we get a little help with a BM. And no guarantee that it's a good BM. Let me tell you. They only want to get paid! That's where we'll spend the money."

"Not so bad," Manny said. "I wonder if a fella can spend a little bit more money and get a pretty young nurse to help with a BM. Good BM. Not so good BM. You know, I would have been embarrassed not so long ago. Now? Not so much."

"You embarrass me," Minnie assured him. "To tell you the God's honest truth, I think you embarrassed Sadie too. What? You think she might get so hotsie totsie wiping dreck from your tuchus, this pretty young nurse, she'll want to take off her white dress for the rest of the show? *Oy, Gott . . .*"

"Embarrassed? What, embarrassed? Sadie was his sister," Julius said. "His sister. What brother ever stopped embarrassing his sister?"

"Sadie was common too," Manny said. "If she didn't embarrass herself there wasn't much more I could do. What am I telling you? Where do you think the son Billy got it from, thin air? No, the apple fell off the tree. Such a trash mouth on him, with the cursing and the smoking. She's no different, the wife, the mother of the girl, what's her name, Eloise. But! And it's a big but . . ." Manny laughed at his own joke, as he had for too many years to remember. But it was still funny! A big but! "A big but. She stepped in on the money *mishegas* when it counted, my sister Sadie,

God rest her soul, when that shaygetz pulled his little no-Jews-allowed routine."

"I never liked him. Never. But he didn't pull the routine. That no-goodnik country club had the Jew rule in place since you-know-when. He didn't do it," Minnie said.

"Have it your way," Manny said. "I know what I know."

"Sadie knew it too. So do I." Julius said, turning to Minnie. "What difference does it make who made the rule? The shaygetz husband knew the rule. The shaygetz husband lived and enforced the rule. Who was surprised? With a name like Douglas Smythe and the Jew baiting those people came up with, just like they came up with their *vacocta* scheduling story as secret code for the Jew rule, as if blond hair and no Jews would keep them superior."

"So?" Manny asked. "What did she ever see in him in the first place? As I recall, she'd already changed from an ugly duckling. She could have waited for better."

"Who knows?" Minnie asked back. "Maybe she was after the money then too."

"I don't think so," Julius said. "She was never so good looking, you know, as a girl. I heard she had a complex. She was quiet. She wanted something different from what she was or what she had, like they all do now. We're not so old. We wanted it too."

"She wanted different from Jewish?" Minnie asked. "That's not what we wanted."

"Nah! She wanted different from tall and gawky and not so busy on the dance floor because nobody came around to ask. She wanted in. Maybe she wanted a brand new shiny shaygetz who could take her for a whirl and bring her up to snuff," Julius ventured.

"Pshh!" Minnie scoffed. "So she was stupid?"

"I don't think so," Manny said. "Who can be so stupid? I think she wanted to try the Jimmy Dean pure pork sausage."

"You are disgusting. Who are you, to call anybody common?"

"What, disgusting? It's on TV! Prime time!"

"Whatever," Julius said. "She got smarter."

"Maybe," Manny allowed. "I don't know. I might pay more for a young one. Pretty, not so pretty. I don't care, as long as she's young."

Julius nodded.

Minnie said, "I hope you get an old one. And fat."

"They don't have fat," Manny said. How can they have fat, with all the bending and *schtuping*?"

"Now you want the schtuping?"

"I said stooping. How can a fat person stoop and bend like they have to do?"

"So you want that a young one should wipe your tuchus?"

"I think so," Manny said. "Let's see. If it's a million two, and we each get a third, that's four hundred grand. Let's say three hundred a night with the pills and the testing and the room service. That's . . . don't tell me . . . okay, what's three hundred into four hundred?"

"It would be three hundred into four thousand," Minnie said.

"Even better! Okay. Let's say it's three point one for every thousand. Multiply by four hundred; you get about twelve hundred nights. That's only three and half years," Manny said.

"Should be long enough," Julius said.

“What if it’s not?” Manny asked.

“We make a pact,” Minnie said. “Anybody leaving leaves the rest to the rest.”

“You’re forgetting the taxes,” Julius said. “It won’t be four hundred thousand after the taxes.”

“What, taxes? I’m not paying any taxes,” Manny said.

“I think that’s okay,” Minnie said. “I think the IRS is comfortable with alta cockers not paying any taxes if they die before the money runs out or the audit, whichever. If she can’t find a Jewish fella, looks like we get about eighteen months.”

“I’ll take it,” Manny said.

“Yeah,” Julius said. “Eighteen months is better than a kick in the noggin. But let’s not forget about that pact. One of us is going to need it.”

“Don’t worry,” Minnie said. “I won’t forget.”

They sat and pondered time, beginning with three times eighteen months but quickly realizing that each passing month would diminish time by two months until somebody . . . They wondered what would be worse, solitary existence with no friends left or another few months of room service.

In a while, Manny asked, “What was the third test?”

Minnie said, “Test? What test? You know, I’m thinking. Helen Schavitz has a son, a doctor, extremely wealthy. Just got a divorce. Even with half, he’s still loaded. Not too old. A doctor. Maybe he’s in town.”

“Call her up,” Manny said.

“Am I missing something?” Julius asked.

Later, Back at JoAnne's, Too Wound Up to Turn In

Giddy with prospects for a payout, JoAnne savored the tiny bonds breaking. Twisting the cap was like turning back the clock. Up late, they sat at a kitchen a table with a joint and a nightcap.

"No, please," Sok said.

"And thank you." JoAnne poured four fingers and a thumb.

Eloise went to bed.

Sylvie followed.

"Great dog," JoAnne said. "Who knew she'd be so mannered? And lovable."

"Who knew you'd be so loving?"

"You did good, Sok. I like calling you Sok."

He shrugged.

"I like the dog. I love the dog. I was always easy that way." He shrugged again in a set piece. "When did you change back?"

"Change back?"

"Yeah, back to sensible. Back to smarts and the real world."

"We change. We hope for improvement on the way. You're

different too. I'd bet Billy also changed."

"But *you* . . . You got so far out there. Nobody knew you. You rarely spoke. Most people thought you were an acid burnout. I thought you were crazy, but you kept going. And now look. You're rational. You speak in sentences. You were always tall and handsome. And smart. But you cast it all aside to be crazy. We didn't stay in touch because . . . We didn't feel anything left to touch. We loved you but heard you hooked up with the orange jammies. We didn't try so hard. We thought you were a goner."

"I get it. When did I come back from so far gone?"

"Yeah. That's what I said."

"I have to think." He closed his eyes.

"Don't do that. Smoke this." She lit the joint, inhaled and offered.

He declined. "Why get so finely buzzed on extraordinary wine and smoke a joint?"

She exhaled. "It' perfect with Boone's Farm. You should remember, even with changes. Man . . ." She took his hand. "We went around the world, didn't we?"

He took the joint for old time's sake. "If I had to pinpoint a come around on the go around, I'd put it at my talks with Hima."

"You mean the man, the Grand Wizard?"

"Yes, him. I've been around stinky people. I avoid them or tell them to bathe or whatever it takes to stop stinking. He stunk, but I couldn't tell him. He knew it anyway. The stink changed things. I still don't get it. Well, it opened my eyes."

"Like ammonia?"

"Yeah, but sinister."

"Did you cringe?"

"Yes, the ampoule restored consciousness. I've thought about it. I've tried to imagine his objective. I can't. How can anybody live with that? I'd seen it before."

"You opened your eyes and realized the cult life stinks?"

"Not exactly. He started confiding in me. It was stupid. People thought he was clever and wise, but he wasn't. He was stinky. I still loved the operation. We had high times. The founder was a nutter, and so were we. It worked. But it stopped working."

"Hey, sugar tit, you were a nutter and smarter than the average professor. Most of the good-grades crowd weren't so sharp at street level. Besides, he wasn't stupid. He skimmed millions and got away with it." She pushed his sleeve up to touch the tattoo.

"Got away with what? He's dust. The money is stuck in South America, never released, some of it."

"Do you hate him?"

"Not anymore. I regret him and me. Evil and stupid. I get doubts, but they go away. He set me up. I let it happen. Cult mentality, and I wonder how things would be, with the money and Hima Luja thriving. It could have worked."

"You'd still be dancing in orange jammies at the airport and tinkling your finger chimes?"

"Cymbals. Probably not."

"What did you imagine?"

"I thought it was good and would get better."

"Why did you do this?" She rubbed the tattoo.

"I got it from Hima."

"It's a concentration camp tattoo."

"That's who he was. Hima Luja. Henry Lawrence. Heinrich Lohrenz. He got one back then, for cover. I asked him to do me up. Twenty oh oh oh one B. Last Jew out."

"You didn't know about him? How could that be?"

"Maybe I . . . He had a charm, early on. It made sense."

"You're more miffed on the money than the Nazi stuff."

Sok shrugged. "I set it aside, the Nazi part. He made light of it. He said his jokes helped people along. That didn't sit well, but we resolved our differences after all on a little prank of my own. Do you mind if I tell you about it later?"

She poured and lit the joint. "We will not pass this way again."

He sighed and began the tale, by which Hima's punchline became his epithet: *You're going to get cooked . . .*

True believers lifted Heinrich Lohrenz to his funeral pyre, talking love, as they lit the fire, as flames leapt and crackled. They cheered but booed when firemen doused the show. "I went in close for a loving touch, to find a pulse in his neck. We took an ambulance to the crematorium. I sat by him, telling the one about Hymie and Thelma and her edible underpants. And the one about the Jewish parrots, which can be quite funny, but I was off. The ambulance guys also thought it was flat. Dispatch to the cooker was slower, with forms and prep, and it was over very fast. Ignition is more like jet propulsion than a bonfire."

He shivered briefly, giddy in summary. "I felt chosen, not good or bad. I delivered. Just a courier. I met the challenge. I opened his eyes. I know what he saw. I think I know what he thought."

She scooted out and came around to pull him up, into a hug. "Tell me."

"Fucking Jews. Something like that. One-up to the bitter end, I think. I thought I'd never share this. It's okay."

"It's more than okay."

"I wish Billy . . . I needed someone to know, someone to say fuckinay. Or something. I'm grateful for you, listening."

"Fuckinay, Sok. He's here. Fuckinay."

"I'm good."

They drank.

They smoked like old times.

"I'm good, but what if I was wrong?"

"About what? Fucking with an old Nazi?"

"Maybe . . ."

"You got balls, Sok."

"What if he was only following orders?"

They laughed.

"They all followed orders. A death camp Nazi with an SS tattoo who killed a few Jews by necessity? Sok. You may have been wrong. I'm good too. Your visit here was your last and first step. I feel it. So do you, I think."

"I think tomorrow is Sunday, and we'll go for a hike. Oh, no, I forgot. Tomorrow is tomorrow, and I'll go far, far away. I think it's late. I could think anything. It's what I do for a living. Used to do. I'm too young to do nothing. But I don't know so much."

She said she loved him more than ever for who he'd been and what he'd become. She loved him being there and being Sok and hoped he would stay, one way or another.

"Yes," he said. "Miles to go before we sleep." He went to the sofa, lay down and slept.

Sojourn South

Eloise's accounting staff made haste. Having tracked to the appropriate banks below the equator, they established rapport, as a potential client might. They gained assurance on a timely withdrawal of funds by a client of record, on presentation of valid documents. Those bankers would further enjoy relief from nonvalid claims and attendant consequence. Both would cease.

Solomon had complied with Hima's insistence on keeping his passport current. *Because . . . you never know. You know?*

Jennifer had also insisted, for the wondrous world awaiting.

Elder Eloise didn't feel presumptuous in making reservations for the next day, Chicago/Bogota, round-trip. She thought foresight fundamental in masterful management and presumed agreement all around, asking neither man what else he had to do.

Too much wine and little sleep helped in their way. Solomon and Rupe dozed for hours in the air, leaving a few hours more to think. Checking into Hotel Si Claro the following evening, they walked a few blocks, relaxed over dinner and turned in.

Talk in the morning was sparse, save a brief review: present the docs, answer questions concisely, sign off and leave. They walked to the bank and went in. Four bankers waited in a conference room.

"Ve haff ze papahs," Rupe said by way of greeting.

Solomon regretted his friend's flippancy, stepping up, as he'd done in the park a long time prior, presenting certified docs with photo i.d. of the Chief Executive Officer, also known as "Member" of the same charitable endowment with deposits in this bank. "I'm Solomon Kursh, the depositor of record."

Three bankers remained emotionless as Vulcans, as the fourth eased back on an impish grin. This was no banker. Viga came into focus, slumped, older, septum bent on pleasures unique to the region. In splendorous wallow, his suit, shirt and tie all silk, he said, "*Qué tal, mein* Solomon?"

Solomon informed Rupert: "Viga."

Rupert stepped up, as he'd done in the park, "We heard your father was drugged. He was made to watch."

"I also heard," Viga said.

"Something to think about," Solomon said.

Viga shrugged. "Always a risk, trusting a Jew."

"Gasundheit. Yes, sad. You look well, but can you trust me saying so?"

"I do. Life is good," Viga said.

"You need to change your noses," Solomon said.

Viga blinked.

The lead banker read the docs. "*The Hima Luja Temple for the Sanctity of Souls Having Fun.*" He looked up. "Is it fun?"

"It is," Solomon said. "How do you know this man?"

The banker said, "Mr. Lohrenz is on our board. It looks like you've had a nice reunion."

"Yes. Lovely. He's a director?"

The banker half-smiled. "Yes. It seemed appropriate, with such significant deposits."

"He's not the depositor of record."

"No. That's you."

"But he made withdrawals?"

"Yes, as stipulated by your co-administrator when these accounts were set up. We would hope that you will reconsider closing these accounts. These funds have been in safekeeping with excellent management. Stable for years."

Solomon wondered how much got skimmed but doubted an easy answer and sensed a delicate balance. Three Columbia bankers and Viga were poised to transfer funds, as encouraged by a formidable faction to the north, to avoid further scrutiny and the World Bank Enforcement Division. Affirmation from the State Department had bolstered the move. Balances remaining totaled between four and fourteen million. Solomon said, "You will wire the funds this morning?"

Three bankers remained stoic.

Viga grinned like a death head and looked like his father without the good cheer.

"German engineering," Solomon said.

"*Si. Es bueno*," Viga agreed.

Sok and Rupe flew home the next day, enjoying the pleasures of the region that night and agreeing that a return to Bogota would be better later, with fewer concerns in the hopper and the women along for the fun. They agreed that Viga would not come north. Why would he?

In the air, after dark, Solomon ventured. "Hima and Viga

spirited the funds to Columbia, using me as a front person, in case of trouble. And I, we, just went and got back the balance of the funds. Is that what you see?"

"Yes. I wouldn't want you to base a political campaign on a promise to retrieve lost money, but that's what we did."

El's accounting staff managed disbursements to Hima Lujans of tenure, including Stanley Sokolov and Rupert Gilley.

Rupert declined, but Solomon insisted. "Technically, I may have been able to do it alone. Practically, we don't know, and I didn't want to go alone. I value your help. You worked it to a tee."

Rupe couldn't argue and agreed to the status of a tenured devotee on disbursements. "But I'm no cultist."

Sok said, "You evolve. You qualify."

And in the End . . .

In youth, Stan Sokolov loved waking up. Unencumbered, unaccounted, unattached, he drifted on the interface of sleep and waking. Without worry, without mope, he knew nothing as nobody, happily. The pitter-patter of little feet signaled Harry the dog . . . happiness surged, as Harry leapt and burrowed in, grunting urgently. *We're burnin' daylight, sodbuster.*

Decades later, up from the rapid-eye depths, he surged to a different nature. A naked woman bedside wrapped cool fingers on his dingdong and leaned into it, "You get what you nee-eed!"

The little concert ended on a petulant wail: "Mother!"

This man, this international courier, this Sok or Solomon or Uncle Stan, would not be shared. Yet again, this was not about JoAnne!

"Sok."

"What!"

"Sh . . . You had a bad dream. Me too." A warmer hand touched his face and peeled the sheet and blanket, "Do you mind?" She eased in. "I don't mean to arouse you. I was scared. And cold. Warm me, please."

"Scared of what?"

"I dreamed nobody would love me. I missed you."

He shifted to avoid the formative. "I was gone two days. People do love you."

"Romantically?"

"You came to me with a trick question?"

"You're touching me inappropriately."

"You put me in an awkward position."

She turned to him. "You know this is it. Real life. Last run. I want to think the best of you, but you keep me at a distance. You insist on distance, and I don't think you want to."

"You don't think I want to insist? Or I don't want distance?"

She propped on an elbow. "I think you're stuck. You have no place in the world. I think we're stuck."

He whispered, "Eloise."

"Yes."

"Eloise."

She met his eyes in first light.

"Eloise."

"Sok. Can you express yourself better?"

"Eloise, I love you?"

"Oh, man."

"Eloise."

"Yes."

"I'm not tied off."

She sighed. "Why did you put everybody through that?"

"I needed to see. I think I do."

"What if we conceive?"

"I think we won't."

"I'm okay either way. I thought about it."

"Babies are starving in poor countries for the sake of brief relief. I read that some diseases cost hundreds of years of human life. Scientists see life on a single species. They don't talk about human diseases saving years of life for other species."

She snuggled. "I have an idea for you."

"Okay."

"We think Billy is here in spirit."

"Yes.

"I think you're here in body but gone in spirit."

He lay still.

"You seek light. You're addicted to it. Your baseline is too high. You're beaming away."

He blinked.

"I think you don't understand love. It begins as less and becomes more. It's an experiment based on instinct and feeling. I had feelings for you." She lay back.

"You make me feel awkward. I love you too?"

She shook her head.

They lay quietly, unsettled.

He mumbled, "*merrily, merrily, merrily, merrily . . .*

"Another song from the '60s?"

"Yeah, the 1860s."

"Are you listening to me?"

"I am. I think we're friends, but I don't know what to think of you. You're sexy, but I . . . I worry."

"This is complicated for you?"

"Yes."

"Men think about sex every seven minutes. Some men. You might call it reflexive, but some men fall in love."

He turned. "Eloise. I saw your beauty on the surface, and I see you again at depth."

"You mean as an aggressor?"

"No. You're persistent. That can be good. I don't know if you can . . . I could be a burden. Failure is a mystical force for me, the most powerful catalyst for success. I do love insight, what you call light, but I have a . . ."

"You're not a burden or a failure. I see you too."

Silence settled.

"It's just that . . ."

She interrupted, whispering, "Have you ever been romantic?"

"I have, I think." He took a moment to scan the files. Surely the years had yielded something more than sunbeams or a pulse and a thump, something to make him wonder where she is now, a trace of spirit and body in communion. Surely, he . . .

He stopped scanning when she oozed over, closed her eyes and put her lips to his for a lingering kiss.

About the Author

Robert Wintner has authored sixteen novels, three memoirs, four story collections and five reef photo books. He has crossed two continents on motorcycles, sailed four of the seven seas, dove tropical reefs around the world and rose from ashes to success in a place Forbes Magazine called the most difficult business arena in America. Profiled in a dozen metro daily papers, interviewed on a hundred radio shows, he declined an appearance on Leno when asked to arrive in mask, fins and snorkel. He is committed to style, story, entertainment and lasting value intact.

Robert Wintner is the nom de plume of Snorkel Bob, Hawaii's biggest reef outfitter. He is a front-line activist in reef defense and lives on Maui with Anita, Cookie the dog, Yoyo, Tootsie, Rocky, Buck, Inez and Coco the cats, and Elizabeth the chicken.

Made in the USA
Middletown, DE
22 February 2023

25056884R00186